Sunshine on Sunday

ജ⚬ଓ

JC Conrad-Ellis

SUNSHINE ON SUNDAY

For information about Provision Press please visit our website at www.blackdiamondseries.com.
Library of Congress Cataloging-in-Publication Data
Conrad-Ellis, JC

SUNSHINE ON SUNDAY/ JC Conrad-Ellis
ISBN 13: 978-1-957593-04-3
Teen Fiction

Copyright Registered: 2022
First Published by Provision Press in the USA

Printed in the USA
January 2022

10 9 8 7 6 5 4 3 2

DEDICATION

This book is dedicated to:

BWE

Love,
YWMOE

ACKNOWLEDGEMENTS

Thank you to the public library system and librarians throughout the world who make books and reading material available to anyone free of charge. My love of reading was conceived and nurtured through the public library system. Thank you for all that you do.

CONTENTS

"The Lord will fight for you; you need only to be still."

Exodus 14:14
The NIV Study Bible
New International Version

Sunshine on Sunday

Chapter 1

It Takes Two

Her eyes panned the ladies' locker room in the private country club, its exclusivity disguised by the shabbiness of the sitting area's furnishings. She toed a large snag in the well worn carpet, and her gaze followed a tear that wound from the Hollywood style make-up mirror to the locker area. She walked into the locker area and admired the postcard size gold plaques on each locker. Each plaque bore the name of a female member, identifying the green locker as her personal domain, a rainbow palette of silk tabs dangled from each nameplate. The rows of lockers were separated by a line of narrow benches. Golf shoes sat atop many of the lockers like crowns. Several lockers had small embroidered birds affixed to the colorful silk tab, and one locker in the row boasted a large embroidered eagle on its tab. She knew from her high school golf class that a birdie was one stroke below par, and an eagle was two strokes below par.

Walking slowly through the aisle, she casually read the members' nameplates and wondered how the lockers were assigned since the names weren't in alphabetical order: Claire Hall, Therese Paulfrey, Carolyn Fambro, Amelia West, Barbara Hudson, Lillie Bishop, Jenelle Merritt, Mrs. William Wardell. She chuckled, amused that someone still listed herself using her husband's name and not her first name. *How old fashioned is that? She's probably really old. Well, she can't be that old if she is still golfing? You can be old and golf, Maria!*

Her eyes kept reading the locker name plaques: Mrs. David George, Sharon E. Kelly, Mrs. Theodore John, Deona Whitney Danick, Angela Blair, Mrs. Karyn Wardell, Michael Bailey, Dr. Rachel Goldberg, K. Neely Elise, Elle Dudley-Barton. She stopped at Elle Dudley-Barton's locker and touched the small bird affixed to her yellow tab. *Finally, a progressive woman who added her husband's name to her name instead of just taking his name. Hallelujah!*

A yawning Maria walked back into the main sitting area and plopped on the large floral sofa, disappointed that the inviting sofa lacked firmness in the seat cushions. She wished she had time to take a quick nap, but the flush of the toilet and creaky water pipes stood her to her feet and back to her post at the make-up table.

"I look like a lemon meringue pie," the voice whined. "I should have worn the cream colored dress instead of this suit," she hissed. "And this yellow blouse makes me look like a dessert! What was I thinking?" she asked as she tossed the embroidered hand towel into a small linen basket.

"You look fine," Maria assured her. "The dress was too casual. The suit looks more tailored and put together," she smiled. "You can barely see the blouse beneath your jacket because the jacket fits you so well. It just looks like a soft, delicate camisole peeking out," she assured. "It's an evening wedding so you want to look elegant, and you do. You look very elegant."

The nervous bride twirled the baby's breath in her hair, pulling it out and repositioning it on the left side. "Does it matter which side I wear the baby's breath?" she panted.

Maria shrugged halfheartedly. "I don't think it matters. But the groom will be on your right, so maybe the baby's breath should be on your left so it's not poking him in the face," she suggested.

"That's a good idea," she agreed. The bobby pins hanging from her lips, she carefully positioned the baby's breath above her left temple.

"Let me help you, Mom," Maria suggested. "You don't want the flower to look like a spaceship landed on your head," she teased. "Sit down so I can reach your hair better."

Without a fuss, Liz Wesley plopped in the wooden chair and smiled at her daughter. "Thank you, Sweetie. I'm just so nervous today," she admitted. "It's my wedding day!" she beamed. "I'm getting married!"

Maria grinned at her mother's reflection as she carefully smoothed the soft curls that framed her mother's face before pinning the baby's breath into a tuft of delicate curls.

"How's that?" Maria asked. "I think that's the look we're after," she commented.

Liz spun around and reached for her daughter's hands, squeezing them softly as she spoke. "You're happy for me aren't you, Maria?" she asked. "You do like Richard don't you?" she pleaded, studying Maria's face for a hint of remorse.

Maria looked at her mother lovingly. "Richard is a great guy, Mom," she replied. "He treats you like a queen, and I've never seen you look happier. I'm happy for you both," she finished.

Clutching her mother's pearls, Liz Wesley exhaled. "I'm so glad to hear that," she admitted. "It would kill me if you weren't happy for me," she shared, spinning around and reaching for her makeup bag. "Richard asked me to marry him three years ago," Liz confessed. "Did I tell you that?" she asked quickly. "And then he asked me again the year you went off to college, but I told him that I thought it might be too difficult for Neal to handle," she continued without waiting for Maria's reply. "You know, having a strange man living in the house might have been too much for Neal," she paused. "But once Neal decided that he wanted to live with your dad, and with you now in college and on your own, I was out of excuses," she shrugged. "And I love Richard. He makes me very happy."

Maria stared at her mother's reflection. "Did you ever think that you'd remarry, Mom?" she asked.

"I didn't," she admitted. "Honestly, I was scared to get married again since I screwed it up the first time," she sighed. "I'm still a little scared about this whole marriage thing, but I'm wiser now," she smiled.

"You were only twenty when you and Dad married, and you didn't screw it up, Mom," Maria corrected.

"Well, maybe not technically," Liz agreed. "But it takes two to tango in a relationship, Maria, so I can't completely blame your dad for all that went sour in our marriage," she paused. "He was wrong to cheat, but I see now that there was a lot that I could have done differently too," she confessed.

Puzzled, Maria wrinkled her eyebrows and stared at her mother's reflection. "Like what, Mom?" she asked.

Liz powdered her nose and reached for her eyelash curler. "I resented your father for making me a housewife," she admitted. "I blamed him for me not having a career, which was wrong. We both decided that I would put my career goals on hold so that we could raise our family, which I don't regret for a second," she assured. "But instead of carving out an identity for myself during that time, I stewed and resented your father's success," she said. "He felt that I didn't believe in him and that I didn't appreciate the life that he was building for his family," she continued. "And I did, but I was so focused on the sacrifices that I was making that I didn't know how to celebrate what he was doing. I lost sight of myself in the glare of his success," she sighed. "And by the time I decided to return to school and get my degree, there was such a rift in our marriage that it was impossible to repair," she sighed. "I don't know if that makes any sense to you," she finished.

Maria eyed her mother curiously. "It makes sense, but it sounds like you're blaming yourself for Dad having an affair, Mom," she said.

"Not at all," Liz corrected. "I don't blame myself at all, but I do acknowledge the role that I played in the problems that we had in our marriage. Now your father made the decision to go outside of our marriage to seek a solution, which was wrong. There was no excuse for that," she clarified. "But with hindsight, I wish that someone had taken me under their wing and helped me see what was happening while it was happening," she shared. "Maybe we could have benefited from counseling before it spun too far out of control," she offered as she curled her long eyelashes. "Do you think I should put on false eyelashes?" she asked.

"Go for it," Maria encouraged. "It's your wedding day! Let's glam you up!"

Mrs. Wesley opened a pack of false eyelashes and carefully applied them.

"Do you still love Dad?" Maria asked.

As though expecting the question, Liz answered quickly. "Of course I do," she said. "He's the father of my children. I will always love him, but I'm not 'in love' with him anymore. Do you understand the difference?" she asked.

Maria nodded her head in the affirmative. "You care about him and care about what happens to him, but there's no passion or emotion."

"Precisely," Liz said. "It took Mama Kaye to help me understand that," she explained. "I only wish that I had sought her wisdom sooner. Not that I regret what happened," she corrected quickly. "I think everything happens for a reason. Had I not been wandering in the wilderness like a lonely doe whose buck was just shot by a hunter, I wouldn't have met Richard," she smiled.

"Mother! Dad was not shot like a buck!"

"I know, but that's what it felt like. A divorce feels like a death in many ways. But my mourning period is over now, and Richard is such a blessing in my life," she beamed. "I am so in love with that man!"

"What did Mama Kaye tell you?" Maria asked.

Mrs. Wesley walked over to the small radio that sat in the corner and turned up the volume, bopping her head to the jazz tune playing from the speaker. "Maria, hand me an emery board from my purse would you? I snagged my nail, and I don't want it to run my pantyhose."

Reaching inside one of the zipper pockets in her mother's purse, Maria pulled out a stack of emery boards and fanned them at her mother. "Really, Mother! Do you really need six emery boards in your purse?" she teased.

"You know how neurotic I am about my nails," Liz defended. "I might lose one, so I need a backup," she laughed.

"A backup is one extra one, Mom, not five extra ones," she laughed.

"Stop teasing me and hand it over," Liz laughed.

"What did Mama Kaye tell you?" Maria repeated.

"Tell me about what?" Mrs. Wesley asked.

Maria stared at her mother with irritation. "You were telling me that Mama Kaye helped you understand the difference between loving someone and being in love with someone," she reminded. "Is that what happens when you get closer to forty? Does your memory just disappear?" she teased.

"I am going to ignore that comment because today's my wedding day, and I'm choosing to ignore all comments that are not celebratory on my big day," Liz said. "But Mama Kaye helped me to see that it was okay to forgive myself for my marriage not working," she explained. "Since my marriage failed, I felt like I disappointed God and my mother's memory and the example that my parents showed me," she sighed. "I felt like a big, fat failure, so I never planned to remarry. I was just going to enjoy Richard's company while it lasted. Mama Kaye was the only person who knew that Richard asked me to marry him a few years ago."

"What changed your mind?" Maria asked.

"Mama Kaye," Liz replied quickly. "She told me that I was being foolish and that I would die a lonely, miserable, old woman unless I learned to forgive myself about getting a divorce, and learn to trust again." Her face scrunched into a soft scowl as Liz imitated Mama Kaye's tone, her index finger waving in the mirror like a school teacher's pointer. "'Elizabeth Jeanine Wesley, you need to marry that man before he stops sniffing around. Stop crucifying yourself about getting a divorce. God has forgiven you, so marry that man or I'll marry him,'" Liz laughed. "Mama Kaye is such a character, but she was right."

"But Daddy wanted to get back together with you," Maria pleaded, sounding every bit like a ten year old girl. "You couldn't trust him, is that why you wouldn't give Daddy another chance?" she asked.

As only a mother could do, Mrs. Wesley caught the longing in her daughter's voice. She turned in her chair and faced Maria. "Are you sure you're okay hearing this, Maria?" she asked softly. "This is probably not the right time to have this discussion."

"I'm fine, Mom," Maria assured. "It's just that I've never heard you say this stuff before," she offered quickly. Maria plopped on the chair facing her mother.

Liz studied her daughter carefully. "Really, Mom," Maria assured. "I really like Richard. I just wanted to hear what Mama Kaye told you," she said.

Taking a deep breath, Liz spoke slowly. "Your dad and I went on a few dates about two years ago," Liz confessed.

Maria's eyes and mouth widened simultaneously. "You did?" she asked. "You cheated on Richard with Dad?" she asked.

"Not exactly," Liz laughed. "We just went out to dinner a few times and talked. We have two children together, for goodness sake, and we had a home that we were trying to sell, so we discussed it over dinner. Twice," she finished.

"But you called it a date, Mom," Maria pointed out.

"I did, didn't I?" Liz giggled. "It felt like a date because your father picked me up. He brought me flowers and opened the car door for me," she remembered. "He was really trying hard to woo me back," she shared. "But it was too late. I was already in love with Richard."

"Well, what did Mama Kaye tell you that helped you make up your mind?"

Spinning back on her chair, Liz continued to apply her makeup. "I confessed to Mama Kaye that I was confused. On the one hand, my ex-husband wanted to get back together with me, but now I was in love with another man," she said. "So Mama Kaye asked me if I would be happier with Neal or Richard," she paused. "She told me to forget about the history that I have with

Neal and the guilt I felt about the divorce and to just think about my happiness. 'Do you see a happier future with Neal or with Richard?' she asked me. And I saw myself happier with Richard," she confessed softly. "Your dad and I had two beautiful children and a good life for a long time," she said. "But I feel something for Richard that I never felt with your father. I don't know if it's maturity or what," she paused. "But I didn't want to look back, and Mama Kaye gave me permission to move forward guilt free," she sighed. "So that's what I'm doing. And I hope you're happy for me, Maria."

"I am, Mom," Maria comforted. "I'm very happy for you and Richard."

"You should make friends with older women, Maria, so you can benefit from their wisdom and experience," she coached. "It's great to have friends your own age, but it's always nice to have women who are wiser to help guide you. Plus, older women aren't afraid of telling you when you're wrong, and sometimes your friends won't tell you the truth because they don't want to hurt your feelings," she cautioned.

"I've heard this lecture before, Mom," Maria groaned.

"But it's true. Mama Kaye always speaks her mind to me. She could care less about hurting my feelings," she laughed. "'Pump your brakes' is Mama Kaye's favorite saying," she laughed. "You know what that means don't you?" she asked.

"It means slow down," Maria groaned. "I'm almost twenty years old, Mom. I've been driving for almost four years."

"When I was growing up, if Mama Kaye saw me doing something that she thought wasn't a good idea, she'd say, 'Elizabeth, you need to pump your brakes.' That's what she told me when I told her that I was having dinner with your father. Older women have traveled the road we're on and see all of the curves and potholes," she said. "And they're not afraid to warn you about them. You'll need that wisdom. And you might not always want to come to me for advice," Liz continued. "I didn't have the benefit of my mother's advice since she died when I was young, so I'm so glad that Mama Kaye stepped in."

"Mama Kaye isn't really related to us is she, Mom?" Maria asked. "I don't remember."

"Nope. She's just a friend from the church where I grew up in the city," she explained. "She was the youth choir director, and she was friends with my mother. They sang in the adult choir together and served on the Petite Matrons Women's Ministry board together. She was at least ten years older than my mother, so she must have been in her mid forties when my mother died," she explained. "The whole church embraced our family and Mama Kaye became a surrogate mother to me. Her husband's name is Papa Willie, but they never tried to befriend your grandfather. Mama Kaye just focused her attention on me," Liz smiled. "And I'm glad that she did."

"I miss seeing Mama Kaye," Maria said. "We used to see her a lot. I didn't realize that you still kept in touch with her."

Liz spun on her chair and fumbled in her make-up bag. "Oh sure, I still talk to her about once a month or so," Liz explained. "I talked to her all the time when your dad and I were first separated, and I usually stop in for a visit three or four times a year. I never call first, I just ring the bell. That's how people used to do it when I was growing up. You didn't call the person and announce that you were coming; you just stopped by for a visit. It was spontaneous and a nice surprise. Now people make appointments to see people they care about," she rambled. "I miss the spontaneity of neighbors just dropping by for a chat. Her schedule hasn't changed in twenty five years. She has youth choir rehearsal every Wednesday night, adult choir rehearsal every Thursday night, and her women's ministry board meeting is on the first Friday of every month," she paused. "Now if the choir is singing at a funeral, she might be at church for that. So if I stop by her house and she's not home, I go to the church to see her."

"I remember going to her house," Maria smiled. "She always gave Neal and me these orange candies dusted with powdered sugar," she remembered.

Her head nodded up and down. "That's her signature treat," Liz smiled. "Those orange hard candies and iced tea mixed with cranberry juice," she laughed. "I guarantee you she has a bowl of those on her coffee table right now just in case company stops by. And she is still one of the best cooks that I know. I miss having dinner at her house," she trailed. "She helped me learn to cook as a young girl. After my mother died, Mama Kaye and I would cook Sunday dinner together at her house and I'd eat with Mama Kaye and Papa Willie, then she'd send a plate of food home for Neal and your grandfather," she remembered. "I'm really looking forward to moving back to the city so I can spend more time with her. She's getting up in years."

"Is she still the youth choir director at church?" Maria asked.

"She sure is," her mom replied. "And two of the children who studied under her have gone on to pursue careers in music," she shared. "She still sings in the choir too. Since we'll be living in Hyde Park, Richard and I are going to attend his church, but I think once a month I'll surprise Mama Kaye and attend early service with her before going to service with Richard," she shared. "She would like that. The men's choir sings on the third Sunday of the month, so she'll be in a pew."

Maria smiled at her mother. "So every third Sunday, you'll sit through two church services, Mom? Isn't that a bit much?"

Liz tossed a wad of tissue at Maria. "No, it is not. Going to church always adds sunshine to any Sunday," she teased. "Besides, when I'm in the sanctuary of my childhood church, it reminds me of my mother," she sighed. "I really miss Mary Jane," she said softly. "Plus, I miss sitting next to Mama Kaye in church. And I know she's not going to be around forever so I want to spend more time with her," Liz admitted. "Hopefully, when I get old, you'll want to spend more time with me," she said.

Reaching across the table, Maria tossed the same crumpled tissue back at her mother, accompanied with a frown. "Don't talk like that, Mom," she whined. "You know I don't like it when you talk about getting older and dying."

"Who said anything about dying?" Liz laughed. "I just hope that you make time for me when I get older and you have a family of your own. That's all," she smiled. "You have to enjoy the people that you love while they're still here, Maria Jane."

"Of course I will, Mom," Maria assured. "Assuming I live in Chicago. I may get a job some place else," she reminded.

"That's true," Liz agreed. "But home will always be home. And there's no place like home," she grinned. "That's what my mother used to always say."

"Mom, if your mother's name was Mary Jane, why did you name me Maria Jane?" Maria asked. "If you wanted to name me after your mother, why didn't you name me Mary Jane?"

Liz smiled at Maria. "Maria is the Spanish word for Mary," she explained.

"Duh, Mom," Maria groaned. "But I know how important

family names are to you. You're named after your grandmother and great grandmother," she reminded.

"Well, your father didn't want me to name you Mary," she paused. "He said that it sounded too plain and old fashioned," she shrugged. "So we compromised and named you Maria. It was Mama Kaye's idea to name you Maria. I went running and crying to Mama Kaye when your dad told me that he didn't like the name Mary, so Mama Kaye suggested Maria Jane," she paused. "Well, what she actually said was that the mother signs the birth certificate and that after carrying you for forty weeks, I had a right to name you anything that I wanted and if my fool of a husband didn't understand that I wanted to honor my mother by naming my daughter after her then to heck with him," Liz laughed. "And then she apologized for saying that and suggested I name you Maria Jane," she added, her look distant and soft, the recollections pouring into her memory like a waterfall. "To tell you the truth, I don't think Mama Kaye really liked your dad very much," Liz recalled. "It's all coming back to me now. I remember the first time that I brought Neal over to meet Mama Kaye, she told me to 'pump my brakes,'" Liz remembered. "Elizabeth Jeanine, pump your brakes with this one," she warned. "I ignored her of course because I was head over heels in love," she added. "And I thought she was just being motherly and discouraging me from marrying my first boyfriend," she paused. "But now that I'm more mature, I think she was trying to let me know that she could see the bumps in the road," she sighed. "But she never tried to stop me from marrying him. In fact, she sewed my wedding gown and helped me put on my make-up on my wedding day," she smiled. "On my wedding day, my mother's sisters didn't appreciate the role that Mama Kaye played, but they saw how close we were, so they backed off and let

Mama Kaye play surrogate mother," she explained.

"But you said that Mama Kaye was really outspoken and always spoke her mind and she didn't care if she hurt your feelings," Maria reminded. "Why didn't she tell you what she thought about Dad?"

"In her own way she did," Liz sighed. "Telling me to pump my brakes was her way of advising me to be cautious," she explained. "I knew what she was implying, but no one was going to stop me from marrying Neal Wesley," she remembered fondly. "I really loved your dad," she smiled. "Mama Kaye was the one who taught me that I have to learn where other people end and I begin," she explained.

"You say that to me all the time," Maria reminded.

"And I learned that from Mama Kaye," she explained. "You are your own person.   And as much as I'd like to control your life and manipulate you like a marionette," she laughed. "now that you're an adult, you have to learn where I end and you begin. You can't be worried about what I do and how it will make you look. The things that I do are not a reflection of you," she reminded. "Learn where I end and you begin."

"I remember the first time you told me that. I was embarrassed by something that you were going to wear to my school," Maria chuckled.

"You stayed embarrassed by my clothing," Liz giggled. "But I wore what I wanted to wear and told you to get over it," she said. "When people give you advice, listen to it and weigh it against your values and judgment. But you have to live your own life. I may not approve of all of the choices that you make," she paused. "And hopefully you'll come to me for advice and heed some of my wisdom, but at the end of the day, it's your life to live and they will be your decisions to make. And if the road that you choose has some bumps in it, so be it. That's life," she smiled. "I don't regret the bumps in my journey, because that journey brought me you and Neal," she smiled. "And now it's led me to Richard."

The grandfather clock, asleep in the corner, chimed on the quarter hour. "Is it already twelve fifteen?" Liz gasped. "I'll be a married woman in fifteen minutes," she smiled without waiting for a reply. With military precision, she scooped her make-up into the large make-up bag and tossed it into the carry on bag at her feet. Standing, she smoothed her skirt and gazed at her reflection. "I am ready to be Mrs. Elizabeth Jeanine Dawson," she smiled.

"You're dropping Wesley?" Maria asked surprised. "I thought you were going to hyphenate your name?"

"I am going to hyphenate it legally and use it professionally," her mother explained. "But socially I'll be Mrs. Richard Dawson, III. Doesn't that have a nice sound to it? Mrs. Elizabeth Jeanine Wesley-Dawson."

"That sounds like a mouthful to me, Mom," Maria groaned. "Why don't you drop Jeanine and just make Wesley your middle name?"

"I thought about it," she paused. "But my mother gave me that name. It was her grandmother's name. Elizabeth was my grandmother's name, and Jeanine was my great grandmother's name," she explained.

"Honor your ancestors by naming your children after them," Maria whined. "I've heard this a million times, Mom," she smiled.

"Good. I'm glad you've retained this bit of wisdom," she grinned. "And don't let your husband talk you out of it. Stick to your guns," she cautioned.

The locker room door creaked slowly. "Liz, are you done yet?"

her father's voice bellowed through the door.

Maria walked over to greet her grandfather. "Hey Paw Paw," she grinned. "The bride is ready," she announced.

"Well, tell her that Richard is here and so is the minister, so let's get this show on the road," he barked. "Mama Kaye told me to come and get you."

"I'm coming, Dad," Liz replied. "I'll be right out."

"Mama Kaye is here?" Maria smiled, walking toward her mother. "I thought you said that you and Richard were having a small family wedding."

"Mama Kaye **is** family," Liz reminded. "Just because we don't have a blood connection, she's as much a part of my family as anyone else. Of course she's here," Liz finished.

"I miss Mama Kaye," Maria offered. "I'll sit next to her at the reception," she shared.

"She'd love that, sweetie," her mother smiled. "Let's go. I want to be standing at the altar with Richard when the clock chimes on the half hour," she said. "You know that you should get married on the half hour when the hands of the clock are rising to signify that your new relationship is on the rise," Liz advised checking her teeth for lipstick one final time and quickly crunching a mint from the crystal dish on the table.

"Got it, Mother," Maria groaned. "I will get married when the clock hands are rising," she smirked, shaking her head at her mother's superstitious ways and dutifully grabbing her mother's tote bag to assume her maid of honor responsibilities. *I'm glad Mama Kaye is here. I need some Mama Kaye wisdom. My love life is a hot mess!*

Chapter 2

The Courtship

"Do you have two of these in an extra large?" Teenie asked, holding the sweatshirt across her chest. Eyes downcast, her tone was indifferent and borderline rude. Without waiting for a reply, she continued. "And if you don't have this one, then see if you have the one with the white embroidered Y in an extra large," she finished. "I need two of them," she paused. "Please." The please tossed in as a last second afterthought, her conscience nudging her to abort her uncharacteristically rude behavior.

"Like the one you have on?" the young clerk asked. "Or like the one that I'm wearing?" he clarified.

Looking down at her chest, Teenie blushed, forgetting that she was wearing the very sweatshirt that she sought to purchase. "Either one could work," she said. "But I'd prefer one like the one that I'm wearing," she smiled, her tone a tad softer.

"Do you want one of each?" he asked.

"Actually, I'd like them to be identical," she replied.

"Let me guess. One sweatshirt is for your dad or your brother, and the other one is for your boyfriend," he chuckled. "Do you really want your dad or your brother to have the same exact sweatshirt as you?" the clerk asked. "All of the freshman girls come in and buy matching sweatshirts for their boyfriends," he paused. "But they usually buy a different one for their dad or their brother," he explained.

Staring at the clerk, she arched her left eyebrow dramatically. "How'd you know that I'm a freshman?" Teenie asked.

"You have that deer in the headlights look plastered across your face," he chuckled. "Plus, the sweatshirt that you're wearing is our most current design. All of the freshies have been buying it. The upperclassmen prefer the vintage Yale apparel," he explained. "Are you sure you want two of the same sweatshirts?" he asked again. "They're the same cost."

"I think so," she stammered. "But let me take a look at what you have," she said softly.

"Suit yourself. It's your money," he shrugged. "But I'm not sure if we have any extra larges left because the larger sizes always sell out first, and since it's so close to Thanksgiving, we've had a run on sweatshirts. The freshman students always buy them to give as gifts," he explained as he walked into the back of the small store.

Teenie followed his head as he bopped to the music blaring from the ceiling speaker, the letters SBX stenciled across the speaker in green. She instantly recognized the artist as Sting, the lead singer from The Police. She'd just purchased a copy of Sting's soundtrack entitled: "The Dream of the Blue Turtles." She'd loved the soundtrack just like he said that she would.

The Student Book Exchange sold the best Yale paraphernalia on campus. And if they didn't have your size, they could special order whatever you needed and have it delivered within three days. She casually fingered the tee-shirts and sweatshirts that held center stage over the textbooks vying for more prominent shelf space.

They sell a few textbooks in here, but it's really more of a tee-

shirt and sweatshirt shop. I wonder why they call it the Student Book Exchange.

She closed her eyes and sang aloud.

The clerk's voice startled her. "You like Sting?" he asked. "This is vintage. They never played this track on the radio. How do you know the words to this song?" he asked, studying her curiously.

"I bought "Dream of the Blue Turtles" last week," she shared. "I play it all the time," she admitted. "What did you find back there?"

"You're in luck," he said. "You must have gone to church today, and God must be smiling down on you, because I have two of the one like you have on, and I have two of the one like I have on," he explained. "Which two do you want? That never happens this close to Thanksgiving," he marveled.

Teenie chewed on her lip. "In fact, I did go to church today, and they say that God always adds sunshine to your Sunday when you go to church," she stated proudly. "Never mind," she offered, waving her hand dismissively in response to the clerk's confused grin. "I'll take your advice and buy one of each," she smiled.

"Good decision!" he chided. "Give the one that matches yours to your boyfriend and give the other one to your dad who pays your tuition," he grinned. "I take it that your boyfriend isn't a Yale man?" the clerk asked. "Where does he go to school?"

Teenie fumbled in her backpack for her wallet, wincing briefly to calculate how much the thick, expensive sweatshirts would withdraw from her scholarship padded bank account.

"Huh?" she asked rhetorically. "He goes to Princeton," she shared. "And the other sweatshirt isn't for my dad," she corrected. "It's for a friend who's in medical school at Howard," she shared.

"Princeton! That's where I'm going next year," he offered.

"Aaaah, you're playing the field aren't you freshie?" the clerk teased. "I didn't even think of that one. You look so innocent," he laughed. "Usually the freshman guys come in and buy identical sweatshirts to send to girlfriend number one and girlfriend number two," he paused. "They usually buy identical sweatshirts so they don't get busted and confused wondering which sweatshirt they gave to which girlfriend. But it's rare that a freshman girl comes in with that scam," he cackled. "You win the prize for surprising me, freshie," he laughed.

"It's not what you think," Teenie pleaded.

The clerk raised his hands in the universal surrender pose. "Hey, I am not here to sit in judgment of the customers," he stated flatly. "I'm a lowly senior in high school, and I'm just here to facilitate the transaction and gouge you for overpriced apparel," he laughed. "But the stories that I could tell working in this store," he whistled. "They would make your head spin."

Feeling defeated, Teenie smiled widely and handed him her debit card. "I can only imagine. Here's my bank card," she beamed brightly.

"You have beautiful teeth," the clerk complimented.

Startled, Teenie blushed slightly before replying. "Thanks," she uttered as she self consciously ran her tongue across her teeth, still not quite accustomed to the smooth feel of her teeth enamel's new emancipated status. She was slowly growing accustomed to the resulting compliments that often followed her wire free, bright smile accessory. "I just had my braces removed about two months ago," she boasted proudly. "By the way, I notice that they sell more Yale paraphernalia than books in this store," she observed. "Why do they call it the Student Book Exchange?" she asked.

"You really are a freshman," the clerk laughed. "Everyone calls it SBX. Don't let anyone on campus hear you call it the Student Book Exchange or they'll tar and feather you," he laughed. "My dad owns this store, and we have to sell some books and have the word "book" in our title in order to get a bigger tax break from the city for being so close to campus," he explained. "But tee-shirts and sweatshirts are our bread and butter," he finished. "This store put my sister through Yale, and it's sending me to Princeton," he grinned. "Good luck with your dating scam, little Miss Freshman with the perfect teeth who likes Sting," he winked as he handed her the shopping bag. "And don't worry, discretion is my middle name," he paused. "I will pretend like I never saw you if you bring one of your boyfriends back into the store," he winked. "I have an older sister, and I watched her scamming with her boyfriends all the time," he laughed.

She winked back and stuck her tongue out at the clerk before slinging her backpack over her shoulder and trudging out the door with her package.

Once outside, Teenie rested the shopping bag at her feet and zipped her fleece jacket, grateful that she'd tied the jacket around her waist before heading into town. Glancing out her small dorm room window before embarking on her shopping pilgrimage, she noticed that many of the students braved the fall temperatures wearing flip flops and tee-shirts, but she knew that the bright sun that shone in the sky was not enough to warm the cool Connecticut temperatures to her liking. Even wearing her standard college uniform of a thick sweatshirt, she usually felt a chill and wondered how the students could parade around with their toes exposed in fifty degree weather, many wearing shorts.

As the sun hid behind a tall building, the wind swirled leaves at her feet, creating a whirlpool effect of rust and gold along the pavement. David's voice sang in her head as she walked swiftly back to campus.

ഇരു

"That telephone grows out of your head, Teenie," her dad observed. "You haven't even put the sheets on your bed yet and you're plugging in that phone. Whose call are you trying to catch?" he asked. "It must be some boy," he groaned.

Teenie exchanged a knowing glance with her mother. "No one in particular, Dad," she stammered. "I just want to make sure that it works." She placed the receiver to her ear. "Bingo! It's working. A dial tone is like music to my ears," she grinned.

"We need to get going so we can take you and your friends out to dinner," Jackie explained glancing at his watch. "And then we're going to hit the road. I want to drive for at least six hours tonight," he explained. "After we get you unpacked, we'll take a quick walk around so Byron and Allen can see more of the campus. I think I remember how to get to the student union from our college road trip," he said.

"Why can't we just stay on campus?" Byron asked, his deep voice resonating off the walls in the small room. "I'm sure there's a college party tonight," he chuckled. "I saw a gaggle of cute girls checking me out when we were moving Teenie's stuff in," he continued. "I didn't realize that smart girls were so hot," he laughed. Byron chest bumped Allen who stroked the peach fuzz on his chin.

"As if college girls would be interested in you two, clowns," Teenie groaned.

Billie smiled at her children. "Tanisha, I know it's hard for you to imagine this," she paused. "But your brothers are handsome young men now. Whenever I'm out with them, I notice the teen girls trying to get their attention."

"Gross!" Teenie groaned. "That's because they don't know how dweebish they are."

"I think those girls were hoping that I was moving into the dorm instead of you, Thunder Thighs," Byron teased. "Just kidding, sis," he offered quickly. "You don't have thunder thighs anymore. But you do have a bat in the cave," he finished.

Her hand rushed to stroke her nostrils.

"She falls for that one every time," Allen laughed. "Good thing they didn't test you for common sense on your Yale entrance exam," he teased. "But Byron's right, Dad," Allen whined, his voice an octave higher than his older brother's. "I wouldn't mind crashing one of these parties myself," he echoed.

"We are going to eat dinner with Teenie and her friends and then hit the road so we can make a dent in our trip," Jackie instructed. "And you need to get your rest Byron because I'm going to have you drive for a few hours tomorrow," he advised.

"I can't believe you don't even have a roommate, Teenie," Byron observed. "That's so sweet!"

Her early admission letter brought with it preferred dormitory selection status, and after consulting with her Yale buddy, she decided to seek housing in a new dormitory that had recently altered its policy and allowed freshman to apply. Teenie had researched the resident colleges but decided that she would prefer the privacy of having her own room instead of sharing a sleeping quarters with three other girls, even if the resident college set-up also offered a small kitchen and a shared television lounge area. To her surprise, she'd been assigned to a floor with freshman boys at one end of the hall while Monica and Laura were assigned to the all girls floor of the building.

Her relationship with Brian Kraft and sojourns to the North Shore had reunited Teenie with Laura, one of her cabin mates from leadership camp. The encounter had surprised them both.

"Laura?" Teenie asked cautiously, tapping the girl softly on the shoulder, unable to recall her last name. "Is your name Laura?" she repeated loudly.

Turning toward the shoulder tap, the recognition was instant. "Teenie!" Laura squealed. "Oh my God! What are you doing at a party in Kenilworth?" she asked as she pulled Teenie into an embrace.

"I'm here with Brian Kraft," Teenie explained. "What are you doing here?"

"The guy throwing the party is my boyfriend's cousin," Laura explained. "I can't believe that you're here. And you're still dating Brian Kraft after all this time?" she squealed. "Mike and I lasted about six months after camp, and then it crashed and burned," she offered casually.

"Actually, Brian and I just started seeing each other again a few months ago," Teenie corrected. "We bumped into each other at prom of all places," she explained. "But before that I hadn't heard from him in two years," she clarified. "So we just started dating again."

"I recognized you right away," Laura smiled. "Your hair is longer, but you look the same. And you have braces now," she noticed.

"You look the same too, except your hair is shorter," Teenie noticed. "That's why I wasn't sure if it was you. I love your haircut!"

Laura fingered her thick bob. "Thanks. I just felt like it was time for a change," she offered. "I've had long hair my whole life, and I wanted a new look. Plus, my mom thought that a shorter haircut would help me look more studious for my college entrance interviews," she said. "Your hair looks great longer," she offered. "But sometimes people don't take natural blondes seriously. They treat you like a dumb ditz," she shrugged. "It's a stupid stereotype, but even in high school I felt like I had to work extra hard to prove to the teachers that I was just as smart as the fat, plain, ugly girls," she groaned. "Not that I have anything against the fat, ugly girl crew," she continued. "But if you're unattractive and wear thick glasses, sometimes the teachers assume you're smarter than someone like me who happens to like math, science, couture clothing, and be runway ready," she laughed.

"I see your ego hasn't shrunk any since our camp days," Teenie laughed.

"Nope! My ego is as healthy and vibrant as ever, girlfriend!" Laura giggled. "Anyway, I didn't want to take any chances since I'm applying to the Ivys," she continued. "If I don't get into at least one Ivy league school, I think my parents will put me up for adoption," she laughed. "My mom suggested that I dye my hair brown until I get my acceptance letters, but I love my blonde hair, so I agreed to just cut it into a sophisticated style," she continued. "My grades and test scores are awesome, so I should get into at least one of my top choices," she sighed. "At least I hope so. Where are you planning to apply for college, Teenie?" she asked fingering Teenie's now shoulder length locks.

"I applied to Yale, Northwestern and the University of Illinois in Champaign," Teenie offered. "I wanted to apply to Wellesley too, but then I changed my mind about going to an all girls' college. What about you?"

"I applied to Yale too!" Laura squealed loudly, ignoring

the stares from some nearby partygoers. "That's my number one choice," she exclaimed. "I also applied to Princeton, Harvard and the University of Pennsylvania. I really wanted to go to Northwestern, but it's too close to home for me, and I wouldn't feel like I was on my own. My parents went to Dartmouth and they were really pushing me to go there, but my brother goes there now and I didn't want to be in his shadow," Laura explained. "I hope we get into Yale together. I'm planning to apply for a single room, but maybe we could live in the same dorm," she suggested. "I'm going to get a beer, do you want one?" she asked.

Shaking her head from side to side, Teenie declined. "I don't drink beer," she offered. "And you shouldn't either. You're only eighteen," Teenie chastised.

"You're such a kill joy," Laura groaned. "You sound like my boyfriend. Fine! I'll have a diet 7 Up. I don't need the carbs from the beer anyway," Laura laughed.

"Where is your boyfriend? I want to meet him," Teenie said.

"He's probably upstairs taking a nap. He's such a total nerd," she laughed. "But we get along great. He hates parties, but since it's his cousin's birthday, his parents made him come," she explained. "I'm the loud crazy one in the relationship, and he's the tall, serious, quiet one. He's a computer science genius. And you know what they say about still waters," she winked. "No more star quarterback types for me. He's the best boyfriend I've ever had! I'll introduce you to him later," she said. "But let's find a pen and some paper. I want to exchange numbers again," she suggested. "And this time let's pledge to keep in touch. I know we promised to keep in touch after camp," she paused. "Everybody always says that at camp, but no one ever does, so don't take it personal. I didn't keep in touch with Monica or Sharon either," she confessed.

Teenie smiled. "Well, that makes me feel better. At least it wasn't a black thing," she laughed.

Swatting Teenie gently on the shoulder, Laura laughed heartily. "You're still a militant little rebel," she mocked. "I still think of your 'black girls eat, white girls don't' theory and it cracks me up," Laura laughed. "Are you still creating little stereotypes about us white people?" she teased.

"No. I've decided to lay off you guys since I'm swimming in your pool now," Teenie laughed. "It's hard to have a white boyfriend and come up with stereotypes about his race," she said. "I feel like a hypocrite."

"Good! You shouldn't judge other people," Laura smiled. "Here comes your little paler nation boyfriend now. Let's see if he remembers me," Laura whispered.

Brian inched behind Teenie and wrapped his arms around her waist. Turning slowly, she pecked him on the lips. "Let's see how good your memory is," she said. "Do you remember who this is?"

"Laura. Mike's girlfriend from leadership camp," Brian said casually.

"How in the world did you remember her?" Teenie asked.

"I'm good," Brian shrugged. "I never forget a face, and watching your reunion from across the room, it was like a flashback to camp, the way you two squealed and giggled," he mocked. "Plus, we ate all of our meals together for two weeks," he reminded. "Your other cabin mates were Monica and Sharon," he continued. "I like your haircut, Laura," he complimented.

"You're good," Laura observed. "I can't believe you remember our cabin mates' names," she said stunned.

"He's a cyborg," Teenie laughed. "That's my Brian," she grinned.

∰∵

"Where are Laura and Monica's parents?" Jackie asked.

"Their parents dropped them off on Friday," she explained. "They wanted to get here early. Thanks for inviting them to dinner with us," Teenie said.

"I'm just glad that you're here with some people that you know," her dad offered. "I can't believe that my little Booger is now in college."

Teenie closed her eyes and clamped her jaws together tightly. When she opened her eyes, the look of loss on her dad's face was apparent, so she smiled softly and swallowed her words, glad that she hadn't blurted out at her father.

"Jackie, you can't call Tanisha 'Booger' in public," Billie cautioned softly. "She's eighteen now. Just think of how that must sound to her friends, sweetheart," she explained.

"I can't even call her that in front of family?" he asked indignantly. "No one heard me," he defended. "I use her nickname 'Teenie' when I'm around her friends now," he reminded.

"But you might slip and call her Booger in front of one of her friends and embarrass her," Billie continued. "Remember we talked about this."

"I'll call Laura and see if they're ready to go to dinner now, Dad," Teenie said. "Plus I have to use the bathroom, so I'll meet you guys in the lobby."

Her parents and brothers were barely in the hallway when the phone rang. "Hello," Teenie smiled.

"Have you met any Yale nerds yet?" the voice asked.

"David!" Teenie beamed. "How are you?" she asked walking over to close her door.

"Hey Teenie with the teenie, tiny bladder," he replied. "Are you getting settled into your postage size room yet?" he laughed.

"Why didn't you tell me that this room would be so tiny?" she whined. "My room at home was tiny, but this room is even smaller," she groaned.

"The single rooms are always super tiny," he agreed. "But at least you won't have a roommate snoring and waiting to use the phone," he advised.

"It's so good to hear your voice," she whined, plopping on her bed, grateful that her parents had left the room.

"You too, princess," he smiled. "Medical school is kicking my butt," he groaned. "I have mad respect for my parents now," he admitted. "And my old man worked part-time while he was in medical school. I barely have time to study and keep up with my labs, so I don't know how my dad was able to stay on top of his studies and hold down a job," he groaned. "And my parents were married and had my sister when my mom was in her third year of medical school," he shared. "So of course I get no sympathy from them about how rough I have it," he said.

"You're not regretting going to medical school instead of law school are you?" she asked. "I remember one of the first things you said to me was that when you became a federal district court judge, I could clerk for you," she reminded.

"I remember saying that," David chuckled. "I really thought I'd sit on the bench one day, but my parents envision that my sister and I will take over their medical practices when they retire, and since my brother went to law school, that left me to get the medical degree," he said. "I don't regret it. I always loved the sciences. My brother will be the family attorney. We plan to open a medical office together, and my brother will be the family practice attorney.

Gotta keep the family legacy strong," he said. "That's how you create generational wealth. Keep it in the family. I don't think I'll take over either one of my parents' practices because I don't plan to live where I grew up," he paused. "But we'll have that discussion in a few years. I'm really enjoying medical school, even though some days I feel like it's kicking my butt!"

Teenie smiled into the receiver. "It's fun to finally hear you stressed about something little Mr. I Don't Have a Care in the World!"

"I'm definitely stressed. My parents laugh when I complain about how tired I am and remind me that I'd be just as tired if I were in law school. But they're not sweating me too tough since I graduated a year early from Georgetown. They're loving that I saved them a year of that tuition," he offered. "But enough about me, why are you in your room? I really didn't think that I'd catch you. I thought I'd get your answering machine."

"You almost didn't catch me," she said. "My parents are downstairs waiting for me so we can go to dinner," she explained. "I was just about to call my friends Laura and Monica so they could come to dinner with us, since their parents dropped them off early," she paused. "My dad is feeling all paternal and wants to make sure that I'm not here lonely," she smiled. "And of course you know I have to go the bathroom," she giggled.

"Know that," he laughed. "When I have a spare moment, I'm going to do some research on how we can reinforce your bladder," he teased. "There's got to be something they can do for you, Teenie tiny bladder," he laughed. "That's the real reason why I chose medical school over law school. I want to find a cure for your tiny bladder, Teenie!" he laughed.

"Finish medical school before you start trying to come up

with cures, Dr. Barton," she giggled.

"Where are you going to dinner?" he asked.

"I have absolutely no idea. My dad did some research and found a restaurant just off campus. I'm sure it'll be a seafood restaurant since my father loves crab," she said.

"Have your parents moved yet?" David asked.

"They're moving next weekend," Teenie replied. "I can't believe that you remembered that."

"My memory is like a steel trap," he grinned. "They're moving to a house in Plum Creek. I remembered that because when I took you home a few years ago when we hung out at Todd's house after he broke his arm, you told me that your family was supposed to move to Plum Creek, but they didn't because your parents got a divorce," he rattled. "My memory is a steel trap, baby!"

"Wow!" Teenie exclaimed.

"They're not moving into the same house that you almost moved into before are they? That would be quite ironic," David offered.

"No. It's a different house, but I like this house better because it gets more sunlight," Teenie explained. "The other house had a lot of trees on the lot, so the rooms seemed dark," she explained. "Not that it should matter to me since I really won't live there. But at least when I come home for breaks I can enjoy the new digs."

"Exactly. Does it feel weird that your parents are remarried now?" David asked.

"Not really," Teenie shrugged. "That's not true," she corrected. "At first it did, but now it feels normal again."

"Well," David yawned. "I'll let you go so you can call your friends and get to dinner," David yawned again.

"Am I boring you?" Teenie teased.

"Not a chance," David offered. "I'm just tired. Medical school is intense."

"I'm so glad you called me," Teenie smiled. "What a nice surprise."

"I'll call you in a few. Feel free to write me a letter if you get bored," he suggested. "But don't be mad when I don't write you back," he cautioned. "I'll call you more than I'll write you. I'm not a writer."

"Aye, aye, Captain," Teenie smiled.

"And don't forget to bring me a Yale sweatshirt when I see you at Thanksgiving," David reminded. "I'll send you a check for it. But don't wait until the last minute because the good ones will be picked over," he cautioned.

"David, you don't have to send me a check for it," Teenie groaned. "I can buy you a sweatshirt," she scolded. "I'm pretty flush these days between the summer job money that I hoarded away, and my scholarship money," she boasted.

"It feels that way now," he cautioned. "But once you start taking road trips, and buying sweatshirts and eating out a lot, your account will start to deflate," he warned. "I'm sending you a check for my sweatshirt. You don't need to buy me any gifts," he barked. "My parents are loaded and I have a trust fund. You are not to spend your money on me. End of discussion, Tanisha."

"You are such a bull headed, male chauvinist pig," she snorted.

"If you want to do something nice for me, you can bake me some cookies and send them to me, or write me letters," he advised. "Now scoot and spend some time with your parents before they leave," he ordered. "By the way, pick up Sting's soundtrack, 'Dream of the Blue Turtles,'" David suggested. "I know you like The Police so you'll love it. Bye, Teenie," he yawned.

"Bye, David," she smiled. "Get some rest." Hanging up the phone, she squeezed her knees together before racing around the corner and into the small bathroom, glad that her room was a mere ten steps from the bathroom's entrance.

∽◌◌

Glancing at her watch, as she walked through the dorm lobby, waving briefly at the evening desk clerk, she noticed that she had just enough time to drop off her packages before meeting her friends at Yesterday's Restaurant for their Sunday night dinner.

"And don't wait until the last minute, or the good ones will be picked over," he'd said.

With just two days before Thanksgiving break, she had indeed waited until the last minute. He'd sent her a check a week after their phone chat, the note barely legible: 'Buy me a cool Yale sweatshirt' he wrote. 'Not a nerdy Yale sweatshirt. Talk to ya later gator – D.' The letters size XL scrawled across the top.

I hope this is a cool Yale sweatshirt. He'll like it. As she walked toward her door, she could see that she had a new message on her message board.

Teenie, We'll meet you in the lobby for chow. Usual time. Laura

Keying into her room, she plopped the shopping bag in front of her closet and walked over to the light on her blinking answering machine and hit play.

"You have three new messages," the machine said. "Message one."

"Teenie, It's David. I never balance my checkbook, but my mom keeps telling me that there's a check out of sequence that hasn't been cashed yet. Did you get the check that I sent you for the sweatshirt? I hope you got me a cool sweatshirt. Cash my check, Tanisha! Call me later. It's Sunday. I'll be in labs all day today. I get home on Tuesday, so let me know if you want me to pick you up from the airport on Wednesday when you come home for Thanksgiving. I'm looking forward to finally meeting your parents."

"Message two."

"Hi Tanisha. It's Mommy. Just checking to see how your week went, and your dad wants to know if you want him to pick you up from the airport. Call us tonight."

"Message three."

"Hey Teenie. It's your Princeton Prince, just checking on his Yale Princess. I've decided not to go home for Thanksgiving. My folks are going to come East and we're going to stay at our place in Manhattan. I know this is last minute, but why don't you come with us? My parents keep an apartment on Riverside Drive and they said that you could spend Thanksgiving with me and my family. We could ice skate in Rockefeller Center and watch them turn on the big Christmas tree lights and catch a show on Broadway. Call me later."

Teenie stared from the phone to the answering machine, her eyes like a pendulum on a grandfather clock. As if on cue, the phone rang. She swallowed hard and stared at the ringing phone afraid to face her fate.

Chapter 3

All Good Things

The dirty blankets hugged his shoulders, a tattered barrier against the autumn wind that whipped from the lake. A stack of hats sat atop his head, his unshaven face was care worn and wind burned from years spent braving the fierce Chicago winters. Transfixed, she wondered at his age, her attention momentarily diverted by the business men and women who quickened their pace in response to the arctic chill, seemingly oblivious to the homeless man. Justine stared in amazement as he unceremoniously discarded the crumpled paper sack onto the pavement and dove back into the steel waste basket, carefully opening a polystyrene food container. Noticeably excited with his culinary treasure, he leaned against the wooden train stairs and used his grubby fingers as a fork, eagerly scooping the contents into his mouth and chewing aggressively. Disgusted, yet curious, she watched as he carelessly tossed the food container into the street and reached back into the trash, sipping on a half filled beverage that teetered on its side. The pink lemonade apparent through the clear colored straw, he gulped quickly before tossing the cup into the street and diving back into his cylindrical buffet. She shook her head in disgust as the white food container took flight and glided down Randolph Street like a square kite.

Saddened by this display of social injustice and irony, Justine turned from the window just as the elevated train barreled overhead, barely audible through the thick glass panes. A businessman in a suit smiled and waved at her through the window. She smiled and waved, hoping that he wouldn't come in and flirt with her. Her monthly quota had long since been met.

Justine had grown accustomed to the male traders, lawyers and bankers who grinned at her through the window, casually returning the next day as if they'd just seen her for the first time. Their left hands were always discreetly tucked into their pocket or gripping a newspaper that shielded the gold or platinum band encircling their ring finger. Her sales were the highest in the department, and she knew this was due in part to her mastery of the game.

Like a spider catching a fly in her web, she'd mastered the art of luring customers into her sweater boutique. The corner location, with windows facing Randolph and Wabash, proved the perfect sales perch to pitch the over priced hand knit sweaters.

When the store manager had first moved Justine from the ladies apparel department, she'd protested vigorously.

"I don't understand why I'm being moved, Miss Cecelia," Justine stated. "I have higher sales than any other associate in the department. My week day full price sales are top notch, and I am the only one who pushes the promotions," she whined.

Her manager resembled Nancy Wilson with her warm honey skin and perfectly coiffed salt and pepper hair. The natural silver frost highlights and perfect waves hinted that she visited the salon every day, a suggestion that she denied vehemently. Nonetheless, not a hair ever dared venture out of place on Miss Cecelia's head. Her thin frame was always draped in the finest couture the store had to offer, and some couture that was sold by the store's biggest competitors on either side of North Michigan Avenue and Oak Street.

Cecelia Cornet was a slave to fashion, and if her tastes could not be satisfied by her store's extensive couture selection, she ventured further down the Magnificent Mile until her appetite was satiated. A fashion matriarch in Chicago, she received employee discount privileges from her vast army of peers in the retail industry, so she never paid full price for anything at any store. She reciprocated this favor at her store. Cecelia was the Field Store matriarch and knew where all of the retail bodies were buried. Plus, she was the best. The departments under her tutelage always led the region in top sales. Always. Cecelia Cornet was a sales master. She smiled warmly at Justine and patted her on the shoulder, her perfectly manicured nails resting on Justine's shoulder.

"You're special, Justine," Cecelia smiled. "That's why I allow you to call me Miss Cecelia instead of Miss Cornet like everyone else," she purred. "You remind me of me when I was just starting out in the business," she winked.

"But I like working in the designer label department," Justine whined. "I don't know if I'll be as good selling in the men's department. I feel like I'll be starting over, and I don't want to lose my competitive edge," she explained. "I'm on track to be top sales leader for the store."

Cecelia had introduced Justine to the little square Essie brand nail polish that she now favored and encouraged her to keep her nails painted a neutral color. Justine had modeled her mentor and begun painting her nails the marshmallow, ballet slippers or East Hampton cottage colors, sometimes mixing the shades for variation as Miss Cecelia had suggested. Reaching for Justine's hand, she smiled approvingly at Justine's neat nails.

"You won't, sweetie pie," Cecelia said softly. "You're my best sales girl. Which is why I need you on the main floor in the men's department," she paused. "I'll teach you the rules of the game. You are to report there tomorrow. I will be there to show you the ropes myself," she winked before walking away.

True to form, Cecelia coached Justine on the nuances of selling apparel to men. "Men aren't like women. Gay men like to buy from gay men," she coached. "But our gay clients will buy from you if you know how to handle them," she advised. "But straight men like a pretty woman to help them select their clothes. Straight men don't like to browse. They want to be told what they'll look good in and guided toward the purchase," she explained.

"I haven't been around that many gay men before," Justine stammered. "How can I tell the difference?" she asked innocently. "How will I know if a man is gay or straight?" she asked.

"Don't worry, baby," Cecelia paused. "You'll be able to tell," she smiled. "In fact, your legs, chest and shoes will tell you," she winked.

She'd been right. The gay customers complimented Justine on her shoes and clothes. The straight customers complimented Justine on her beauty. She felt like she was on display, like a caged animal in the small corner sweater boutique. The music blaring through a speaker perched on the corner. The music made them look toward the window, and her short skirts made them take a double take, like the women parading in the windows of the red light district of Amsterdam. The short skirts had also been Cecelia's idea.

"I remember when my legs were perfectly toned and stretched

up to my waist," Cecelia smiled.

"Your legs are still slamming, Miss Cecelia," Justine smiled. "Your legs look like Tina Turner's legs, and so do your arms."

"My legs are still my best feature," she agreed. "And they say that the legs are the last to go," Cecelia bemused. "But back in the day, my legs were like Dorothy Dandridge. You have legs like a Soul Train dancer," she winked. "And your arms are perfectly toned like mine. Don't hide your best assets," she coached. "Work with what God gave you."

Justine wished that she'd been tracking her sales based on the length of her skirts. The shorter the skirt she wore, the more they bought. The monochromatic shoe and tight look was her favorite, her legs resembling two long licorice sticks. White men, black men, Asian men, it didn't matter. When she smiled at them in the window, they came into the store. She could imagine the mental gymnastics as they calculated the next Metra train that they would take, and the story they'd concoct to their wives as they walked in with an expensive hand knit sweater.

Justine imagined that their stories were always the same. "I've been thinking about buying one of these sweaters," they'd say. "You can tell the kids to give me this sweater for father's day or my birthday," they'd suggest.

Anticipating the client's entrance into the store, Justine would pop a mint in her mouth as she prepared to invade his personal space.

"Let me guess," she'd purr, her peppermint breath caressing his skin as she gripped the client's bicep gently, yet firmly. "You're an extra large sweater, right?" she'd grin, her long eyelashes batting overtime.

"I am," he'd smile. "You're good."

"I'm the best," she'd wink. "You have a warm fall glow to your skin, so I'd recommend a burnt orange sweater to compliment your natural tonality," she'd suggest. "Have you had your color chart read?" Justine would ask.

"No, I haven't," he'd stammer.

"You should. Your color chart tells you the colors that work best with your skin tone and chemistry," she'd offer. "You should always stay in the warm family: oranges, reds, soft yellows, café," she'd suggest. "The grays, blues and blacks are for men with a winter tonality," she'd explain as she tossed him a bright colored sweater.

"I've never owned a yellow sweater in my life," he'd protest.

"Try one on," she'd encourage. "Let's see how it looks," she'd coax as she gripped his briefcase and helped him remove his suit jacket, her fingertips gently caressing his back. "The fitting room is right in there. Start with these two. Come out when you have them on," she'd smile.

Moments later, she'd sold two sweaters that were days from being placed on the clearance rack.

"Would you like to have lunch sometime?" he'd ask nervously, his left hand still discreetly shielded by something in his hand. "I'd love to learn more about the color analysis techniques," he'd say as he handed her his platinum American Express card.

Justine would grin widely as she swiped the card. "You're so nice to offer," she'd reply. "I'd love to do a color analysis for you. Let me take your business card. Call me at the store next week and we'll get together," she'd grin.

"Great!" he'd blush. "I can't believe that I've never had a color analysis," he'd stammer.

"Well, everyone should have their color palette explained so that they know what flatters them," she'd smile. "Although with your skin tone, you can wear almost all of the colors on the palette," she'd suggest. "What do you do for a living, George?" she'd ask reading his name from his credit card.

"I'm a banker, lawyer, trader," he'd offer, his chest poking out an extra inch as he paid for the two hundred dollar sweater. "I'll call you next week, Justine."

After placing an identifying comment on each card, Justine would toss the card into the drawer adjacent to the register. George was given a large MbbY in small letters which stood for mustache, bad breath & bought yellow sweater. She'd decided to curate the business cards by profession and had placed tally marks in each section. During slow times in the sweater section, she studied her business card file to refresh her memory on her client's features. The bankers outnumbered the lawyer cards that she'd collected by a slim margin. When sales were really slow, she would call a customer to let him know that a sweater in a color that he'd admired had gone on sale.

Usually, her sweater sales conquest would call her two or three times to schedule a lunch, and each time, she'd be too busy to talk to him. Sometimes, the bold ones would return to the store wearing the sweater on casual Friday. She would fawn over how good they looked in the sweater and greet them by their first name, which always surprised the customer. Her tone filled with honey, Justine would apologize for not being available to dine with him, gripping his bicep softly and assuring him that she'd try to be available the next time he called. She would seize the opportunity to show him a new sweater that arrived and usually nailed another sale. It was usually on this second trip to the store that she would casually notice the band on his ring finger. She always feigned shock and dismay.

"I didn't realize that you were married. How long have you been married, Oliver?" she'd ask, a hint of sadness in her tone.

"I thought you saw that I was married," he'd say softly.

"I just noticed your ring," she'd comment. "And I'm sorry, Ted," she'd pause. "But I don't do lunch dates with married men."

"It's not a date," he'd stammer. "I just want you to read my color palette."

"Tell you what, Brink," she'd say coyly. "Invite your wife to join us for lunch and I'll read both your color palettes," she'd offer.

The calls and visits usually stopped after that.

She decided to straighten the sweaters on the shelf, repositioning the colors to coincide with the new window display.

I hope my replacement is on time today. If I'm late for class tonight, my professor is going to peel my head. I hope this test is easy.

Justine walked behind the register and pulled out her notebook. The Blue Demon glaring back at her from the wire notebook's cover, menacing and mean looking.

I can't believe that I paid two dollars extra for these DePaul notebooks. This Blue Demon thing is scary looking. It's what freshman do, Justine. Get in the spirit of your school, cheapskate. You work, and you're clocking serious cash now. You can afford the logo notebooks!

Justine doodled in the last page of her notebook. She'd recently dropped one of her classes which changed her status from full-time to part-time. AM's voice rang in her head.

"Don't get so caught up making money that you lose sight of your goal. Remember, it may seem like a lot of money now," he warned. "But in five years, when your cohort has their college degree, their salaries are going to outpace you," AM advised.

"But it's fun," she defended. "It's a challenge to see how much I can sell. I'll still maintain my full time status," she said.

"Are you still upset that you didn't get accepted to Boston College?" he asked.

"Not anymore," she lied. "And I'm not mad at you that you took your scholarship to Harvard Med," she offered. "How can you turn down a full ride at Harvard Medical School? It would have been foolish to take out loans to go to Northwestern when Harvard is giving you free money," she finished.

The farewell had been difficult. She looked forward to seeing him over Thanksgiving break, but had just learned that she would have to work the entire weekend.

"It's black Friday," Miss Cecelia advised. "This is the busiest shopping weekend of the year. You will have to work all weekend, Justine," she warned. "All associates are scheduled for a full shift from Wednesday through Sunday." For the first time in the store's history, Field was open on Thanksgiving Day from nine o'clock a.m. until one o'clock p.m. Miss Cecelia was running several door buster specials during this peak time and would be unveiling the store's Christmas window displays. "You'll receive double time on Thanksgiving Day and time and a half on Friday, Saturday and Sunday," she explained. "That should motivate you not to call in sick," she winked.

ಎಃಜ

"Justine, what's going on?" AM asked. "We agreed that we would spend Thanksgiving together. We haven't seen each other since I left in August," he stated.

"I know," she whispered. "And you can still come, but I'll have to work," she suggested.

"Why are you whispering?" he whispered. "Why am I whispering?"

Justine chuckled softly. "A whisper always begets a whisper, as Tanisha says. But I'm whispering because I'm at work. They called me in to work today because someone called in sick," she explained.

"But don't you have an English lit class on Thursday afternoons?" AM asked.

Smiling at how quickly he'd memorized her schedule, she winced. "I do, but it's a lecture so I can get the notes from someone over the weekend," she assured. "When you come for Thanksgiving, you can study while I'm at work, and then when I finish my shift, we can hangout," she offered.

"But you'll be tired from being on your feet all day," he reminded. "And I wasn't planning to bring my heavy books on the plane because I was looking forward to taking a much needed break from my studies over the long Thanksgiving weekend," he said. "I'm ahead in all of my labs and need to get away from the books for a few days."

"Well, you can tour all of the museums," she encouraged. "You can visit the Art Institute of Chicago and the Shed Aquarium and Field Museum," she suggested. "I know how much you love the museums."

"It's a holiday weekend, so the museums will be full of tacky tourists," he said. "Besides, I don't want to go alone. The point of me coming to Chicago is to spend time with you, Justine," AM reminded.

Justine sighed softly. "AM, I have a customer waiting," she said softly. "So I'm going to have to call you back. I'll call you tonight."

That night, they'd talked on the phone for over an hour. She'd been unprepared for AM's attitude.

"This isn't working, Justine," AM blurted. "I'm not a long distance relationship type of guy," he continued. "That's why I really wanted us to go to school in the same city."

"What are you saying, AM?" she asked. "Are you breaking up with me?"

"I think I am," he said. "I don't see any other way. With my crazy study and lab schedule, it's impossible for us to talk on the phone," he said. "And when I have a break in the middle of my day," he paused. "You're at work at Field and can't talk. And now I can't even see you at Thanksgiving. This just isn't working for me," he finished. "We need to take a break. Let's pull back from each other and reassess how we're feeling in a few weeks," he continued. "I need to get through my next set of exams, and this relationship is causing me too much stress right now. Let's plan to talk over the December break."

"So that's it?" she said. "We've been apart for less than three months, and because I have to work, you want to break up?"

"That's just it, Justine," AM said. "You're choosing to work. You don't have to work. There's a difference," he paused. "You are supposed to be a college student, not a sales associate. You're spending more time working than studying. Your priorities have shifted, not mine," he finished.

And so it went. Every argument she presented, he posed a counter argument. After sixty minutes of word volley, he ended the call abruptly, telling her that a few weeks apart to sort out their feelings would do them both some good. AM promised to call her during his Christmas break, and then he hung up the telephone.

Her body numb, Justine faked a stomach virus so she wouldn't have to face her family at dinner. Her brothers might not notice, but she knew that eagle eye Andrea would know that she'd been crying, and Justine didn't want to explain the puffiness around her eyes to her mother. Turning her body toward the wall, she buried her face in her pillow when Nurse Andrea came in to check on her. Content that Justine was not running a temperature, and believing her when she'd said that she'd already taken an antacid to soothe her stomach, Justine exhaled when her mother left the room. Using her pillow as a silencer, Justine quietly sobbed herself to sleep in her clothes. Awaking a few hours later to pee, her stomach churned from hunger. She squinted at the alarm clock teetering on the edge of her armoire, the numbers a fuzzy red haze. Reaching for her glasses, she breathed deeply and placed her spectacles on her nose. The clock read ten thirty two. She reached for the phone to call AM before he unplugged his phone at eleven o'clock. Her finger poised to dial, she stared at the phone and remembered that they'd broken up.

It had taken her almost three days to confess the break up to her mother.

"AM and I broke up," Justine mentioned while chopping an onion for dinner. Her tear ducts already moist from chopping the onion, she knew that her mother wouldn't be able to discern the onion injected tears from the heartbreak tears.

"I'm sorry, Sweetie," her mother replied seriously. "What happened?"

Justine gave her mother the Cliff notes version of the break up, stopping short of sharing that she'd dropped a class changing her status from full time to part-time. She needed sympathy from her mother, not a lecture.

Andrea had continued to prepare the meatloaf and listened quietly. "All good things sometimes come to an end," she said casually. "It's a sad fact of life. One person changes and the other person feels left behind," she paused. "People grow apart. If there's one thing that I know it's that in order to stay in a healthy relationship, you have to take the people you love with you," she suggested.

"But I didn't get into Boston College, Mom," Justine whined. "So it wouldn't have made sense for me to move to Boston."

"I don't mean physically take the person with you, Justine," her mother corrected. "But you have to be evenly yoked with your partner. You have to be willing to reinvent yourself so that you have new and fresh experiences to share with your boyfriend or mate," she said. "Within reason of course," she added.

"So if AM started riding motorcycles and getting tattoos all over his body, in order to keep him interested in me I'd need to do the same?" Justine asked sarcastically.

"Not necessarily. But people don't really change that much, Justine," her mother explained. "If AM was going to be interested in tattoos and motorcycles you'd know it by now. What I'm talking about is more basic," she said. "He's in medical school right now, and you're spending more time working at Field than studying at DePaul," she said gently. "It sounds like you've altered the rules of your relationship game," she said as she sautéed the ground turkey. "Maybe AM wants his girlfriend to be a full time student and a part-time sales clerk and not the other way around."

Stunned, Justine stared at her mother, wondering if she'd been listening to her conversation.

"Your father and I are paying your tuition, Justine," Andrea offered. "I just got the letter that you dropped one of your classes which makes you a part-time student now. When were you going to tell us?" Andrea asked as she peppered the turkey.

Her head down, Justine reached for the yellow pepper and began to chop it. "I was going to mention that to you, Mom," she stammered. "But I've been upset about breaking up with AM," she confessed.

"I don't want to pick on you while your heart is broken," Andrea offered. "And you're an adult now, so I don't mean to be all up in your boyfriend business," she paused. "But AM is a very practical, goal oriented young man so I wouldn't be surprised if he became concerned that your priorities have shifted from your academic pursuits to a life as a retail maven," she said. "Not that there's anything wrong with a career in the retail industry, but you don't have to work, Justine. Your father and I are paying your tuition," her mother reminded. "You're choosing to work. Besides, if you decide that a career in retail is something that you want to pursue, you'll have to work weekends and evenings," she reminded. "You won't have time to be in a relationship, especially if your boyfriend is in the medical profession. AM might be thinking way ahead of you."

Justine continued to chop silently, wiping a tear with the sleeve of her sweatshirt.

"You have your entire life to work, Justine. This is your time to focus on your studies and the life experiences to be learned from being a college student," Andrea advised gently. "I don't want you to miss out on the young adult college experience because you enjoy making money. There will always be money to be made," she coached. "You do realize that your father and I are only paying for college until you're twenty-two?" Andrea reminded. "And then you're on your own. Now I expect you to make up this class over the summer so that you can achieve sophomore status next fall,

Justine. In fact, your father and I are thinking that it might be best if you applied to a school further away so you can live in the dorms," she suggested. "I was a commuter student because my parents couldn't afford to pay for my room and board. But I think living in the dorms is an experience that you should have. Your dad wants you to think about Notre Dame," she finished.

"Notre Dame!" Justine blurted. "Just because Daddy attended Notre Dame, doesn't mean that I want to go there," she whined.

"At least give it a thought," Mrs. Wellington encouraged. "It doesn't have to be Notre Dame, but we want you to start your sophomore year at a new school. And as for AM, if it's meant to be, it'll work itself out, sweetie," she paused. "Affairs of the heart always do."

Justine chopped the yellow pepper as a tear slid down her face and on to the tip of the cutting board.

"I can finish making dinner," her mother said gently, removing the knife from her hand. "Why don't you go to your room and study?"

Without a word, Justine walked down the hall, the floorboards creaking softly beneath her bare feet. She leaned against her door and stared at her textbooks.

Chapter 4

Hot Cross Buns

Carefully folding the large, yellow bath towel into a tight tri-fold, she placed it on top of the laundry basket before inhaling deeply, her nose enjoying the sweet smell of fabric softener. She remembered to bend at the knee before lifting the clothes. Rashanda cradled the basket in one arm, as she turned the door handle with her free hand. Sighing loudly, the three flights of stairs loomed like Mt. Everest. Bracing herself for her climb, she mounted the stairs with the bravery of Sir Hilary and ascended the cement mountain one step at a time.

At least this dorm has a laundry room in the basement. I shouldn't complain, because I could be dragging the laundry to the Davis Street Laundromat in the frigid cold.

Once at her destination, she balanced the basket against the door and leaned down to insert the key that dangled from the chain on her neck, an adornment that she wore daily to prevent herself from the typical freshman dorm room lockouts. As the door swung open, she was greeted by a cool breeze billowing from the window. A welcome respite from the hot laundry room, but the sweet lake air was no match for the thick heat that fumed from the radiator. Sighing, she placed the laundry basket on a chair and fanned herself.

The following week, Evanston had experienced an unusual cold spell for late September, with temperatures dropping into the low forties. The students complained loudly, but unless the temperatures dipped below thirty two degrees Fahrenheit, the dormitory furnace could not be turned on until October 1st without special written approval from the office of the President. Days later, in typical Chicago fashion, October 1st was one of the warmest days on record, with temperatures in the low eighties. The students now pranced around the dorm in tee shirts and shorts, complaining about the incessant heat which blared through the radiator like a cruel joke. The second summer had lingered for five days, with the cool Lake Michigan breeze providing occasional relief from the sweltering heat that spiraled through the hallways.

Almost daily, a new note was plastered on Ian's message board door. Rashanda laughed at some of the more clever wordings from the witty Northwestern students who displayed their prose proudly. "The heat is so intoxicating that I feel like a dizzy blood clot on a gyrating floor," read one. Another boasted, "Sir Ian, Please summon the power that you have with the bourgeoisie academic establishment so that the lowly proletariat doesn't die of heat exhaustion. Signed your humble heat exhausted servants." "I have a cousin who lives in the projects of Boston, and their apartment was always ghetto hot. I feel like J.J. on Good Times! Adjust the heat, dude!" One female student wrote, "Will I be written up for parading around the dorm in my bikini? I usually don a bikini when the temps are in the eighties, whether indoors or out." When the message board was full, the students plastered his door with index cards affixed with tape or chewed bubble gum. Rashanda had decided to stick the notes into a photo album scrapbook, carefully removing the bubble gum with a napkin.

Rashanda laughed as she read, amused by the students' creativity. Ian ignored the postings, chuckling slightly as she read them aloud.

"I'm not God," he shrugged. "I can't control the weather. Two weeks ago they were begging us to turn on the heat," he reminded. "And now that it's on, they want it turned down. If I have the super adjust the boiler, and the temps drop into the thirties next week, it'll take forever to warm up this old dorm again," he paused. "Then they'll be complaining that it's too cold. They'll get over it. Students just need a cause du jour," he finished.

"But it is really hot in here, Ian," Rashanda agreed. "Can't he just adjust it temporarily and then adjust it back up when it gets colder?" she asked.

"It's not quite that simple. The boiler is almost forty years old, and it's very temperamental. We're lucky that thing is still pumping out heat. I don't want him to tinker with it now that winter is upon us. Besides, they're running a capital campaign to raise funds to replace the old boilers in the older dorms this summer. Hopefully they'll be able to raise the money so they don't have to increase tuition," he explained. "Which dorm do you want to dine at tonight, pretty lady?" he asked.

As the resident hall coordinator for Courtyard, the off-campus dorm that overlooked the Ryan Football stadium, Ian was accustomed to student complaints. He'd spent his sophomore and junior year as a resident assistant, consoling the homesick freshman, and coaching the type A, grade conscious students through their first set of midterms and finals while helping others navigate the financial aid labyrinth to design creative ways to help pay their tuition costs. He'd been named RA of the year and chosen as the resident hall coordinator for Courtyard, one of the larger dorms on

Northwestern's campus. Rashanda was proud of him.

The year before, while visiting Ian for the day, Rashanda had watched in awe as he expertly averted an employment crisis when the freshman girls hired to work in the mailroom threatened to quit. Over the two week Christmas break, there were no arrangements made for mail sorting, which meant that the young girls returned from their brief respite home for the holidays to fourteen gray bags the size of an eight year old child, each brimming with mail and packages. To complicate the dismal situation, some of the less patient dorm residents were awaiting mail and harassing the mail clerks to sort faster. The situation was ripe for mutiny. The students and mailroom clerks raced to Ian's door to voice their fury. Rashanda watched as Ian stepped into the hallway and listened to each complaint. As though he'd been anticipating the conflict, he calmly and quickly posed a solution that silenced each complainant.

"As the RA in charge of mail distribution," the irate student argued. "You should have had them here to sort the mail to avoid this issue," he finished arrogantly. "Or they should be down there working around the clock until our mail is sorted and in our boxes. This is ridiculous!" he ranted.

"I see," Ian said. "First of all, since the dorms were closed over the Christmas break, it would have been against university policy for anyone to be in the dorms. The alarm system was engaged and the heat was turned down to fifty eight degrees," he offered calmly. "The dorm room mail was stacked in the main lobby where the alarm system is bypassed," he explained, lifting his hand swiftly to silence the student who was poised to interrupt.

"Secondly, why should the mailroom clerks have to give up their holiday to do their job when no other work study students were asked to do the same?" he asked, continuing without a reply.

"That would have been ludicrous. And as I'm sure you're aware, these ladies are students just like you, which means that they have classes and have to study just like you," Ian grinned. "Besides, there is only so much money in the work study budget to pay the students and I can't have these ladies working crazy hours or they'll eat through all of their work study money before the quarter is even over," he paused, again raising his hand with a grin to silence the aggressive student. "But there is a solution to this dilemma that will work for everyone," he grinned.

"The way I see it," Ian paused. "This is a dorm problem. And everyone who is concerned about how quickly the mail gets sorted needs to get involved in the solution. It's a team effort."

"But it's not my job to sort the mail," another student blurted loudly. "They're paid to sort the mail. They need to do their job!"

"And they'll sort the mail in a reasonable amount of time," Ian assured. "If you don't mind my asking, what are you expecting in the mail that has your blood pressure boiling over how soon the mail gets sorted?" Ian asked.

"My grandmother sent me a check forgetting that I would be home for Christmas break," the student explained. "And I really need that check," he said, his arms folded across his chest.

"Tell you what," Ian offered. "I'll loan you the amount of your grandmother's check, right now and you can pay me back when you get your check."

The student stared at Ian softly. "Dude, the check was for five hundred dollars!" he exclaimed. "You're going to loan me five hundred dollars?"

"Sure. I'll write you a check today. But you're going to sign a promissory note that will be signed by both of us and the mail clerks as witnesses that you will pay me back within one week. If not, you will owe me my principal plus five percent in penalties," Ian explained.

"Wow!" the student grinned. "That would really help me out. I need to pay to have my car repaired, and without that car I can't get to my off campus internship," he explained. "The repairs cost three hundred, so if you could loan me the three hundred until we find my check, I'd really appreciate that," he smiled warmly.

"Done. Does anyone else have a dire financial issue that needs to be addressed today," he paused. "I'm not a bank, but I'm willing to help if I can." His eyes panned the small mob before continuing. "Now the mail clerks normally spend two hours sorting and stuffing the dorm mail each day," Ian shared. "Which means that we currently have twenty-eight hours of mail sorting to do," he paused. "Now, all of the students in our dorm signed a covenant that we would perform eight hours of community service each month," he shared.

The angry mob stood silently and listened intently as Ian continued. "And as the RA, I have the power to approve the community service projects that my dorm students choose. And in my opinion, fourteen bags of mail certainly qualifies as a project that impacts our dorm community," he continued.

"But I was planning to volunteer at the soup kitchen for my community service obligation," one of the mail clerks offered.

"And you still can," Ian assured. "But I'm willing to give you credit for sorting the mail, so technically you'll be getting paid for sorting the mail and fulfilling your community service obligation at the same time," he explained. "It may seem like double dipping to some of the students, but I want to provide an incentive for both of you to give as many extra hours as you can, and you'll need to train some of the other students to serve as shift leaders.

We'll have different sign up times so that students can sort when it's convenient for them," he continued. "In fact, I'm going to put up flyers in the lobby to see how many students we can get to help us," he said.

"I'm an art major, so I can draft up some flyers quickly," one student offered. "And I'll place them around the dorm tonight."

"Fabulous!" Ian grinned. "With enough laborers, we'll be caught up on the mail sorting in a couple of days," he smiled. "Or sooner, if we have a few night owls who want to work a midnight shift," he said. "I'll spring for snacks and sodas from my student activity budget," he shared. "We'll have a mail sorting party!" he grinned.

Ian's suggestion had worked brilliantly. Before proceeding, he'd quickly shared his idea with the dean in charge of student housing for her approval. Not only had she approved of the idea, but she'd encouraged all of her dorm leaders to do the same. The Daily Northwestern student newspaper had run an article touting Ian's creativity in devising a campus wide solution that had plagued each dorm for years. The following year, the school planned to sponsor a competition between the larger dorms to see which dorm could sort and deliver their dorm's holiday mail the quickest.

So it was no surprise when Ian had been named the youngest Resident Hall Coordinator of the Courtyard dorm as a senior, a responsibility typically reserved only for graduate students. The coveted role came with an enviable one bedroom apartment that boasted a tub bathroom, galley style kitchen and a terrace.

Rashanda reached for a tissue and wiped her nose, not surprised when the tissue was stained red. The heat and humidity had made her nose bleed again. She walked into the bathroom and quickly sniffed from the bottle of alcohol, a trick that Grace's mother had suggested. "Just take two sniffs from a bottle of rubbing alcohol, and it'll dry that nosebleed right on up," Mrs. Dudley said. Staring at the light pink tissue, Rashanda grinned at the wisdom garnered from the old wives tales that reminded her of her grandmother, Big Momma.

The door slammed quickly while she was in the bathroom. She wiped her nostril with a tissue.

"Hey there," she sang into the hallway. "I'm in the bathroom," she offered. Content that the nose bleed had stopped completely, she quickly washed her hands.

"Make sure you spray," he yelled down the small corridor, his voice filled with laughter.

"Ha ha! You're back early," she said. "I thought you had a tutoring session today."

"I did, but the student cancelled," Ian explained. "Which is fine by me because when they don't give me twenty four hours notice, I still get paid," he grinned.

Rashanda walked into the living room and plopped on the sofa, resting her feet on the small wooden coffee table that came with the furnished apartment. Ian rifled through the mail, tossing the envelopes on the dining room table. When his eyes noticed the large laundry basket resting on a chair, he turned and frowned at Rashanda.

"Rashanda, I told you that I would take care of the laundry tonight," Ian said. "You shouldn't be lifting heavy things any more," he scolded.

"It wasn't that heavy," Rashanda dismissed, shifting her weight on the sofa and placing a throw pillow beneath her feet and behind her back. "And I knew you had tutoring so I thought I'd just do the laundry," she explained.

"But the doctor said that with the spotting, you should take it easy and not lift heavy things," he reminded. "Listen to the doctor, Rashanda," he scolded. "Were you spotting?"

"No," she replied. "But I had another nose bleed," she shared. "But it was a light one."

Ian walked over and opened the patio door. "This heat wave shouldn't last too much longer," he assured. "And I'll buy a humidifier tomorrow to help keep the air moist," he suggested.

"Or we could just put a pitcher of water near the radiator," she offered. "Grace's mother told me that a pitcher of water works just as well as a humidifier," she finished.

"She's right," Ian agreed. "That's a good idea. Back in the day people didn't just run out and spend money on things the way we do now," he paused. "They didn't have it to spend so they had to improvise and come up with creative solutions," he continued. "Necessity was definitely the mother of invention. And unfortunately, the creation of wealth has made people lazy and fat," he sighed.

Rashanda smiled at Ian from the sofa, watching as he absentmindedly sorted through the mail. "Obesity is on the rise because people are spending more time watching people play sports on television than participating in activities themselves," he ranted. "At the clinic today, this overweight woman came in trying to get the doctor to give her a handicap sticker so she could park in handicap spots when she goes to the store and work," he chuckled. "She told the doctor that she needed it because she has high blood pressure," he paused. Rashanda listened intently and placed another pillow behind her lower back.

"Can you believe that? If she would park farther away, she might lose a few pounds which would lower her blood pressure," he continued. "And that's exactly what the doctor told her. Of course, the patient was not too pleased," he said. "It's ridiculous. I'm not even finished with medical school yet, and I know the correlation between diet, exercise and hypertension," he boasted. "Reduce your caloric intake, increase your time spent exercising and your blood pressure will lower. It's really not rocket science," he continued. "And childhood obesity is on the rise too because these kids spend more time playing video games than they do playing outside," he trailed.

"Ian, I'm hungry," Rashanda interrupted.

As though snapping out of a trance Ian raced to Rashanda's side and sat by her on the sofa. "I'm so sorry, I was having a moment," he offered. "You know how worked up I get about health issues. I'll get the car and we can have dinner at 1835 Hinman today," he suggested.

"But then you'll lose your good parking space," Rashanda reminded. "Let's just go to Elder," she suggested. "I don't mind walking, and the food at Elder has gotten better."

"Are you sure?" Ian asked. "What if your nose starts to bleed again?"

"I'll be fine, but I'll bring some tissues just in case," she laughed. "It usually only bleeds in this sauna of an apartment," she said.

"I don't mind moving the car," he repeated.

"But then we'll have to find parking near Elder," she reminded. "Which is almost impossible," she paused. "Besides, it's only about a half mile up the street, let's just walk. I need the exercise. While I was doing the laundry, I ate another one of those hot cross cinnamon buns that we had for breakfast," she confessed. "And now I feel like I need to burn a few extra calories after hearing you rant about the obesity epidemic," she laughed.

"You shouldn't be eating junk like that," he reminded. "But are you sure you feel okay walking?" Ian asked again.

"Ian!" Rashanda groaned. "Enough! The doctor said that I can do everything that I was doing before," she reminded. "I won't lift the laundry basket again," she assured. "The next time I'll just drag the duffel down the stairs. I can do my homework while I wait for the load to finish, and then I'll leave the clothes folded in the basket on the folding table," she offered. "And you can bring them up when you get home. How does that sound?" she asked.

"I could live with that," he smiled. "I don't think anyone in the dorm will steal our clothes," Ian concurred.

"Now I'm really starving," Rashanda reminded. "I'm eating for two, remember, Mr. Hall?"

"How could I forget, Mrs. Hall," he grinned widely. "Today is the four month anniversary of our due date," he smiled. "You look so cute with a little bun in the oven," he grinned. "And for the record, you always ate for two," he teased, pulling her into an embrace from behind, his arms cradling her small belly as he nuzzled his head in her hair.

Chapter 5

Lipstick and Lace

Her name was Muffin. Technically, Muffin was her nickname. But no one called her by her real name, or at least that's what she'd explained to the group during her giggly introduction. When asked, she'd flatly refused to share her real name. Now the mystery of her name hung in the air like a jar of jelly beans in a guessing game. Pretending to listen to Muffin's monotone, Grace stared at her intently. She noticed the Miss America smiles plastered on the other girls' lips. Forcing herself to smile, Grace carefully studied Muffin's appearance. She measured the width of the wide, white headband that appeared to be half the size of Muffin's small head. She was confident that Mary Tyler Moore had worn a similar headband on an episode of The Dick Van Dyke Show or the Mary Tyler Moore Show. As Muffin rambled on, Grace's eyes rested on the small strand of pearls encircling her neck barely skimming the soft yellow cashmere sweater set that she wore atop an A line denim skirt. Muffin's legs were bare inside burgundy penny loafers that appeared new from the sheen that glistened from their tips. Shiny copper pennies were tucked inside the half moon of each small shoe. Grace did a double take when she noticed how small Muffin's feet were. She allowed her eyes to roam the room and noticed how many of the girls were dressed like Muffin, the pledge mom.

Penny? I bet her name is Penny. Penny in penny loafers. No, Penny is a cute name. It's probably something old like Edith, Ethel, Beulah, LulaBelle, or Bethel. I bet it's something hideous like that. Muffin looks like she's from old money. People from old money always name their children after their relatives so they'll leave them more in their will when they die. She's probably named after a rich ancestor. Or it could be Margaret. No. Margaret isn't a bad name. They'd call her Meg or Peggy anyway. Why is Peggy the nickname for Margaret? Why is Dick the nickname for Richard? An uncontrollable chuckle slipped from her lips, momentarily distracting Muffin's flow. She turned her attention to Grace.

"Pledge Dudley, is there something that you'd like to share with the rest of the group?" she smiled. "I'm sure your pledge sisters could use a laugh too."

Leaning back on two legs of her chair, Grace shrugged her shoulders. "I was just wondering what your real name is," Grace replied. "Since you're explaining how the pledge process for Kappa Gamma Mu will make us sisters," she paused, resting the chair on all four legs. "If we're your sisters, we should know your real name, dontcha think?" she asked cockily. "I was going through a list of names in my head trying to guess what your name is, and some of my choices made me giggle," she admitted boldly.

A few gasps could be heard from the group as the girls turned to stare at the girl seated in the back row, her golden bronze skin standing out like a licorice jelly bean in a bowl of rice. Color flushed Muffin's cheeks as she pursed her thin lips into a fake smile, her eyes darting between the fourteen other pledges, some of whom covered their mouths with their hands, while others sat frozen in their seats, shocked at Grace's brazenness.

Unfazed, Grace continued on her quest. "I mean really," she continued. "How bad could your real name be, Muffin?" she asked, tilting in her chair again, her head leaned against the fireplace. "And are you really going to go through life having people call you Muffin?" she asked. "It's a cute nickname now, but by the time you're forty, it's going to sound absurd!" she laughed.

"My real name is a family name that's been in my family for generations," Muffin stammered. "And I just prefer to keep it private," she finished.

Feeling empowered, Grace continued. "And when you get a job do you really think you'll be taken seriously with a name like Muffin?" Grace prodded. "On second thought, you look like you come from old money so you probably won't work outside of the home. You're probably getting an MRS degree majoring in husband searching 101 and minoring in housewifery," she challenged. "And if you do work for a minute, you'll work for your family's company so your nickname won't matter," she ranted. "Besides, you'll marry someone and be at home raising your children as soon as you feel the first gestational flutter in your belly," Grace giggled. The room was stunned silent.

"That's enough, Pledge Dudley," Muffin stammered. "You're out of line. That's extremely inappropriate."

"Well, if you won't tell me what your real name is," Grace mocked. "At least tell me what size shoe you wear. You have the feet of a ten year old. I wear a size 9AA shoe," Grace offered. "Now you know my shoe size, so what size do you wear?" she asked.

"I wear a size 5AAAA," Muffin shared quickly. "All of the women in my family wear quads. We have to have our shoes custom made," she boasted.

As if on cue, all of the girls stared intently at Muffin's delicate feet. Grace stood and faced the girls who sat in two neat columns in the sorority house's meeting room, the chairs lined up neatly in four rows of four. "Am I the only one who wants to know Muffin's real name?" she asked. "If we're going to establish a sisterhood bond, shouldn't the bond start by knowing the real name of our pledge mom?" she continued.

"I don't see why that should matter," Muffin defended.

"It matters because we're curious," Grace shot back. "Or maybe I should just call my attorney and have him suspend the annual donation that my grandmother's trust pays to Kappa Gamma Mu," she threatened.

"That's blackmail," Muffin gasped. "I can't believe that you would do that. Your grandmother was a charter member of this house," she whimpered.

"And now she's deceased, and there are certain codicils in her will that can be amended at my discretion," Grace grinned.

Another loud gasp was heard in the room.

"I don't think we're off to a good start. You have a copy of my transcript from high school, my SAT scores, and I've shared my first semester grades. You practically know my entire life story thanks to my grandmother's legacy," she paused. "I don't know your grades and I don't even know your legal name, Muffin," Grace said. "It's a very reasonable request, and I can't believe that you won't share this trivial bit of information. That's not very sisterly," she mocked.

A few of the other pledges shrugged, their head bands nodding in agreement. "Pledge Dudley is right," one girl whispered softly. "She makes a good point," another offered.

"Olive," Muffin mumbled softly. "My real name is Olive."

"Olive?" Grace repeated. "Oh my," she giggled. "I'm so sorry. It's worse than I thought!"

A collective gasp was heard in the room that was quickly replaced by a sea of hushed giggles. Two pledges that sat in the row ahead of Grace's chatted between themselves.

"I can't believe Pledge Dudley just said that," Pledge one murmured. "That was so crass!"

"I can," Pledge two whispered. "Her grandmother's trust money is what keeps this house running. She can say whatever she wants," Pledge two finished.

"Her grandmother was a Kappa Gamma Mu?" Pledge one asked.

"I didn't think they let black girls in the house," Pledge two mumbled. "I wonder if she was adopted. What do you think?"

"I'm not sure, but I think she's biracial, Claire," Pledge one whispered. "Can't you tell? She's pretty light for a black girl."

"I hadn't really noticed, but now that you mention it, she isn't as dark as the black girl who went to my high school," Claire observed.

"You had a black girl at your high school?" Pledge one asked.

"We had one. I wasn't friends with her though," Claire clarified. "I really didn't pay much attention to her."

Grace glared at Claire and her friend and slanted her eyes. She watched as they shifted in their seats. "Whose idea was it to name you, Olive?" Grace asked. "And how did you get Muffin as a nickname?"

Defeated, Muffin stepped back from the table top podium and plopped in the wing back chair positioned in the corner. "Olive is my great grandmother's name," she continued. "She had sons and always wanted a daughter so my grandfather convinced my dad to name me after his mother," she paused. "But no one has ever called me Olive," she cautioned. "My mother hated the name and protested, but clearly my dad won that battle. I planned to legally change it to Olivia when I turned eighteen," she continued.

"Why didn't you?" Grace asked. "It's not too late," she offered. A fresh wave of giggles flooded the room.

"There is a clause in my grandfather's will that if I change my name, I forfeit my trust fund," she sighed. "Actually, my grandfather was the only one who called me Olive," she corrected.

"I can relate to that," Grace shared. "My grandparents had a lot of stipulations in their will too. I have a detailed list of do's and don'ts that I have to follow in order to maintain my trust fund," she offered.

Claire's jaw dropped as she stared at Grace in disbelief. Grace's eyes honed in on Claire's like radar and she leaned in so that only Claire and her friend could hear her. "And for the record, Claire, I was adopted." she stated boldly. "My birth mother, Lydia Moore, was the only child of Michael and Amelia Moore. My mother died when I was two, and my grandparents passed away shortly before that," she continued. "I was adopted by the couple that worked on my grandparents' estate for years. My mother raised my birth mother, and my father was their chauffeur," she said as Claire shifted in her seat. "So yes, I was adopted, but I am a blood line Moore, and heir to the Moore fortune. And yes, my skin is a golden copper hue, the same hue that you try to obtain when you worship the sun in search of a tan," she smirked. "The chair that your narrow tail is resting on was purchased with my family's wealth," she gloated. "You need to learn to whisper better, Claire," she finished before directing her attention back to Muffin.

"I think family names are a nice way to honor our ancestors. I recently learned that I'm named after my maternal grandmother," Grace offered. "I'm sorry that I was so flippant before, Muffin,"

Grace apologized. "It was wrong to suggest that you're getting a MRS degree. I was just teasing you and trying to lighten the mood a little bit," she explained. "Olive really isn't a bad name at all. It's not like Beulah or LulaBelle or Ethel," she smiled. "What's your middle name?"

"Jean. My legal name is Olive Jean Crown," Muffin shared. "I can't believe that I'm telling you guys this," she blushed.

"Is the Crown Student Union named after your family?" someone asked.

"Yes it is," Muffin beamed.

"She's loaded too," Another girl whispered. "And she's fourth generation Kappa Gamma Mu."

"Why didn't you use Jean as your first name?" Grace asked.

"My parents tried," Muffin sighed. "Jean was my maternal grandmother's name, and my mother tried to just call me Jean," she paused. "But my grandfather was still alive and my father didn't want to offend his intentions," she explained. "So my mother came up with a pet name for me," she continued. "She told my grandfather that she craved carrot raisin bran muffins when she was pregnant with me, so she nicknamed me, Muffin," she explained. "I actually love carrot raisin bran muffins, but they're so high in fat that I don't dare eat one," she finished. "But the nickname worked. My grandfather didn't have a problem with my parents giving me a pet name. In fact, sometimes my grandfather called me Olive Muffin," she giggled. "Saying it aloud now is kind of funny. I can't imagine a muffin made of olives," she laughed.

"Sounds pretty gross," Grace admitted, walking toward the front of the room, her long legs striding confidently to the podium near Muffin's wingback chair. "Can I talk to you privately for a moment, Muffin?" she asked.

Muffin stood to her feet and smoothed her skirt. "Absolutely," she said. "Ladies, we're going to take five. Please return to your seats in five minutes," she instructed. "Feel free to go on the veranda and get some fresh air or walk around the garden. We also have light refreshments in the formal dining room. Help yourselves!"

Muffin escorted Grace to a small alcove beneath the large mahogany staircase in the main foyer. Two small desks were squeezed together with two wooden chairs that appeared very stern and uncomfortable. "This is our serious study nook," Muffin explained. "We also have a larger study room on the fourth floor with twenty desks, and the old living room sofa and chairs, but it gets kind of loud up there at times. Is everything okay, Pledge Dudley?" she asked.

"I apologize for trying to embarrass you in the meeting," Grace offered. "It was wrong for me to suggest that you're getting an MRS degree," she admitted again.

"Apology accepted," Muffin assured. "It's not the first time that I've heard that one," she smiled. "I know that the pledge process can be a bit stressful," she continued. "And you were right. If we're going to be sisters, I should trust you with my secret name, Pledge Dudley," she smiled.

"Please stop calling me that," Grace stated. "Just call me, Grace."

"Our by-laws state that we are not allowed to call the pledges by their first name until after the induction ceremony," Muffin explained.

"I don't think I'll be making that," Grace said flatly.

"But you must," Muffin exclaimed. "If you don't go through the formal induction ceremony you won't receive your sorority pin," she said. "It's on a weekend day, so it won't conflict with any of your classes."

"I'm ending the rush process," Grace blurted. "I'm not cut out for this sorority stuff. The pearls, lipstick and lace just aren't my thing. I'm just not feeling it," she sighed leaning against the wooden desk and folding her arms across her chest.

Muffin quickly opened the door of the study hall room and stuck her head outside checking to see if anyone was within earshot. "If you don't complete the pledge process, the house will blame me," she whimpered. "I should have told you my name right away," she admitted. "I'm really sorry about what just happened in the other room."

Grace stared at Muffin in amazement. "What are you talking about, Muffin? I am the one who owed you an apology," Grace challenged. "You have a right to maintain privacy about your name. Besides, I can't alter my grandmother's will," she giggled. "I was just bluffing. Or at least I don't think that I can alter my grandmother's will," she corrected. "I'm sure if I investigated it long enough and paid enough in legal fees I probably could challenge it, but I was kidding."

"Then why don't you want to continue the pledge process?" Muffin asked.

"I just don't feel like I'm cut out to be a sorority girl," Grace explained. "I know my grandmother was a Kappa Gamma Mu, but I'm not feeling it."

"Is it because you're the only black girl who rushed our house?" Muffin whispered. "We've never had a black girl in the house before, but most of the girls are super excited that you're here," she assured. "And not just because you're a descendant of one of our charter members," she clarified. "Some of the girls in the house don't know that you're her granddaughter. They know that her granddaughter is rushing our house, but because your last name is different and you're black, it's not obvious to some of them who you are. And because you're so fair, some of them don't realize that you're a black girl," she whispered again. "You won't stand out in the pledge class picture at all."

"Muffin, you don't have to whisper black girl," Grace explained.

"I didn't want to offend you," Muffin explained.

"I know that I'm black, Muffin," Grace replied. "And I know that you know that I'm black, so it's not offensive to me when you notice that I'm black," she explained, raising her hand and smiling to silence Muffin's next comment. "The truth is that even though I'm biracial, I identify as an African American, so I am feeling out of place in a room full of white girls," Grace admitted. "My mother died when I was two, I never knew my grandparents, and I didn't hang around that many white girls in high school," she sighed. "So just going through the pledge process has felt like I'm learning a new language," Grace admitted. "Don't get me wrong, everyone in the house has been very nice," she paused. "I'm just not feeling the sorority thing."

"But it's in your bloodline, Grace," Muffin pleaded. "Your grandmother was a charter member! You're a Kappa Gamma Mu," she grinned.

"No. I'm really not," Grace replied. "Now what do I have to do to undo this process?" she asked firmly.

"Well, since you haven't paid your pledge fees yet," she explained. "There's really nothing that you have to do officially. I'll just tell the other girls in the house that you changed your mind," Muffin said. "But as your pledge mom they're going to press me for a reason," she said. "We're the most popular sorority on campus. We've never had a pledge decline an invitation to join our sisterhood," Muffin sighed. "There go my hopes for winning president of the house."

"What are you talking about?" Grace asked.

"I'm running for president at the end of the semester, and this will be viewed as a black mark against my candidacy," Muffin shared. "The fact that I couldn't convince you to stay will be used against me by my opponent."

"But it's not your fault," Grace reminded. "I'm just not feeling it. They shouldn't hold that against you."

"But they will," Muffin sighed. "Polly Higginbotham will use this to her full advantage."

The voices in the hallway got louder. Through the small glass pane in the door, Grace could see the pledge class dutifully walking back into the meeting room, many carefully balanced china coffee cups in one hand and plates with petite scones or fruit in the other.

"We'd better get back," Muffin said.

"I'm so sorry, Muffin," Grace offered. "I've caused enough of a distraction today, so I'll sit through the rest of the meeting quietly, and then I just won't show up for the induction ceremony," she decided. "I'd be happy to talk to the girls in your house and assure them that my decision had nothing to do with you," she suggested. "Is there any reason that I could give that wouldn't be viewed as a black mark against you?" Grace asked.

Muffin shrugged with her hands. "Well, I think the only thing that wouldn't be held against me is if you were to announce that you've spent time in prison or that you're gay," she smirked. "They couldn't blame that one on me," she laughed. "Let's get out of here. This room has no air circulation." Muffin turned the handle and opened the alcove door. The cool air from the hallway greeted the girls as they walked back to the meeting.

Grace watched in admiration as Muffin smoothed her skirt and reached for the small silver bell on the tabletop podium. She flicked her thin wrist three times, and the room fell silent. "I hope all of you were able to enjoy some fresh air," she smiled. "And I see that many of you are enjoying our fat free scones. I'd like to thank Pledge Dudley for creating a reason for a moment of respite. I get so carried away at this podium that I forget to pause and take five," she grinned. "Remember, don't share my proper name outside of your pledge circle," Muffin winked, waving her index finger at the group. "My own pledge sisters don't know my real name. Now let's pick up where we left off because I promised that I'd have you out of here in less than two hours and we only have twenty minutes left for me to stay true to my word," she grinned staring at her notes.

"Excuse me," Grace said softly from the back of the room.

Muffin stared at Grace curiously. "Pledge Dudley, do you have a question?"

"Not exactly," Grace inhaled. "But I don't think that I'm going to be able to complete the meeting today," she said. "I'm not feeling very well."

"Are you feeling light headed from our little meeting in the alcove?" Muffin asked. "That room is so stuffy. And you didn't have a proper break. Shame on me!" Muffin scolded. "Feel free to help yourself to a snack or walk outside for five minutes if you'd like," Muffin suggested. I'll open the window and create a cross breeze," Muffin offered.

"That's not it," Grace said. "I think I'm gay."

Chapter 6

Like a Woman Scorned

He had called it a promise ring. The stone was three carats. Liz had called it gaudy, excessive, and inappropriate, insisting that the ring be returned. Maria had flatly refused. Liz then suggested that she not wear the ring until it could be added to their homeowner's insurance policy, just in case. Her daughter had ignored that bit of motherly wisdom too. The ring twirled on Maria's thin finger like a hula hoop. The platinum band struggling to support the massive pear shaped diamond. In the cafeteria, the size of her ring was a topic of discussion both in Café Cocoa and outside its unofficial borders.

In the heart of West Philadelphia, on the University of Pennsylvania's campus, Café Cocoa was the black section of her dormitory's cafeteria. It consisted of six tables just outside of the food line, and it's where most of the black students generally ate their meals. The administration frowned upon the black students' self imposed cafeteria segregation, encouraging the African American students to enjoy their meals at other tables in the large dining hall. Occasionally, the administration would be so bold as to place closed signs on the tables in Café Cocoa, forcing the black students to sit in other areas. The forced integration was always short lived, and never achieved its intended purpose.

Irritated, the black students would disperse to other areas of the cafeteria and form a temporary Café Cocoa in protest. As a sign of solidarity and support, the white students (who always honored the Café Cocoa borders) would shift their tables and leave open seating for the black students to sit together. In an odd showing of solidarity, or at best a sympathy strike, the white students always refused to sit in the Café Cocoa section of the cafeteria, some choosing to stand at over crowded tables to eat their meal rather than cross the artificial picket line by sitting in the Café Cocoa section, even at the insistence of administrative personnel encouraging them to do so.

At least once each year, the student newspaper ran an article on Café Cocoa, and criticized the African American students for isolating themselves during meal times. The president of the Black Student Union always submitted the same editorial reply, reminding the newspaper that the administration ignored the daily, collective gathering of ten or more white students at meal time, and questioning why when black students choose to sit together, it was viewed as isolationism and self inflicted segregation.

Maria's ring had become a topic of discussion on campus. The preppy, narcissistic sorority girls (who normally scurried nervously past Café Cocoa with their trays of rabbit food) now boldly walked into the Café Cocoa section of the cafeteria. Their eyes squinting as though navigating through thick fog, they nervously panned Café Cocoa to find the girl who matched the description they'd been given: olive tone skin with long, straight, jet black hair. Upon spotting their prey, they would march over and ask to see her ring. The instructions were always delivered more in the form of an order than a request that could be declined. "Are you the freshman with the big ring? Let me see it!" Without so much as an introduction,

Maria's paw would be swept into theirs as they gazed at her ring like a Smithsonian artifact. Eyeing her ring suspiciously, most boldly raised Maria's thin finger to their faces to validate the ring's authenticity, as though their pupil possessed a jeweler's lube. Their jaws usually fell slack when they saw the crystal clear clarity and color of the beautiful diamond floating in the six prong platinum setting, a Tiffany trademark. Maria knew the drill, and this latest encounter started out as familiar as all of the others.

"I told you it was huge," Girl A whispered. "It's bigger than my mother's rock!"

"Do you mind if I ask you how big that stone is?" Girl B asked boldly.

"The center stone is three carats," Maria sighed.

"Three carats?" Girl B repeated loudly.

"Yes. Three carats," Maria repeated.

"You're a freshman and you're wearing a three carat diamond from Tiffany? What does your fiancé do?" Girl A asked.

"He's not my fiancé," Maria corrected.

Girl A and Girl B exchanged curious glances.

"Well, why did he give you a diamond for your left hand?" Girl A asked suspiciously.

"It's a promise ring," Maria explained. "And it's for my right hand, but it's too large for that finger so I'm wearing it on my left hand until I get it sized," she finished. "Not that it's any of your business."

"It's such a beautiful ring," Girl B stammered, ignoring Maria's sarcasm. "And it's so unusual for a freshman to have such a large ring," she continued. "Most girls don't get their ring until senior year, and then it's usually not that large out of the gate," she giggled. "And it's usually not from Tiffany!"

"I know," Girl A concurred. "My mom told me that you have to have at least one baby before you can get in the three carat league," she offered. "Unless your husband makes partner," she continued. "My mother didn't upgrade her stone until my parent's tenth wedding anniversary," she paused. "My dad's practice was doing really well, so he let her upgrade her stone from Cartier. She still has that red and gold box that it came in," Girl A sighed. "Personally, I like the jewelry from Cartier better than Tiffany," she added arrogantly.

"Cartier, Tiffany, who cares?" Girl B giggled. "Your mom's stone is beautiful and so is this one! I hope I don't have to wait ten years to get a big rock," Girl B sighed still gripping Maria's hand and squinting intently. "Is it real? They're making cubic zirconia that almost looks real these days," she stated.

"Of course it's real, dingbat," Maria winced, jerking her hand away in disgust. "Can't a black girl have a big ring?

"I didn't mean to offend you," Girl B offered weakly. "But a lot of women have nice fakes that they wear so they don't wear the real thing all the time," she added. What does your boyfriend do?" she asked. "If you don't mind my asking," she added.

"Actually, I do mind you asking. That's really none of your business either," Maria replied. "But he's a professional athlete."

"Oh," Girl B sighed with relief. "That explains it."

"Explains what?" Maria asked.

"That explains why your ring is so large. We know how black athletes always like their bling. What team does he play for?" Girl B asked.

Maria quickly rose to her feet. "You have a lot of nerve," Maria replied. "You don't even bother to introduce yourselves to me, yet you come over here and interrogate me with your nosy questions like I'm your friend," she growled. "And then you insult me? What do you mean you know how black athletes like their bling?" she repeated. "Get out of my face! This interview is over, haters!"

Girl A and Girl B each took a half step back. "What'd she call us?" Girl A asked stunned.

"I think she called us haters," Girl B replied.

"I called you haters. Now get your insolent, jealous, boney butts out of my face so I can enjoy my meal!" Maria screeched.

Flushed, Girl A and Girl B stared at Maria in disbelief, their eyes roaming nervously from left to right as though noticing for the first time that they were in Café Cocoa surrounded by a sea of caramel and mocha tan faces staring at them. "Calm down, girlfriend. You don't have to get so defensive. We were just trying to pay you a compliment by admiring your ring," Girl A explained nervously.

"First of all, I am not your girlfriend," Maria snorted. "Second, you were not trying to pay me a compliment. You were being nosy! We live in the same dorm, and you don't even know my name. I've seen you both in the laundry room every week, and you never bother to speak to me. And when I've spoken to you, you look at me like I'm invisible. I hear you slicing and dicing your sorority sisters in the laundry room like witches," Maria blurted. "You're like the evil witches from the Wizard of Oz! Now be gone before someone drops a house on you too!" Maria growled, waving her hand to shoo them away like swarming gnats.

"No need to get ghetto on us," Girl B mumbled before rolling her eyes and turning on her heels.

The chocolate milk wave hung in the air like a waterfall, dripping from Girl A's blonde tresses. The blue cheese dressing splattered Girl B's nose before she knew what hit her.

"Eeeek!" Girl A screamed. "I'm vegan! I can't believe that you threw milk on me!" she shrieked.

Maria felt arms encircling her waist. Her friends rose and restrained her as she lunged toward the girls, like a cornered cat, back arched and teeth hissing. Her arms securely pinned at her sides, Maria screamed at the top of her lungs, "Get out of my face before I slap the taste out of your mouth!" she shrieked.

Visibly shaken, with food dripping from their heads, both girls retreated to a chorus of laughter and chuckles as the cafeteria manager raced over to intervene before a full blown food fight ensued.

ഇൻൽ

"Café Cocoa Hostile to Outsiders"

She crumpled the paper and tossed it at the foot of her bed. That was the headline in the student newspaper the next morning. The story that ran accused Maria of throwing food at the girls for walking into Café Cocoa. The reporter who ran the story never bothered to contact her to get her version of what happened. The quotes from Girl A and Girl B appeared under a photo of the disheveled girls taken by the cafeteria manager, who was looking for a reason to disband Café Cocoa and limit the number of black students who were allowed to sit together in the cafeteria. There was no mention of the girls' invasion of Maria's personal space, the rude personal questions that they'd asked her, their insulting remarks or the ghetto comment. It was a classic case of biased journalism at its best.

Friends who'd witnessed the exchange urged Maria to meet

with the president of the Black Student Union so that he could add her version of the conflict into his rebuttal editorial piece and demand that the newspaper print a retraction and sanction the reporter who'd run the imbalanced story.

Maria climbed the stairs of the Black House. The large, white Victorian House that stood on two lots was officially known as the African American Studies Department, but the African American students still referred to it as the Black House. Upon walking into the large foyer, she braced herself for a sneeze. The house smelled of mold, mildew and moth balls and always triggered an allergy attack. For this reason, she limited her visits to the Black House.

"Atchoo, atchoo, atchoo," she sniffled. She always sneezed in threes.

When she opened her eyes, a white tissue was waving in her face like a surrender flag.

"Thank you," she smiled, grabbing the tissue.

"You must be Maria," he smiled. "I'm John," he introduced. "Is it possible to sneeze with your eyes open?" he asked. "No. Let me rephrase that. It's possible to sneeze with your eyes open, fact or fiction?"

"Huh?" she replied.

"Fact or fiction?" he repeated. "Is it impossible to sneeze with your eyes open? Yes or no?" he grinned.

"I've never given that much thought," she shrugged, wiping her nose with the tissue. "Is that a trick question?"

"Nope. Take a guess," He urged. "Fact or fiction?" he asked, handing her another tissue.

"No," she shrugged. "It's not impossible to sneeze with your eyes open."

"Honk! Honk!" he snorted. "Wrong answer. It's impossible

to sneeze with your eyes open. The next time you sneeze, pay attention and you'll notice that your eyes automatically close during a sneeze," he explained. "So it's fact. The correct answer is fact."

"Okey, dokey," she giggled.

"It's a game that my family played at dinner when I was growing up," he explained. "Someone would tell a story or make a statement and you had to guess if the story was fact or fiction," he smiled. "It's fun. Before you walked in I was having a homesick moment and thinking about our dinner ritual," he offered. "We're going to meet in here," he led, pointing to a small alcove office near the main foyer. "Have a seat," John smiled.

Maria wiped her nose and tossed her backpack on the floor, quickly surveying her surroundings. The tiny office was crammed with books from floor to ceiling. A metal desk was stuffed against a large oval shaped window portal that overlooked the front porch. A tattered love seat was perpendicular to the desk and almost as wide.

"My real office is on the third floor," John explained. "But when the staff goes home I come down here and work from the secretary's office so I can hear the door open and see who's coming and going from this window," he explained. "I heard the stairs creaking and saw you sneezing as you walked up the stairs."

"My allergies are off the chain today," Maria sniffled.

"What are you allergic to?" John asked.

"The better question is what am I not allergic to," she replied. "I'm allergic to pet dander, mold, mildew, dust mites, grass, cottonwood," she listed. "You get the idea."

John handed her a box of tissues and nodded. "My brothers have bad allergies too, and so does my dad. My mother and I were spared. Thank God!" he smiled.

Maria's head turned as a golden retriever wearing a red bandana around his neck, sauntered into the room and boldly placed his head on her knee. Her body tensed.

John leaned slightly and rubbed the dog's head from his chair in the tiny room. "Buddy, this is Maria," he introduced softly. "Plotz!" he ordered. Buddy laid at Maria's feet, his large head now resting on her shoes. "He's the house mascot and he wouldn't hurt a fly. In fact, Buddy would slobber on any burglars who came in here," he laughed.

Maria sat back as Buddy smelled her feet, nudging her shin with his golden head, encouraging her to pet him.

"He's really friendly," John explained. "He thinks he's still a puppy. I'm surprised he didn't jump right in your lap. He naps on that sofa during the day," John giggled before his face turned serious. "Wait, you're allergic to pet dander too aren't you?" John asked. "I think I heard you say pet dander, right? Beat it, Buddy!" John ordered.

Maria's reply came in the form of a sneeze. "Atchoo! Atchoo! Atchoo!" she nodded. "I always sneeze in threes," she explained. "Do you have any statistic about people who sneeze multiple times?" she asked, as she reached for another tissue.

"I don't have any data on that," he offered. "I'll send Buddy upstairs," John offered as he stood. "He'll keep coming in here if I don't." John rose, snapped his fingers and pointed to the stairs. Buddy obediently raced up the stairs.

"You were right!" Maria blurted quickly. "My eyes closed when I sneezed. I tried to hold them open, but I couldn't," she laughed, reaching for another tissue.

"I told you," John winked. "It's a natural reflex. When you sneeze, your eyes close," he explained. "You know what?" he asked.

"Let's get out of here because between the mold, mildew, dust mites, dog hair and pet dander in this old house," he chuckled. "You're going to sneeze your head off or go through my entire box of tissue," he smiled. "Let's chat on the front porch. There are chairs out there that we can sit on," he finished. "Or we can walk to the library and meet inside."

"I'll be fine on the porch," Maria sniffled. "I took my seasonal allergy pill so being away from the mold, mildew and dog should help," she smiled.

John quickly grabbed her large back pack and walked through the foyer into the enclosed vestibule. With his free hand, he pulled the large door open and stepped to one side to allow Maria to walk out ahead of him.

Once outside, he placed her back pack near a chair and turned the other chair on an angle to face her.

"Now tell me what happened in the cafeteria," he encouraged, his left knee crossed over his right knee and his finger gently stroking his chin. "You don't seem like the type of girl to just throw food at some girls for crossing the Café Cocoa border," he shared. "Give it to me straight, no chaser. I want to hear the whole truth, and nothing but the truth, so help you God," he laughed. "I've heard the story from several different people on campus, but I want to hear it from the horse's mouth," he smiled.

Maria relayed her version of the cafeteria food throwing incident to John who listened intently without taking notes.

"Typical," John muttered when she finished. "I knew there was a lot more to that story when I read it," he said. "Even without having met you, it just didn't sound like the type of thing that a U Penn student would do," he offered. "Once again, the biased media has sensationalized a story to stir up controversy. It must have been another slow news day at the paper," he chuckled. "Because if the reporter had bothered to contact you or any other witnesses, they would have realized that there was no story to print," he continued. "When in fact there is a story to print, the story is the sense of entitlement that exists with some people in the majority culture," he paused.

"Who's the majority culture?" Maria asked. "Do you mean white people?"

"You got it," John said. "It's a term I coined because it sounds less in your face than saying 'white people' when I want to make a point. Where was I?" he asked absentmindedly before continuing. "No one wants to print the white privilege story," he explained. "Those girls violated your personal space, they insulted you and your boyfriend with that 'black athletes like their bling' comment," he paused. "And you were well within your rights to get upset and react. Now, throwing food at them was a wee bit over the top," he chastised. "But in the heat of the moment, they're lucky you didn't smack them. Yet another example of privilege, but if the reporter had printed that story, the campus would accuse you of being too sensitive," he paused. "That's what they accuse us of when we hold a mirror to their face and show them how their behavior is out of order, discriminatory, privileged, racist or just plain wrong. 'Why are blacks so sensitive?'" he mocked in falsetto. "That's what they'd all be saying on campus. I've been to this dance before," he sighed. "It's their world and we are just squirrels trying to get a nut," he sighed again, shifting his posture slightly, his hands gesturing animatedly as he spoke.

"I'm going to use this angle for my rebuttal comments," he announced. "I am very familiar with the white privilege theory. When I was at Cornell, in upstate New York, I was so tired of people asking me who I was and what my parents did for a living," he groaned. "I was the only black hockey player on the team, and every time I met another student's parents or friends, and they found out that I played hockey, I got the usual barrage of questions," he paused. "'Where'd you grow up? What do your parents do for a living? How'd you get interested in hockey?'" he chuckled in falsetto once again. "It got to the point where I wanted to have business cards printed with this information," he sighed. "And the thing that used to piss me off is that they never asked those questions to the white boys on the team," he continued. "Even white boys who would transfer in, they never got the third degree the way that I did," he finished. "Because it's acceptable for a white boy to play ice hockey, and it's odd for a black boy to play ice hockey."

"Well, there aren't that many black guys who play hockey," Maria offered.

"That's true, but it was the feeling that I had to explain myself to people over and over again," he replied. "I'm not naïve, I get that it's unusual to see a black guy playing ice hockey, but I still don't understand why people think they have the right to interrogate me and judge whether or not I'm worthy to play a sport based on where I live and what my parents do for a living," he said. "It's like they're segregating sports. If I were playing basketball, football, baseball, or running track, they wouldn't ask me those questions," he paused. "But because I play a sport that blacks don't traditionally play, they believe they have the right to give me the third degree," he said. "My mere existence challenges the long held stereotypes that people hold. 'Blacks don't play hockey. Blacks don't ski. Blacks don't golf. Blacks don't play water polo. Blacks don't play lacrosse. Blacks don't swim,'" he mocked in falsetto. "It pisses me off. They don't do that for white people. Whites are allowed to play any sport they want and excel at it. You don't see some reporter quizzing a white basketball player asking him what his dad does for a living and how he got interested in basketball," he paused. "If you were a white girl with a big rock on her hand, I doubt the other white girls on campus would be asking you what your boyfriend did for a living," he finished. "They would assume that your boyfriend came from old family money."

Maria nodded and shrugged. "Maybe or maybe not," she added.

"And it's not just whites who ask those questions," he corrected. "I've had blacks ask me the same questions too," he added. "And when I say something about it, I'm accused of being too sensitive. Everyone wants to be able to judge people so that the world makes sense to them," he paused. "To the world, a black boy isn't supposed to be able to afford to play ice hockey," he stated flatly. "So when they meet one who does, it throws them for a loop. It destroys the order of the universe as they know it. Or at least it destroys the narrow socioeconomic stereotype that they've created to explain who's supposed to do what. Plain and simple," he continued. "Have the black girls on campus made a big deal about your ring?" he asked.

"A lot of people have noticed my ring, but only the white girls have been asking me what my boyfriend does for a living," Maria noted.

"That's my point," John confirmed. "It's one thing to notice a beautiful piece of jewelry, but it's something totally different to pepper your interest with a barrage of personal questions. I call it the privileged mentality of the majority culture," he sighed. "Your big ring completely destroys their natural order of things, and they feel they're entitled to an explanation that makes sense to them, in an effort to restore their order," he observed. "And you are obligated to provide answers. It's white privilege. I'm going to write my senior thesis on it," John shared.

"I don't disagree with your white privilege theory," Maria offered. "But I have to admit that I can kind of relate to some of their curiosity," she shared. "Not too many blacks live in areas that have indoor ice rinks," Maria added. "Most blacks wouldn't even know what a zamboni was or the penalty box for that matter," she stated.

John stared at her curiously. "I'm not saying that it's right," she paused. "But my younger brother played ice hockey for a few years, and he would get some of the same questions," she added. "I grew up in a suburb of Chicago and there was an ice arena about two miles away from our house. There were a few blacks who played on his hockey team," she added. "But not that many," she corrected. "My brother is very fair so people assumed he was adopted or biracial until they saw my parents. My brother told me that some parents used to ask him if one of his parents was white, not because he looks white, but because he played hockey so well," she finished. "It was difficult for them to believe that a black kid could excel at a sport that is so traditionally white," she paused. "He stopped playing in high school, but I think the fact that you stuck with it and played for Cornell is amazing."

"I loved playing hockey, but I'd had my fill of living in Ithaca," he explained. "It was a beautiful campus, and I was getting an amazing education," he added. "But living in Ithaca was a bit too isolating. Plus, I was tired of fighting the white boys on the ice who would sometimes call me nigger just to incite a fight," he growled. "I'm a really good hockey player, and the other team knew that all they had to do was say nigger and I'd be in the penalty box, or get thrown out of the game," he stated. "I think their coaches would tell them to do it," he sighed. "My coach told me to ignore them, but I couldn't. Whenever they said it, a switch was flipped in my brain and I turned into a different person. In my last game, I tried to bash this kids' head into the ice. Fortunately, I only broke his nose, but I tried to slam his head as hard as I could," John recollected. "His parents wanted to pursue criminal charges against me, and called me a street thug on ice," he said. "The athletic director and Cornell staff attorney got involved and no charges were pressed because we all sign a waiver stating that we're playing at our own risk. And everyone knows that hockey players fight," he shrugged. "It's only by the grace of God that I didn't kill that kid. I wanted to," he admitted. "That's how angry I was. My parents made me stop playing before I killed someone out there," he stated, his eyes staring off into the distance. "They're the ones who made me transfer to the University of Pennsylvania," he sighed. "It was a good move because I had a rage building inside of me and probably could have killed someone on the ice," he offered.

"Wow!" Maria said. "You seem so gentle and mild mannered, I can't imagine you slamming someone's head into the ice."

"I'm usually very mild mannered until 'that' button gets pushed," John said. "I'm just glad that I didn't lose any of my teeth to my sport," he smiled widely showing perfectly straight teeth.

"Did you see anyone lose their teeth on the ice?" Maria asked.

"All the time," John offered. "It was a regular occurrence at games," he laughed. "It was like a badge of honor to have a tooth knocked out," he laughed. "But enough about me," he grinned. "This is about you. You've given me more than enough information to write my rebuttal. If I get it to the paper by six o'clock tonight, they'll print it in tomorrow's paper. I'm going to demand that the reporter print a retraction," he finished. "Can I quote you?" he asked.

"Yeah, sure," Maria shrugged. "But you weren't taking notes," she pointed out.

John tapped his head. "It's all up here," he grinned. "I listen better with my eyes and my head," he smiled. "Although it's hard to focus with that big rock on your finger blinding a brotha's vision," he chuckled. "That thing is huge! I can see why the sorority quad girls are willing to wander into Café Cocoa to scope that thing out. And it's easy enough to find you with that satellite on your finger beckoning them like a beacon," he laughed.

Twirling the ring with her thumb, Maria stared at it self consciously and giggled.

"I can tell by the color and clarity that he paid a nice chunk of change for that beauty," he said. "It's about three carats, right?" John asked.

"How'd you know that?" she nodded. "And most guys don't know anything about color and clarity," she added.

"My old man bought my mother a big rock for their twentieth wedding anniversary, and I had the four c's explained to me in excruciating detail," he explained. "Color, cut, clarity & carat weight. He got her a three carat round solitaire and I was with him when he picked it out. My dad is the king of frugality, and he's still talking about how much he paid for that trinket," he grinned. "But my mother loves it, and I see her staring at it all the time," he smiled. "I got a mini course in diamond buying from my dad's jeweler. He also gave me the father son lecture on buying gifts for the woman in your life," he explained. "'Son, hell hath no fury like a woman scorned. Treat your woman like a queen and she will be more inclined to forgive you when you stumble along the way. And always remember that it's cheaper to keep her,'" John explained in a deep bass voice this time. "My dad has always bought my mother really nice jewelry," he added. "And sometimes my mother buys herself really nice jewelry that she tells my dad is a gift from him," he laughed.

"You have that thing insured don't you?" John asked. "You shouldn't be wearing it until it's insured."

"You sound like my mother," Maria sighed. "My friend is sending my mother the appraisal paperwork so it can be added to our homeowner's policy. I don't wear it everyday," she explained. "But I feel like it's safer on my finger than sitting in my dorm room."

"Your friend?" John teased. "He's clearly more than a friend if he bought you a rock like that," he whistled. "The least you could do is call him your boyfriend," John suggested.

"He was my prom date," she explained. "But Dante and I are really just friends. It's a promise ring."

"A three carat promise ring?" he teased. "Wait a minute, did you say Dante?" he repeated. "Is your friend, Dante, the first round draft pick from Notre Dame who now plays for the Cleveland Browns, and was rookie of the year, Dante?" John asked.

"That's the one," Maria sighed. "How'd you know that was him?"

"Somebody told me they saw him on campus a few weeks ago zipping around in a black Ferrari," John said. "He came up here to see you in the middle of the season?"

"They had a bye that week, so he came up to see me for the weekend," Maria explained. "And that's when he brought me the ring," she mumbled. "I told him not to rent such a flashy car, but he wanted to test drive one before he bought one," she sighed.

"He must really love him some you," John whistled rising to his feet and handing Maria her heavy backpack. "Thanks for coming, Maria," John offered. "I'm going to go in and shoot this letter off so I can make the paper's deadline. It was nice to meet you, Maria, and I'm sure I'll see you around campus," he offered. "Take care!"

"You too," she smiled. Maria walked down the four wooden stairs and replayed John's words. "He must really love him some you. He must really love him some you." As John's words ran through her head, her thoughts stayed stuck on Todd.

At Liz's wedding reception, Mama Kaye had listened intently as Maria shared her Todd story, including the telephone break up with theme music playing in the background. When she'd finished, Mama Kaye had compared Maria's relationship with Todd to a soiled band-aid that's stayed on too long, the glue now black with oil and dirt. "The band-aid isn't serving any purpose, sugar. And if you keep it on too long, it'll just get infected and filled with pus. It's better to rip the band-aid off throw it in the trash and let the wound heal," Mama Kaye had advised. "Put some antibacterial cream on the sore and just let it heal. If you don't pull that band-aid off, you'll get an infection that'll stay with you for a long time." That was the only advice she'd offered on the subject.

Maria smiled at her ring. "I have a three carat band-aid."

Chapter 7

Starve a Fever

The bath towel draped over her head, she leaned over the plastic shoe box and inhaled deeply, closing her weary eyes. She'd tested the shoe box in the bathroom, filling it half way with tepid warm water and swirling it around. Not noticing any leaks, she partially filled the box with a hot water head start and carried it to her room like an eight year old toting a prized carnival goldfish. Teenie placed the liquid box on the center of her desk as her illegal electric hot pot steamed in the corner. She remembered to move her books and papers from the desk to her bed. Her fingers fumbled in her backpack until she located the small metal teaspoon that she'd borrowed from the cafeteria for such a time as this. She scooped in a heaping teaspoon of Vicks vapo-rub and carefully poured the hot water into the clear container. She scooped another teaspoonful for good measure before slowly stuffing her hair inside her shower cap. Her nostrils burned. The doctor at the student health center said that it was the beginning of a sinus infection and had summarily ignored her plea for a prescription, instead encouraging her to get rest, drink fluids and take a Sudafed. With the doctor's bright, white hospital jacket mocking her misery, Teenie wanted to smack the gloating doctor in training. She raised her heavy head from the bowl and lifted her towel. Feeling only slightly better, her head still felt like it would explode.

Her packing complete, she glanced at her large, weekend duffle in the corner, a sign of respite and tension. The sight of the bag intensified the pressure in her head. The mere thought of traveling with a cold caused her to grimace in agony. But there was no looking back. Tickets had been purchased for her Thanksgiving break.

She was tired and needed a nap. The fumes burned her nostrils, but the home remedy spa was working. After two nightly steam treatments, her sense of smell had improved and she could smell someone cooking popcorn on her floor. Now two weeks later, Teenie's head congestion had returned. Leaning in for round two, she closed her eyes and forced herself to breathe deeply as her mother had instructed.

སྱༀ

"Are you okay, Tanisha?" Billie asked. "It sounds like you have a cold," her mother observed through the phone.

"I do," Tanisha admitted. "I went to the doctor, and she told me to just get some rest and take Sudafed," she shared through her stuffy nose. "My head is killing me," she whined.

"You sound horrible," her mother agreed. "Do you have a temperature?" Billie asked.

Tanisha smiled at her mother's use of temperature in place of fever. "No, or at least I didn't when I went to the doctor," she corrected. "I feel warm, but my dorm room is always hot," she offered.

"You might have a sinus infection now," Billie suggested. "Do you have a thermometer? I know I packed one in your first aid kit," Billie reminded. "You need to take your temperature. A temperature is a sign of infection," she added.

"I'll take it when we get off the phone," Tanisha assured.

"And if you have a fever, you should drink plenty of fluids and eat something really greasy," Billie continued. "Feed a fever, starve a cold," Billie sang. "You should layer yourself in plenty of blankets and sweat that cold out of your system," she offered.

"How will eating something greasy get rid of my fever?" Tanisha doubted. "That sounds stupid."

"Tanisha Denise, you know I don't like the word stupid," Billie scolded.

"But it does, Mom," Tanisha chuckled. "Explain to me how eating something greasy will take away a fever."

"I can't explain it," Billie said. "But it works. If you have a fever, you feed it grease. Simple as that. That's what I used to do with you and your brothers when you were little," she paused. "I would fry some French fries and make you eat a greasy hamburger with it," she said.

"I remember those burgers that used to soak through the bread," Tanisha chuckled.

"I would deliberately not drain any of the fat out of the burgers," Billie explained. "And you'd eat it and you'd usually feel better the next day," she finished.

"But how do you know it was the grease that took away the fever," Tanisha giggled. "Can you prove that?" she challenged.

"Can you prove that it wasn't the grease?" Billie shot back. "It's probably just an old wives tale, but it's been passed down for generations," Billie shared. "Your Grandma Bootsy told me this one."

At the mention of Grandma Bootsy, Tanisha raised an

eyebrow and reconsidered the home remedy. "Is it old wives tale or old wise tale, Mom?" Tanisha asked.

"I've always said old wives tale," Billie replied. "But it could be wise tale. Who knows? All I know is that the home remedies are sometimes better than what the doctor tells you to do," she said. "And it's free advice. A doctor wants to charge you an arm and a leg to tell you to take two aspirin, get rest and drink fluids."

Tanisha rolled her eyes into the ceiling and nodded her head.

"Another one that works like a charm is to eat a half teaspoon of Vick's too. The phlegm attaches to the Vick's and comes right on out. I know I packed a tub of Vick's vapo-rub in your first aid box," Billie finished.

"Now you sound like a witch doctor, Mom!" Tanisha offered. "I am not eating a teaspoon of Vick's. That's just gross!" she shrieked. "Ain't gonna happen!"

"Not a teaspoon, a half teaspoon," her mother corrected. "But suit yourself," Billie sighed. "When you were little and had chest congestion or a cough, I would mix it in your hot tea. You wouldn't even notice it with the honey and lemon," Billie laughed. "And you turned out okay. It sometimes gave you a little diarrhea, but it didn't kill you," she chuckled. "I think the runny stool pulled those cold germs out quicker," she finished.

"You are really grossing me out!" Tanisha shrieked. "Where do you get this quacky stuff?" Tanisha laughed.

"These tips get passed down in the family," Billie stated. Tanisha could hear the family pet barking in the distance.

"Does Butch like having a fenced in backyard now?" Tanisha asked.

"He loves it. But your brothers don't like going out there and scooping that poop," Billie shared. "I don't want the yard smelling like manure so I make them scoop it every day. Butch is barking because he wants to come back inside."

"Has Butch finally started being nice to Dad?" Tanisha asked. "Or does he still growl at him?"

"Butch is still not too sure about your father," Billie shared. "But now your dad feeds him every day, so Butch has stopped growling at him. Instinctively most dogs will not bite the hand that feeds them," she finished. "I think he's treating your dad like the alpha dog in the family."

"I always thought that was just a saying," Tanisha said. "I didn't think there was much truth to that."

"Absolutely," Billie replied. "Dogs are pack animals and when you're trying to bond with an adult dog, you have to establish yourself as the alpha dog in order for the dog to be submissive to you," she explained. "If you don't, the dog will think that he's running the show," she finished.

Tanisha sighed. "Not the alpha dog theory, Mom. I've heard that before. I meant the 'dogs won't bite the hand that feeds them' theory," she restated, propping another pillow behind her aching back.

"Oh yeah," Billie said. "Your father was raised with dogs so he knew that if he took over the feeding responsibilities for Butch, he'd eventually warm up to him, and it's working."

"Did you paint my room yet?" Tanisha asked quickly. "Did they have that yellow that I picked out, the color that's in Aunt Helen's sun room?"

"They did. Your Aunt Helen had the name of the paint, so your father had them mix it up at the hardware store. It looks really nice," Billie paused. "We had a paint party the weekend before we moved in. Your uncles came over to help and we played music and painted and then had pizza and beer," she said. "I didn't have a beer, because I can't drink alcohol with my medication, but your father and uncles did," she corrected. "I saw your dad give your brother Byron a small glass of beer too," she added. "I don't like the idea of Byron tasting beer, he's only sixteen."

"He's almost seventeen now, Mom, and I hate to be the one to break it to you, but I'm sure he's probably tasted beer before," she offered. "He's a junior in high school now."

"You don't know that for sure," Billie corrected. "He may not have. Anyway, we aired the house out, but it still smells like paint to me," Billie continued. "I'm so glad to be in my own house where I can paint the walls any color I want," her voice smiled. "I'm going to wallpaper the bathroom in my room, just because I can," she said.

"You might want to rethink wall papering a bathroom, Mom," she paused. "The steam from taking hot showers and baths will make the wallpaper peel," Tanisha suggested.

"Really? I hadn't thought of that, but I guess that makes sense. Maybe I'll just wallpaper the powder room in the basement then. I'm wallpapering something," she said. "You're going to like the new furniture that your dad and I picked out," Billie offered. "The living room and dining room look like a model now," she beamed sounding like a giddy school girl.

Tanisha grinned into the phone. "I'm sure it's nice, Mom. I can't wait to see it," she offered. "By the way," she paused. "I'm not sure, but I might be bringing a friend home to meet you guys over Thanksgiving weekend," she said softly.

"That's fine. We have plenty of space now," Billie beamed. "Is this one of your Yale classmates?" she asked.

"Not exactly," Tanisha replied. "He's a friend that lives in

Morning Side," she paused. "He's in medical school at Howard University," she added.

"Oh," her mother replied. "Did you say Harvard or Howard?" Billie repeated.

"I said Howard. His name is David Barton," Tanisha said. "He went to Georgetown and now he's a first year medical student at Howard."

"Oh," her mother repeated. "How'd you meet this new boyfriend?"

"We met when I was in high school," Tanisha offered. "And he's not my boyfriend, Mom. He graduated from Homer Glen, so he was friends with some of my friends that went there," Tanisha stammered.

"What happened to the boy that you were dating last summer? He's at Princeton, right?" Billie asked.

"His name is Brian Kraft," Tanisha said. "And yes, he's at Princeton," she sighed.

There was a long silence and Tanisha could hear water running. "Are you cooking dinner?" Tanisha asked.

"Uh huh, I'm making spaghetti," Billie replied. "Tanisha, I don't mind meeting your friends, but you know that your father doesn't want to meet any of your random boyfriends after what happened with that other boy," she whispered. "I can't remember his name, but the boy with the earring and gap who took you to prom."

"His name is Glen Horton, Mom," Tanisha groaned. "And David isn't a random boyfriend, Mom. We've been friends for almost five years," Tanisha blurted.

"Five years?" Billie repeated. "And why are you just now interested in having us meet him?"

Tanisha took a deep breath, willing herself to choose her words carefully. Because I was embarrassed about you and didn't want David to meet you when you weren't on your bipolar medication? The words sat lodged in the phlegm in her throat.

"Because we were just friends, Mom," Tanisha whined. "We're still just friends. David has a girlfriend, and he knows that I was dating Glen," she explained.

"Then why do you want us to meet him?" Billie challenged. "You remember how your father gave Glen the third degree when he took you on a date?" she reminded. "And I know you remember how your father threatened him when you told us that he was stalking you," she finished.

This time the sigh was loud and exaggerated. "He wasn't really stalking me, Mother," Tanisha corrected. "But Maria and Rashanda and my other friends suggested that I involve Dad so he would stop calling me so much," she reminded.

"And he was trying to transfer to a school in Connecticut to be closer to you after you broke up with him," Billie reminded. "Sounds like he was stalking you to me, but you can call it whatever you like," Billie continued. "Now why are you willing to let your father meet this David character and not this Brian boy that you call your boyfriend?" Billie asked.

"It's complicated, Mom," Tanisha sighed.

"Is David black or white?" Billie asked. "Is it because Brian's white?"

"What difference does it make?" Tanisha shrieked.

"It doesn't make a bit of difference to me," Billie said calmly. "But I'm just wondering why you want your father to meet him and you haven't offered to introduce us to Brian Kraft?" Billie goaded. "I'm guessing David is black since he goes to Howard

Medical School."

Tanisha marveled at her mother's liberal use of the word us and how comfortable her mother felt referring to herself as part of a couple now that her parents had remarried.

"White people can go to Howard too, Mom. And David just wants to meet you guys," Tanisha offered. "It's really no big deal," she groaned.

"I don't mind meeting him, but don't expect your father to be nice to him," Billie warned.

"You know what, I might not even be coming home for Thanksgiving," Tanisha blurted quickly. "Brian's family invited me to come to New York to spend Thanksgiving with them," she shared. "I haven't bought a ticket home yet, so I might just train to New York," she barked.

"You haven't bought your plane ticket yet?" Billie asked. "But your father put the money in your account two weeks ago so you could get a good fare," she reminded.

"The twenty eight day advance fare was the same as the fourteen day advance fare, so I still have time to get a ticket," she said gruffly.

"Oh," Billie replied. "Well, you know the family is looking forward to seeing you at Aunt Helen's for Thanksgiving, Tanisha," Billie reminded softly. "All of your cousins will be home from college," she reminded. "But you're an adult now, and we can't force you to come home."

"I'm not sure what I'm going to do. Right now I feel like just staying in bed, my head hurts so much," Tanisha whined.

"Boil some water in your hot pot and drop some Vick's vapo-rub in there," Billie instructed. "Wrap a towel around your head and inhale the vapors. It'll help open up your sinuses," she instructed.

"And eat something greasy, and swallow a half a teaspoon of the Vicks," she continued.

"Mom, I'm not eating Vicks," Tanisha said. "I'm just not. And I cook noodles in my hot pot," she paused. "That's gross. I'm not going to want to use it to cook food if I boil Vick's in it," she finished as Laura and Monica walked into the room.

"Boil Vick's in what?" Monica asked.

Teenie waved her hand and covered the mouthpiece of the phone.

"Then pour it into a bowl, Tanisha," Billie suggested. "But you need to place your head over some steaming Vick's," her mother encouraged. "The sooner the better. That's the only way you're going to feel better."

"Okay, Mom. Listen my friends are here so I need to let you go," Teenie said. "I'll let you know what I decide to do about Thanksgiving," she nodded. "Love you too, Mom," she whispered.

"What is Vick's and why does your mother want you to boil it?" Laura asked plopping on Teenie's bed and splattering her books to the floor.

"I can't believe you don't know what Vick's is," Teenie replied. "It's a menthol rub."

"My mother always rubbed it on our chests when we had colds," Monica added, making a rubbing motion over her heart.

"Exactly," Teenie sniffled. "My mother told me to drop it in some boiling water and inhale the vapors to open up my sinuses," she added. "It feels like my head is going to burst," she whined. "Do either of you have a bowl?" Teenie asked.

Laura and Monica stared at each other and nodded their heads no. "I could buy one for you. We just stopped by to see if you needed anything, Teenie," Monica said. "We're going into town and thought we'd check on you. Do you want me to see if I can find a bowl at the drugstore?"

"Or you could just use that plastic shoe box that has your pens and pencils in it," Laura suggested pointing to the clear plastic box above Teenie's desk. "That's probably waterproof."

Teenie glanced at the shelf and nodded. "Good idea. I hadn't thought of that," she confessed. Teenie wrapped the afghan that her grandmother had given her as a graduation gift firmly around her shoulders.

"Do you need us to score some medicina for you, chica inferma?" Laura giggled in Spanglish. "We have a hook up man on campus," she teased.

"Nope. I'm fine. I picked up some medicine from the health center," Teenie said. "But if you go near the greasy spoon diner, you could pick me up a cheeseburger with everything and fries," she suggested. "My mother swears that eating something greasy will make me feel better."

Laura laughed. "Teenie you know I don't do greasy spoons," she stated. "I'm not trying to gain the freshman fifteen. In fact, I'm thinking about becoming a vegetarian," she announced.

Teenie and Monica stared at each other and grinned. "It's not about you, Senorita Self Absorbed," Monica chided. "This is about making Teenie feel better. If she wants a greasy burger, we'll bring her one," Monica assured. Leaning against Teenie's desk, she'd removed the plastic shoe box from the shelf and positioned the pens and pencils in a straight line parallel to Teenie's books. Monica took a paper towel and wiped the pencil shavings from inside the box.

Teenie pulled a ten dollar bill from her wallet and handed it to Monica.

"Fine! You're going in to get it, Monica. I do not want to be seen walking into a greasy spoon diner! In fact, let's get out of here before we catch Teenie's cooties," Laura grimaced covering her mouth with her hands. "No offense, but I hope you're not contagious, Teenie. I don't want to be sick over Thanksgiving break."

"Speaking of Thanksgiving break, have you decided what you're going to do, Teenie?" Monica asked. "Are you going to go home to see David or are you going to meet Brian in New York?"

☙◗◖❧

Two weeks later, Teenie stared at the luggage, her ticket peeking out of the zippered part of her carryon bag. He hadn't taken the news well. She expected him to be disappointed, but she hadn't expected him to be heart broken. The reaction that she received when she shared that he wouldn't see her over Thanksgiving break was clearly heart break. Even over the phone she could feel the heart break in his tone.

She leaned her head over the bowl for what she hoped was her final round of the Vick's steam facial.

Chapter 8

Take Me with You

I live in Dallas, Texas. I live in Houston, Texas. Her mind said each sentence with an exaggerated Texas drawl. The words felt odd on her tongue. It had been a long time since she'd played the choice game. She ran the rules through her head: rock breaks scissors, paper covers rock, scissors cut paper. Two out of three. She'd decided on Dallas, for no other reason than Dallas spelled backwards was salad with an extra L. She'd recently developed a love for chicken Caesar salad with anchovies. It was a stupid reason to choose a city, so she decided to try a more scientific approach. Rock-Paper-Scissors. If he wins the rock-paper-scissors tournament, I'll ask him which city is his favorite. Whatever his reply, that's where I'll go. I'll claim it as fate. If I win, I'll go to Dallas. I'll claim that as fate too, it sounds better than choosing a city because it reminds me of food.

She and her brothers had played the child's game as far back as she could remember. Rock-paper-scissors served as the family's official arbitration judge. Its outcome was official and binding in all dispute resolutions. The winner earned the honors to choose which television program would be viewed, which flavor of ice cream would be purchased for dessert and which movie they would see at the theatre on their weekend visits with their father, outings that had become less frequent now that the children were young adults.

"It's not that serious, Justine," Kendal hissed. "If you want to go to the food court to have a chicken Caesar salad, we can go there for lunch, honeychile," he purred. "I'll just get a miso soup like I always do. I just want to fill you in on my latest conquest," he giggled. Kendal pulled an emery board from his pocket and filed his perfectly manicured nails.

"But I always choose our lunch spots, Kendal," Justine countered. "We'll play rock-paper-scissors. Whoever wins gets to decide where we go for lunch. It'll just take ten seconds," she assured.

"Girl, you know I don't know nothing about these childish games," Kendal groaned, waving his hand dismissively. "How does this work again?"

Justine slanted her eyes at Kendal suspiciously. "Everyone knows how to play rock-paper-scissors. You just forgot the rules. We both place one hand behind our back and at the count of three you put your hand in front and either make a fist which is rock," she demonstrated. "Or show two fingers which represents scissors," she showed. "Or lay your hand flat which represents paper," she explained. "Rock breaks scissors, scissors cut paper, and paper covers rock. It'll make sense once we do it. We'll do two out of three," she finished.

"What if we both show the same thing?" Kendal asked.

"Then we do it again until we are each showing something different," she assured. "It's easy. It's like riding a bicycle, you'll remember how to play once we do it," Justine giggled. "This game saved me and my brothers from many a knock down drag out fight."

"Justine, you know I was raised in a foster home, and we didn't play no games, girl. It was dog eat dog. Kill or be killed!" Kendal said somberly, his voice an octave deeper. "I was lucky to get enough food to eat in there. If I turned my back, the other kids stole my food. This must be some white people game that you learned in Newberry East," he said softly.

"It's not a white people game, silly. It's a child's game, and everybody plays it. And don't even try it. You were not raised in a foster home," Justine giggled. "Your father is a lawyer, and your mother is a teacher. You were raised in Hyde Park and went to the Latin School," she reminded. "You went to school with the children of corporate tycoons so I know you played rock-paper-scissors!"

"I did," Kendal confessed. "But I'm auditioning for a part as a foster child who becomes a crack head," he explained. "It's a Steppenwolf production, and the competition is intense so I was trying to do some method acting to become one with my character," he explained, clutching his hand to his throat for dramatic effect. "It wasn't convincing was it?"

"Not at all," she admitted. "Is the crack head gay or straight?" Justine asked.

"I think he's straight," Kendal paused. "But I'm not sure. I've never seen a gay crack head. What difference does it make?"

"It doesn't. But it's going to take you longer to learn how to method act a straight crack head than a foster child crack head," she laughed.

"Chile, I know that's right," Kendal giggled. "I've been trying to butch up for this role, but it's just not working," he admitted seriously, filing his nail. "It's more challenging than I thought to play it straight. But I'm going to give it my best shot because I really want this part. Or maybe I should just take creative liberties with the part and play it as a gay crack head!" he suggested, waving the emery board like a pointer.

An aspiring actor with a dancer's soul, Kendal worked at Field to pay the rent. Justine smiled at her friend. Since working at Field, he'd become one of her best friends. He was a senior sales associate in the men's apparel department and had helped Justine master the art of merchandising and floor display set-ups. Kendal was a slight build with chiseled cheekbones that popped from his face like wings on an angel.

A Julliard graduate, he loved Manhattan. Ten years earlier, Kendal had auditioned for the Alvin Ailey Dance Troupe. He'd mastered the intricate choreography and made it to the final round of auditions, garnering an audition in front of the beautiful Judith Jamison. Days before his audition, a hairline stress fracture in his left foot reared its ugly head. Undaunted, he rested, iced and medicated, determined to perform through the pain. Once on stage, his alter ego took over. With the confidence of a lion, he locked eyes with Madame Jamison. Seduced by the majesty of the moment, he leapt like an impala, his lithe body suspended in air. He'd performed this move countless times. It was his trademark. He had entered the realm where the dance had become a hypnotic drug, and he found himself in a trancelike state. He was having an out of body experience. Suddenly, he felt his body descending involuntarily. By the time the pain raced from his foot to his brain, it was too late to adjust in time to minimize the impact of his fall. Like skiers and ice skaters, dancers are trained on the correct way to fall. His eyes locked on Judith Jamison's, the bronze goddess of all things dance. In that perfect instant, his years of dance training failed him. His body slammed the stage. Kendal collapsed to the floor writhing in pain. Paramedics were called.

In the recovery room, he was told that he had torn his Achilles tendon and fractured his knee cap and femur. His injuries resembled those of someone who had fallen from a two story window and miraculously landed in a bush that served to slow the descent and cushion the fall just enough to prevent death. They told him that it was a miracle that he hadn't fractured his spine or broken his neck and been paralyzed. Kendal fainted when they told him that.

That night, his parents flew to New York and his mother slept on the pull out bench in his room every night. His third day in the hospital, Judith Jamison sent a beautiful, rare orchid and invited him to audition after his recovery. He treasured the card that he knew had been signed by her personally. They decided that it would be best for his mother to stay with him during his convalescence. He didn't argue. He could barely walk. The recovery was long, painful and arduous. His parents paid for the best physical therapy that money could buy. In his heart, he felt he was being punished. A plastic surgeon was flown in from Beverly Hills to hide the surgical scars. As spring morphed into fall, his mood shifted. He was feeling better. Bored of his mother's helicopter hovering and insistence that he enroll at Columbia Law School, he threatened to go on a hunger strike unless she moved back to Chicago. It worked. She left, and he trained harder and was dancing fifteen months post accident.

A fire burned in his belly. His skill, though slightly dulled, was still sharper than expected. During his long recovery, Kendal had continued his disciplined dancer's diet. His body was as lean and toned as ever. His practice times increased, but in his heart he knew the truth. His dance career was over; at least the platinum level, Alvin Ailey dance career that he'd dreamed about since childhood. That was over. A dream deferred. After a proper period of mourning, he switched to acting. He landed a few small roles in off Broadway productions, and waited tables in Soho to support himself. But walking the streets of New York proved too painful for him. He needed a fresh start. His parents lured him home with a new Saab convertible and a condominium in the Printer's Row neighborhood. It worked. Sweet home Chicago.

When Justine first met Kendal, she'd liked him instantly. As thin as a muscular mannequin, his clothes were tailored to fit his athletic frame, and his grooming was impeccable. At their introduction, he'd insulted her in a loving way.

"Nice to meet you, Justine," Kendal smiled staring at her with a puzzled expression, his left pinky perched on the tip of his lips. "Chile, if you're going to work in my department, you have got to get those eyebrows cleaned up. They look like two shedding caterpillars on your forehead," he squinted. "Are you growing them in or out? I can't tell, but they are a hot mess," he observed. "This will never do!"

Startled by his honesty, she'd raised her hand to her eyes and blushed. "I was, I mean, I haven't had time to tweeze them," she defended. "I normally tweeze them."

"Tweeze them, schmeeze them," Kendal dismissed. "You need to have those puppies waxed. It's a cleaner look. I prefer thicker eyebrows on ladies, not that I prefer ladies," he corrected. "But thin eyebrows look ghetto. Your eyebrows frame your face and should be groomed at all times. Now, let's take you upstairs to the salon. My girl Clarice will hook you up. It's one of the few perks of working in this forsaken place. We get free salon services. Clients are not going to buy from associates who look a hot mess," he finished gripping her elbow and escorting her to the beauty salon. "Clyde will cover your department. This is an emergency," he insisted. "Clyde, it's a code 13," he yelled across the floor as he rushed Justine toward the elevator.

They'd been friends ever since. His clients, mostly Halsted Street dwellers, began to trust Justine's sense of style and came to see her if Kendal wasn't available, which was rare. His clients knew his schedule and only shopped at Field when he was working.

They entered the elevator and pressed the employee lounge button. Kendal had won the rock-paper-scissors tournament, two out of three.

"Which is your favorite city, Dallas or Houston?" Justine asked quickly.

"Dallas or Houston?" Kendal repeated. "I've never been to either. Why do you ask?"

"But if you had to pick one, which would you choose?" Justine tried again. "Have you heard better things about Dallas or Houston?"

"Neither. I've never heard anything particularly good or bad about either one," Kendal admitted. "It's hot and humid in both, and you know my hair does not do well in humidity," he grinned at Justine suspiciously. "Wait a minute. What's going on, Justine?" her friend asked.

Justine bit her lip and watched the elevator numbers, trying desperately to avoid eye contact with her intuitive co-worker. "Nothing," she bluffed. "I just asked you a simple question."

"It wasn't a "simple" question, Miss Thang," Kendal challenged. "Something's up. You better dish, fish!" Fish was the pet name that he used for all of his female friends. "And you better tell me the truth or I will pull this emergency stop button," he threatened. "And you know how claustrophobic you are."

"I think, I mean, I might be," she stammered.

"You might be what?" he challenged. "Cause I know you ain't fixin' to tell me that you're thinking about moving yo' narrow behind to no Dallas or Houston, I know that ain't what you fixin' to tell me, up in here, girlfriend!" he shrieked.

She could feel the urge returning. She inhaled deeply and tried to redirect her thoughts the way the therapist had suggested. Justine stretched her fingers and clasped her hands together, willing herself to take deep, cleansing breaths. In the end, the urge won. Her hand traveled to its familiar comfort spot like a swallow returning to nest in the same tree year after year. Her thumb and index finger gently caressed a few strands of her long hair before settling at her scalp and rubbing gently with her index finger. The subtle nervous habit had returned the night she and AM broke up. She'd rubbed a small bald spot as she cried herself to sleep each night.

Justine had first started the hairline rubbing fixation after her parents announced their decision to divorce. That time, she'd created a small bald spot the size of a quarter in the front of her hair and had been forced to wear bangs to conceal the damage that her nervous habit created.

Frustrated, she clenched her jaws tightly and removed her hand, balling her fist in anger. The urge sparring with her will as her hand traveled back to her hair, and the rubbing continued.

"What's wrong, sugar?" Kendal asked softly. "Don't rub your hair. The spot is growing in now, and you don't want the patch to return," he cautioned. "Pull out your stress ball. I saw it in your purse when you were looking for a mint."

Startled, Justine remembered that she'd confided in Kendal when he noticed the spot along her hairline, after her recent and futile attempt to cover it with a new hairstyle. Like a small child being scolded gently by a parent, Justine obeyed her friend's command, silently pulling out the lime green stress ball that helped her redirect her left hand. She never used her right hand to rub her head, only her left index finger.

"Are you thinking about moving to Texas?" he asked gently.

Unable to speak, Justine nodded her head in the affirmative.

"Do you have family in Texas?" Kendal asked.

"My dad's aunt lives there," she choked. "His mother's sister. I haven't seen her since I was ten. She never had children," she added. "I was named after her."

"Hmmph," Kendal grunted. "Family is family, but what are you gonna do in Texas with somebody your grandmother's age?" he asked.

"I just feel like I need a change," Justine whined as they walked into the employee lounge. "This city reminds me of AM," she whispered as they breezed by other sales associates on their lunch break.

"The wound is still fresh, Justine," Kendal reminded. "I'm not saying that a fresh start is a bad idea," he paused. "But take it from me. Wherever you go, you're going to take your broken heart with you. Moving to Texas is not going to help your heart heal quicker. That's just geography."

"But a change might be just what the doctor ordered," she countered. "Learning a new city, transferring to a new school might prove enough of a distraction to help me get over it."

"You know what's going to help you get over AM?" Kendal chuckled.

"No, what?" Justine replied. "And I'm glad you think my life is so comical."

Kendal grabbed two trays and handed one to Justine. Groaning, he reached for a napkin and wiped his wet tray furiously. "You know me well enough," he smirked. "You should be able to finish my sentence," he chided. "What's going to help you get over AM, girlfriend?" he asked seriously.

Following Kendal's lead, Justine wiped her damp tray with

napkins and stared at Kendal. "My mind is drawing a blank," she confessed.

"Another AM," Kendal blurted quickly. "You need another AM," he paused. "Or a PM or a Tom, Rick or Harry," he laughed. "Pick one. That's the only thing that's gonna help your wounded heart heal. And you know I know what I'm talking about, fish!" he laughed. "You need to find yo' self another man, quick, fast and in a hurry," he stated. "And while you're at it, see if he has a friend for me," he giggled.

Justine smiled weakly at Kendal. His words reminded her of her mother's advice. Andrea had told her that when you fall off a horse, you have to pick yourself up and get right back on the horse or you'll never conquer your fear of falling.

"But why Texas?" Kendal asked as he scooped a ladle of steaming miso soup into his large bowl. "If you're going to move," he paused. "Why don't you move some place exciting like New York city or even Atlanta?" he asked, with a furrowed brow. "I'm confused that you would choose dull Dallas. Blah," he shivered.

"I don't know anyone in New York or Atlanta," she admitted. "At least I have an aunt in Dallas. I don't know if I'm ready to move to a new city where I don't know anyone at all," she confessed.

"I take that back," Kendal corrected. "I've never been to Dallas, so I don't know if it's dull, but it just seems like it would be hot, slow and boring! Cowboys wearing boots and big hats all the time, and talking in that slow way that Texans talk," he stated. "How yawl doing?" he mocked. "Not my cup of tea."

Justine made her salad and crowned it with anchovies. She decided to forego her usual soda fountain treat and instead reached for a bottle of spring water. With the increased stress in her life, her adult acne had returned. She knew that her condition was not helped by the carbonation and sugar that she consumed twice a day. She was trying to train herself to appreciate the taste of coffee.

"I'm glad to see you drinking water, fish," Kendal observed. "It's the best thing for your body. Next I'm going to have you drinking green tea and doing yoga with me," he grinned.

"You're pushing it," Justine smiled, slumping into her seat.

"Sit up straight, chile," Kendal scolded. "You are not auditioning for a part as the understudy for the letter C. Sitting up straight engages your abs. Sit up straight or drop and give me twenty push-ups," he finished.

Obediently, Justine adjusted her posture and scooped a forkful of salad into her mouth. Food still had no taste to her.

"The truth is this, Justine," Kendal sighed. "You can't run from heart ache, girlfriend. Heart ache has to leave on its own. Trust me, I know what I'm talking about," he paused. Kendal scooped the steaming miso soup into his mouth in rapid swoops.

Staring in admiration, Justine marveled at how he could consume the hot soup without scorching his tongue. She took another bite of her salad, and pushed the lettuce around on her plate.

"You can move to Dallas, Texas, Kokomo, Indiana, Paducah, Kentucky or Timbuktu," he said. "But wherever you go, your drama is going right there with you. Like a bad suitcase. It'll be waiting for you on the other end," he assured. "It might even get there before you do and help you find an apartment," he chuckled.

"Be serious for a minute. Tell me what to do, Kendal," Justine whispered. "I'm tired of feeling like this. At least a move would provide a distraction for me. Give me something to focus on other than my broken heart," she sighed, slamming her fork into her plate. Her daily dose of tears welled in her eyes waiting for their cue to enter the scene.

Kendal lifted his near empty bowl to his lips and slurped down the last corner of soup. "If I had the cure for the broken heart flu, I'd be a rich man," Kendal offered. "I wish I could tell you what to do, but only time will heal your blues, my friend. Time and a new bus," he chuckled. "Or a new horse. Whatever your mama said is right. You need to get on a new horse."

"But I still have feelings for AM," Justine whined. "I don't want to get on a new horse."

Kendal shook his head from side to side. "Pathetic. You sound like a pathetic, little puppy dog. Tsk. Tsk. 'I don't want to get on a new horse,'" he mocked, sarcastically.

"Why does that make me pathetic? Because I still care about the guy who dumped me?" Justine whimpered. "I still have feelings for him and that makes me pathetic?"

"Because you haven't learned anything from the experience," Kendal corrected.

"Get the cover for your salad and eat it at break. You're pushing that food around on your plate like a five year old. You're done," he observed. "And I want you to come with me to run a quick errand," he said as he stood.

"What was I supposed to learn from this?" Justine quizzed pulling the lid from beneath her plastic salad box. "I don't get it."

Balancing on one foot and stretching his arms above his head like a lithe exclamation point, Kendal sighed. "My point exactly, you don't get it."

She stared at him like he was an ancient Egyptian code that she was trying to decipher.

Still balancing on one foot, he leaned into her personal space and slowly pressed his nose against hers. His breath smelled like miso soup and Calvin Klein cologne, a dab of which he methodically placed on his tongue, behind his ears, on his wrists and other places Justine blushed when hearing. When questioned, Kendal couldn't remember why he'd begun using fragrance as a breath freshener.

"You must reinvent yourself, Justine Wellington. You must become the woman that he fell in love with again," he whispered softly. His words were slow and deliberate, almost robotic. "You must be the same you, only better," he purred. "And I will help you." Kendal used his thumb and stroked her perfectly manicured eyebrows. "I will transform you into the best of you," he smiled as he slowly lowered his foot to the ground. "I know what you need better than you do," he winked. "I will transform you like Professor Henry Higgins did Eliza Doolittle," he finished.

"Liza Doolittle?" Justine frowned.

"Eliza Doolittle! From the movie 'My Fair Lady.' I know you saw that movie," Kendal groaned.

"New topic!" he stated before Justine could reply. "How's your friend, Grace?"

The look was fleeting, but telling. "What was that?" Justine asked. "Why'd you just look at me like that when you asked about Grace?" she quizzed.

Winking at the cafeteria worker clearing the table, Kendal left two singles on the table and grabbed Justine's salad container. His arm across her shoulders, he guided her to the escalator. "Nothing. Nothing at all. You just haven't mentioned her since she came to the store that time before she left for school," he stammered. "I was just making conversation," he smiled.

"She's fine. I'm supposed to visit her next weekend," Justine shared. "So I'm scheduled off from Friday through Sunday. I'm going to drive down Friday afternoon."

"Maybe I'll go with you," Kendal offered. "I haven't done a college road trip in a minute, and Grace and I really clicked. It could be fun!" he giggled. "But first, I need your opinion on a birthday present for my mother. We don't have to punch in for fifteen more minutes so I want to show you this sweater that I think she might like."

"You actually want my opinion on apparel?" Justine choked. "This is a first."

"And don't make it a last, fish," Kendal giggled. "I just want you to tell me if you think that it's mom looking enough. My old man always says that the stuff that I buy for my mother is too flashy," Kendal framed his face with both hands and fanned all ten of his fingers for emphasis. "He's crazy. He and I both know that I have great style. I've picked out my mother's clothes since I was in junior high," he giggled. "That should have been their first clue that their little boy was special," he chuckled. "That and I used to choreograph fashion shows with my neighbor's dolls. Anyhoo, I'm tired of hearing his mouth when I present her gifts so I want you to choose. And I know you have an eye for boring ladies' fashion," he stated flatly. Kendal stepped off the escalator just in time to miss Justine's swipe.

"Take me with you. I could use a quick road trip. I've got unused vacation time, so let's head to the University of Illinois next weekend!"

Chapter 9

Great Expectation

Her face caressing the coat, Rashanda squeezed the jacket into her body and inhaled. Sniffing the coat made her homesick. Her eyes roamed the familiar space nostalgically. Her long fingers caressed the well worn garment. She slipped her arms through the sleeves. Wearing the coat made her smile. She knew it wasn't scientifically possible, but she felt her mother's warmth, her body heat radiating through the sleeves like a hug. Rashanda buried her face in the sleeve and took another exaggerated deep breath. Her mother's scent was undeniable. She'd worn the same perfume for as long as Rashanda could remember: Heaven Scent, an inexpensive drugstore fragrance. She hadn't noticed it before, but it smelled as though the coat had been dipped in Heaven Scent. Rashanda wondered if the well worn garment had ever been professionally cleaned. She was glad that she hadn't spritzed her wrists with her own cologne. Lately, she hadn't been able to tolerate perfumes of any kind, but she was enjoying her mother's scent which hung in the air like a fragrant bouquet of spring flowers.

The coat gripping her shoulders, her legs crossed at the ankle, she shifted her feet and crossed her legs the other way. Crossing her legs at the knee always cut off her circulation and increased the swelling in her feet. Exhaling, she kicked off her shoes and placed her feet on the sofa remembering the doctor's suggestion to keep her feet elevated. Just as quickly, she slipped her loafers back on. The last time she'd taken off her shoes, she'd had to struggle to squeeze her swollen feet back into them. With her shoes still on, she placed her feet on top of the coffee table, a forbidden resting place in the Jordan household.

She'd convinced Ian that it would be best for her to face her parents alone. He strongly disagreed.

"We're married now, Rashanda," Ian reminded. "We're a team, and there's no I in team. I'm coming with you," he said firmly.

"I need you to trust me on this one, Ian," she pleaded. "I know my father. He needs more time. It hasn't been enough time yet. Once he gets to know you, he's going to love you," she assured. "But we have to take it slow. My father is a stubborn man, Ian. Liking you has to be his idea and it has to happen on his terms."

Her neck craned back as far as it would stretch, Rashanda gazed into Ian's eyes. In her bare feet, she stood almost eight inches shorter than her tall, young husband.

"Don't forget, I'm his first daughter. And I know you remember how intense he was when you took me to prom?" she reminded. "So the idea that you're my husband now is really going to take some getting used to for him."

"Well, he better get used to it," Ian stated flatly. "I'm your husband, and I'm not going anywhere," he stated. "I'm not going to let you take the train and I don't want you driving by yourself."

"What if we compromise? You can take me, but let me talk to them alone first. You can study at the library for a few hours while I visit them. How's that?" she asked.

Ian's shrug was non committal. "I do have a lot of work to do," he agreed.

"It's a win-win situation. You can study while I feel them out. Just plan to call me about two hours after you drop me off and I'll give you a pulse check," Rashanda instructed. "If the coast is clear you can come over for dinner," she paused. "And if it's not, we can go to Aurelio's for pizza. I actually have a taste for pizza, because under the circumstances, I have a feeling that my father is not going to be happy to see you," she mumbled softly.

The garage door gently shook the floor. Dozing slightly, the rumbling startled her awake. Like a frightened child, Rashanda removed her feet from the coffee table and walked swiftly to the foyer to hang up her mother's jacket. Her heart thumped in her chest.

Rashanda Rochelle Jordan Hall, you are a grown, married woman. Calm down! Get it together and calm down! If you act like a child, they're going to treat you like a child!

Pacing, she wondered if she should meet them in the garage or stay put. She decided to stay put. A car door slammed. Seconds later, she heard her sister, Tiffany race inside and ascend the stairs.

Afraid that she might frighten her timid sister, Rashanda greeted her before she reached the front door landing.

"Hey ghetto girl," Rashanda teased. "I see you're still as smelly as ever!" she smiled.

Through the banister slats, Rashanda watched as Tiffany froze in her tracks. Startled to hear a voice in a house presumed empty, yet calmed by the familiar tone and pet name, Tiffany peered cautiously through the banister railings. "Oh, my God!" she said in slow motion. "Shanda? Is that you, Rashanda?" Tiffany squealed as she raced up the remaining steps. "What are you doing here?"

Embracing her younger sister in a bear hug, the girls squealed in animated delight.

"Do Mom and Dad know you're here?" Tiffany asked. "Where's Ian?"

"I thought I'd surprise them," Rashanda said. "Ian's at the library. What's taking them so long to come inside?" she asked.

"Dad bought some new shelving for the garage, so they're unpacking the car. Some of it was strapped to the roof. I had to use the bathroom," she paused. "I can't believe that you're here. It's sooooo good to see you," she purred.

"You too, ghetto," she teased, tossing Tiffany's long hair. "Before they come in, is Dad still super mad at me?" Rashanda whispered.

"Well, that depends," Tiffany offered softly, smoothing her ruffled mane. "He doesn't really talk about it much. You know Dad. He's a man of few words."

"That's what worries me," Rashanda sighed.

"But you didn't answer my question, where's Ian?" Tiffany repeated.

"I did answer your question, psycho. He's at the library. He dropped me off so that I could spend some time alone with you guys," she shared. "If the coast is clear, he's going to pick me up later. If it's not clear, I'll meet him at the mall and you can drop me off there. I can't believe you're driving now, squirt!" Rashanda giggled.

"Believe it, girl. And I only drive the Lincoln. I do not drive Mom's car. My profile is too tight to be seen in a raggedy hoopty!" Tiffany laughed, blowing air on her nails and tossing her long hair over her shoulders. "I think they're planning to buy me my own car!" she boasted.

"What? Dad lets you drive the Lincoln? And they're planning to buy you your own car?" Rashanda repeated. "That's so unfair.

I never got to drive that car," she whined like a spoiled teenager. "Why are they buying you a new car? I was the straight A student, and they didn't buy me a car!" Rashanda argued.

"I don't make the rules, I just benefit from them," Tiffany giggled. "Dad got a promotion at work, and he's tired of having to drive Mom's car so that I can drive the Lincoln," she explained.

Rashanda stared at her younger sister in disbelief. "So Dad leaves the Lincoln for you to drive?" she asked.

"Yup," Tiffany shrugged. "When Dad drove Mom's car for a few days, he realized that Mom's car was a clunker, and he doesn't think it's safe for me to drive. They're looking at a Toyota Corolla. I saw the brochure on Dad's nightstand."

"How do you know it's for you? Maybe they're buying Mom a new car," Rashanda challenged. "What makes you think you'll be driving a new car while Mom is driving a ten year old car?" Rashanda asked incredulously.

"Because Mom's getting a Mercedes station wagon," Tiffany shared casually.

"Mom's getting a Mercedes?" Rashanda asked loudly. "How do you know that?"

"Because I went with them to pick it out," Tiffany explained. "It should be here next week. Dad's not going to give up that Lincoln, so I deduced that the Toyota Corolla brochure must be for moi," she grinned. "You know I won't be pushing Mom's new Benz," Tiffany finished. "Which is fine by me, because it's a station wagon. It's adorable, but it's still a grocery getter," Tiffany added.

"Mom's always wanted a Mercedes," Rashanda admitted. "What kind of promotion did Dad get?"

"I guess it was a good one," Tiffany grinned. "Looks like you already put on the freshman fifteen, fatty, and your hair is getting so long, Shanda," Tiffany noticed.

Rashanda self consciously wrapped an arm around her mid-section and blushed. "Do I look fat?" she asked sheepishly.

"Not fat," Tiffany corrected. "You're just not as boney as you normally are," she shrugged. "But tell the truth, Shanda, was Ian too chicken to face Dad?" she asked. "Because at your wedding, I saw Dad sitting in the back of the church and I thought Dad was going to take Ian out!" Tiffany laughed.

Rashanda playfully smacked her sister's shoulder, the bitter sweet memory of her wedding day gleaming front and center in her mind.

ෂාආ

"She's too young," Mr. Jordan barked. "How did this happen? Why didn't I see this coming, Alice?" he groaned, pacing like a caged cougar.

Mrs. Jordan wrung her hands. "She's almost nineteen. She's an adult. Technically, there's nothing we can do," Mrs. Jordan reminded. "She loves the boy, Bill."

"But she's soooo young," he repeated.

"We were eighteen when we got married," Mrs. Jordan reminded.

"But that was different. Everyone got married young back then," he defended. "Times have changed now. Rashanda is so smart. She has her whole life ahead of her," he groaned. "She's too young to get married."

"You said yourself that you liked Ian, remember?" Mrs. Jordan reminded gently.

"I liked him as a boyfriend for her, not a husband," he

stuttered, the word husband barely audible. "I had such great expectations for Rashanda," he mumbled.

"Well," Mrs. Jordan sighed. "They're in love. He did the honorable thing and asked your permission, which is very respectful," she added. "What are you going to do? She doesn't need your permission to marry the boy, Bill. They're going to get married whether you like it or not," she shrugged.

"I know that!" he screamed. "Don't you think that I know that?" Mr. Jordan plopped on the bed, his head cradled in his hands. "I'm sorry for that," he offered. "But I just wasn't expecting this," he sighed. "What do you think about all of this?" Mr. Jordan asked.

"I don't know what to think," she admitted. "I really don't." Mrs. Jordan shrugged, stroking a porcelain figurine that her daughters had presented as a mother's day gift several years before. Her finger instinctively rubbed the crown of the mocha ballerina. Outfitted in a pink tutu, the ballerina's porcelain crown had a mysterious chip that Rashanda and Tiffany assured they had not caused. Her best interrogation techniques resulted in the same story from each of them. Their air tight alibis and her mother's intuition confirmed that her daughters were innocent of the infraction. Although she suspected that Mr. Jordan had bumped the trinket from her dresser, she knew better than to confront him. "I think he's a very nice young man, Bill," she continued. "He's smart. He's got a promising future ahead of him, he treats Rashanda like a princess, and he loves her," she listed. "She could do a whole lot worse for herself."

"I'm not asking you to sing the boy's praises, Alice! What do you think about this marriage foolishness? Get to the point, woman!" he growled. "Do you think she should marry this boy?

And why now? What's the rush?" he asked. "You don't think she has to get married do you?" he asked softly.

Like most traditional couples reared in the south, Alice and Bill Jordan had managed to avoid any delicate discussions regarding the maturation of two teenage girls. When Rashanda still hadn't started her menstrual cycle her sophomore year in high school, Alice Jordan tried to gain information about her husband's sisters. "Rashanda is concerned that she hasn't started her period yet. Did your sister's start their cycles late?" she asked casually one evening. "Alice! I don't concern myself with lady business!" he blurted. "Don't ask me questions like that, woman!" Mrs. Jordan comforted Rashanda's concerns without involving her husband. When Rashanda's cycle finally started during her junior year in high school, Alice withheld this delightful news from her husband. She'd also not shared when Tiffany started her cycle a few months after the arrival of Rashanda's. Mr. Jordan was not comfortable talking about "lady business."

Mrs. Jordan had heeded Big Momma's advice and taken over responsibility for maintaining the girls' shared bathroom. Stating that she preferred this chore to the nightly ritual of cleaning the kitchen after dinner, the girls eagerly agreed to allow their mother to clean their toilet, a task that both found extremely distasteful. With her new chore providing an opportunity for her to peruse the trash receptacle on a regular basis, she was confident that Rashanda did not have to get married in the way that her husband implied.

She sighed deeply and considered her words carefully. "No, Bill," Mrs. Jordan said softly. "Rashanda does not have to get married," she assured confidently.

"Well, what could it be then?" he asked. "What's the rush?"

Mrs. Jordan paused carefully at the crossroads. She knew that her honest reply was not what her husband sought. She struggled for the words to explain to her husband that she suspected that his daughter wanted to get married so that she could have sex with the boy that she loved. She chewed her lip and prayed for wisdom. The knock was firm and confident.

Jumping to his feet like a gazelle, Mr. Jordan snatched the door open. Standing on the other side of the door was Rashanda.

"Sorry to interrupt, Dad," she said confidently. "But Ian and I have to head back to Evanston. He has a tutoring session tonight," she shared.

Mr. Jordan scowled at Rashanda without speaking. Gently pushing past her husband, her mother stepped into the door frame. "Rashanda, can you stay the night?" Mrs. Jordan asked. "We'll take you back in the morning."

"I don't think so, Mom," Rashanda said softly. "I'm leaving with Ian."

ဆာလ

His refusal to walk her down the aisle hurt the most. Big Momma had called him a stubborn mule. She'd taken Amtrak up from Mississippi to attend her oldest grandchild's wedding, and her own son refused to walk his daughter down the aisle.

The wedding had been thrown together in haste, taking place in the church that she'd attended her entire life. Admittedly, her family's church attendance had been sporadic, but it was still their home church.

Rashanda and Ian had agreed that the ceremony would be quaint and limited to very close relatives and friends. Her sister Tiffany served as the maid of honor and Ian's cousin Mark served as the best man. Though there was no need for such a role, with less than forty guests and a red velvet cupcake and punch reception in the church basement, Teenie, Maria, Justine and Grace served as hostesses. They energetically escorted guests to the front of the church and passed out the brief wedding programs that Maria had designed by hand. The hostesses wore the matching white ensembles that they'd worn to Lori's funeral.

Mrs. Jordan had been the voice of reason, convincing Rashanda and Ian that they shouldn't get married at city hall in front of a justice of the peace. She understood their desire to have a small ceremony, and assured them that they would appreciate a small church wedding much more than a visit to city hall. She'd also insisted on making a wedding gown for Rashanda. She'd purchased a beautiful white silk fabric and sewn a simple Vogue pattern gown with a tight fitting bodice and matching shoulder length veil. Tiffany wore Rashanda's prom dress, the dress she'd worn when Ian presented her with her cherished promise ring. Tiffany thought the dress was ugly and out of style, but she agreed to wear it for her only sister's wedding.

The family's next door neighbor for over fifteen years, Mr. Hampton insisted on recording the ceremony using his video camera. He also served as the photographer. No other neighbors were invited, not even the hostesses' parents. But Mr. Hampton considered himself family, and he was.

As the wedding date loomed, Mrs. Jordan was forced to confirm Rashanda's suspicion that her father refused to walk her down the aisle or attend the ceremony. The news was not received well. Rashanda's body entered a quiet state of shock and denial. The man she'd loved her entire life was asking her to choose between him and the man that she wanted to marry. Ian insisted that they attend marital counseling at the church that they attended on campus in Evanston. During one of the counseling sessions, Rashanda's quiet state of shock was transformed into anger and rage. The pastor explained that her feelings were part of the normal stages of grief. Like dealing with a death, even though her father had not died, his decision to shut her out felt like a death. He assured her that in time her father would come around. He counseled that when he did, the Christian thing to do would be for her to forgive him.

Rage boiled in Rashanda's heart. She vowed to hate her father forever. Like a favorite uncle, Mr. Hampton offered to escort Rashanda down the aisle. Mrs. Jordan politely refused his generous suggestion, knowing that this gesture would be viewed as a wicked act of betrayal by her stubborn husband. Maria suggested that Rashanda be escorted down the aisle by Lori's Angels. Rashanda gladly agreed.

It rained on her wedding day. She feared that the rain and dark sky were a bad omen. The wedding was devoid of pomp and circumstance. Ian and Rashanda arrived at the church in Ian's old car, ignoring Teenie's squeals that it was bad luck for the groom to see the bride before the ceremony. The hostesses quickly ferried Rashanda to the pastor's office to change into her wedding gown. Maria plugged in a lighted make-up mirror, the very mirror that the girls had given Grace as a birthday gift, and applied Rashanda's make-up. Ian wore his only suit and a new tie purchased by his parents for the occasion. As the guests arrived, the atmosphere in the sanctuary was giddy and festive. Ian's cousin played soft piano music in the background. In line with the couple's wishes, the wedding ceremony was scheduled to start promptly at three thirty in the afternoon. Big Momma had told Rashanda that it was customary for a wedding to start when the hands on the clock were on the rise and not the decline.

Guests had been asked to arrive no later than three fifteen. Rashanda made a beautiful bride, with two hostesses flanked on either side of her, each carrying a pink rose with a white silk ribbon. Rashanda carried a bouquet of thirteen pink roses each representing a special person in her life: one each for her five best friends: Maria, Teenie, Grace, Justine and Lori. A rose for her sister Tiffany, and one each for her mother, Big Momma, Ian's mother, Ian, herself and a single rose for their shared future. The thirteenth rose represented her father. Tiffany led the wedding processional down the small church aisle carrying two pink roses wound tightly with a white silk ribbon that represented the unbreakable sisterhood bond that she and Rashanda shared.

Ian's parents had been less than thrilled about their young son's decision to marry while still in college, but they liked Rashanda and wanted their son to be happy. They'd welcomed Rashanda into the family and embraced her tighter when they learned of her father's disapproval. Their gift to the couple was the honeymoon suite at the Conrad Hilton Hotel. Rashanda smiled when she realized that they'd be spending their wedding night in the hotel where Ian had presented her with her cherished promise ring.

The wedding ceremony had taken less than ten minutes. Instead of sitting in the pews, the guests were invited to stand at the altar and cover the couple in prayer. The circle of prayer had been Ian's mom's idea. Staring into her husband's eyes, a single tear slid down Rashanda's cheek. Ian kissed the tear, smiled and swiftly kissed Rashanda's hand. The endearing gesture caused a chorus of "awwws" to resonate throughout the small church. Blocked by the semi-circle of prayer, Rashanda noticed someone sitting in the back row of the church. Her contact lenses slightly moist with tears, she squinted to confirm what her heart hoped. It was her father. Dressed in his only suit, a suit usually reserved for funerals, she tried to get his attention but was quickly swarmed by well wishers. As her eyes spanned the small church, she watched in agony as her father slowly stood and left the church. That was the last time she'd seen her dad.

৪৩৫

"Who are you talking to, Tiffany?" Mr. Jordan bellowed. "You haven't been in this house five minutes and you're already running your mouth on the phone?" he chuckled. "I thought you were going inside to pee and then you were going to help us unload those shelves, girl," he stated, his husky voice appearing even deeper as he approached.

Holding hands, Rashanda and Tiffany glanced at each other and stared toward the stairs. Squeezing and releasing her sister's palm, Rashanda took a step forward and stuffed her hands in her pockets. She squared her shoulders as Mr. Jordan's head slowly rose up the steps, his thinning hair more apparent from her higher vantage point.

"I should have known you would skirt out of helping us unload the car," his voice trailed. "If there's work to be done I can count on you to run the other way," he teased.

"Hi Dad," Rashanda interrupted. "You got a haircut."

With his right hand on the banister, his left gripping a brown grocery bag, Mr. Jordan ascended the last step and turned his head toward the voice. "Rashanda?" he stated, his eyes lighting up. "What are you doing here? I mean, I'm surprised to see you. Does your mother know you're here?" he asked in rapid succession.

She shook her head. "No," she replied timidly. "I thought I'd surprise you guys."

Mr. Jordan looked at Tiffany for any signs of betrayal. Tiffany shook her head from side to side and shrugged her shoulders. "Don't look at me," she pleaded. "I didn't know she was coming either, she scared me half to death when I walked in. I almost peed my pants!" she confessed. "In fact, I still haven't been to the bathroom yet," she shared racing down the hallway.

Her hands still buried deep in her pocket, Rashanda gazed softly at her father, a goofy grin frozen on her face. Unsure of her next move, she studied him like a chess board, wishing that she'd heeded Ian's advice and allowed him to come with her. She felt uncomfortable under her father's gaze. Mr. Jordan was never much of a hugger, and now she didn't know the appropriate protocol for greeting your father when you arrive for a surprise visit home after your dad refused to walk you down the aisle at your wedding and stubbornly chose to observe the ceremony from the back row of the church before leaving abruptly.

"Tiffany told me that you bought new shelving for the garage," Rashanda stammered. "You've talked about that project for awhile," she smiled nervously.

"Yeah, I have," her father mumbled. "I figured there's no time like the present," he smiled just as nervously.

"Rashanda? Is that you?" Mrs. Jordan asked standing beside her husband, slightly winded from her slow trek up the stairs.

"Hi, Mom!" Rashanda beamed loudly, walking toward her mother with arms outstretched. "I didn't even hear you walking up the stairs."

"What are you doing here?" her mother asked squeezing Rashanda in a tight bear hug. "Why didn't you tell us you were coming home? Is everything all right? You and Ian haven't had your first fight have you?" she asked rocking Rashanda in her arms.

"No, Mom," Rashanda smiled. "Ian and I are fine. I just thought I'd come for a quick visit. That's okay isn't it?" she asked. "Or do I have to wait to be invited home now?"

"Of course not. This will always be your home too. Even though you're a married lady now," Mrs. Jordan giggled.

Rashanda noticed that her father was staring at her.

"So how's married life?" he asked quickly. "You look like you've put on a few pounds," he observed. "It looks good on you. You were too skinny."

"Thanks, Dad. I have gained some weight," Rashanda blushed. "The cafeteria food in the dorms is pretty starchy. They serve lots of potatoes, rice and pasta," she shared. "And they have fresh desserts available for lunch and dinner," she continued. "I was eating chocolate chip cookies for dessert at lunch and cake or pie for dessert at dinner. I've cut out sweets now, because my jeans were getting a bit snug," she explained. "I've actually lost a pound of what I'd gained," she stammered.

Ding, dong, ding dong. Ding, dong, ding dong. Dong, Dong, Dong. The Westminster chime signaling a visitor at the front door rang softly.

"I'll get it," Tiffany announced bouncing back into the room. "It's probably for me anyway," she finished.

"Well, I need to get dinner started if we're going to eat tonight," Mrs. Jordan announced taking the bag from Mr. Jordan. "And Bill, I'm sure you want to spend some time talking to Rashanda," she suggested. "Tiffany, I don't know who's at that door, but you need to help me put these groceries away and chop the vegetables for dinner before you can go anywhere or have company," she said walking toward the kitchen. "Who's at the door anyway?" she asked, standing in the doorway.

A goofy grin plastered across her face, Tiffany stepped to one side to reveal the visitor standing in the foyer. "Hi, Mrs. Jordan," the deep voice replied. Rashanda and Mr. Jordan turned toward the voice at the same time.

Like a knight in shining armor, Ian glided quickly up the six steps leading into the living room. Without waiting for an invitation, Ian embraced the stunned Mrs. Jordan and pecked her on the cheek.

Spinning on his heels, Ian turned quickly and greeted Mr. Jordan. "Hello, sir," Ian said confidently, extending his hand.

Ian's presence felt like a twelve pound gorilla had been lifted from Rashanda's chest. She hadn't noticed that she'd been holding her breath, but with Ian in the room, her breathing became deeper and more controlled. She watched as her father met Ian's outstretched hand with his, the soft smile that he'd held for Rashanda replaced by a skeptical scowl. Ignoring Mr. Jordan's hostile glare, Ian pumped Mr. Jordan's hand a few times before releasing his grip. He turned to his bride, wrapped his arms around her and squeezed tightly before lifting her off the ground. Rashanda felt like butter in his strong arms.

"What are you doing here?" she whispered in his ear.

"I didn't go to the library," Ian confessed. "I parked across the street and saw your parents come home. I wanted to be here with you when you talked to them," he said. "So I decided I'd give you a few minutes alone with them." Ian turned to face Mr. and Mrs. Jordan. "I saw you unloading the material in the garage," he admitted. "I wanted to offer to help you, but I didn't want to startle you," he shared. "I knew you probably weren't aware that Rashanda was here yet. Did you fall asleep, Shanda?" Ian asked.

Rashanda wanted to cry, he knew her so well. "I dozed for a few seconds," she confessed. "But I was upstairs talking to Tiffany while my parents were in the garage, know-it-all. I wasn't asleep," she smiled. Her confidence had returned ten-fold with Ian in the room.

"What are you building, Mr. Jordan?" Ian asked.

"I'm redoing the shelving in the garage," he grumbled tersely.

"That's what I thought," Ian grinned. "I felt like I was doing undercover police work," he confessed. "I pretended to be reading, but I was really watching you guys," he laughed.

"If your medical career doesn't work out, maybe you could become a police detective, Sherlock," Tiffany teased.

"That's what I was thinking too," Ian grinned.

Ding, dong, ding dong. Ding, dong, ding dong. Dong, dong, dong. The Westminster chime rang again.

"Now who in the world could that be?" Mrs. Jordan asked. "Tiffany, you may not have company tonight. And you're not going anywhere so don't even ask," she finished.

"It's Mr. Hampton, Mom," Tiffany shared.

Wearing his trademark overalls, an oil stained tire jack slung over his shoulder, Mr. Hampton walked up the stairs and stood beside Mr. Jordan.

"Everybody okay in here, Bill?" he asked. "I saw someone watching your house when you came home and then I saw him ring the bell, so I just thought I'd check and make sure you folks were alright," he said.

"We're fine, Hamp," Mr. Jordan said. "Rashanda surprised us and came for a visit," he said. "That was her fella spying on the house."

"Well, I'll be," he chuckled handing the tire jack to Mr.

Jordan. "I should have recognized you from the wedding video, young man," he said pulling Ian into a tight embrace and pumping his hand. He turned to Rashanda. "Howdy do, Shanda? Howdy do?" he teased as he pulled Rashanda into a tight embrace.

"Uh oh," Mr. Hampton winked. "You've got one in the oven," he chuckled. "Am I the last to know? How many months along are you, girl?" he said loudly, his hand resting boldly on Rashanda's stomach. "I guess you're about three months."

Ian and Rashanda exchanged nervous glances.

"Months along?" Mrs. Jordan repeated. "Are you and Ian expecting, Rashanda?" she asked quickly.

Rolling his eyes into his head, Ian reached for Rashanda's hand and squeezed it tightly.

"That's what I came to tell you, guys," Rashanda smiled. "Ian and I are having a baby."

"Oh my God!" Tiffany squealed. "You're having a baby?"

Mr. Jordan's scowl softened slightly.

Seemingly oblivious to the fact that his announcement was a news flash to the others, Mr. Hampton continued rambling. "Look at how God works. I just today got the video from the wedding. And I was going to bring it over this evening after supper so we could watch it together," he chuckled. "And here it is the bride and groom are right here. Whatcha cooking, Alice? Heck, it don't matter to me none. Mrs. Hampton is on the west side visiting her sisters tonight so she told me I needed to eat leftovers, but you know I ain't never been no fan of leftovers so whatever you're cooking fresh is fine by me," he continued. "Just set another plate for me, when you set the table, Tiff. You know I don't eat much. I'll go fetch that video right now. I also have the wedding pictures developed too, but they're not in an album yet. Just give me a few minutes and I'll put them in an album and bring those over too," he finished. "I'll be right back," he announced as he walked out the front door. "I'll come back through the back door like I always do," he added. "The front door is for visitors."

"Don't forget your tire jack, Hamp," Mrs. Jordan reminded taking it from Mr. Jordan and handing it to Mr. Hampton.

"Thank you, Alice," he chuckled. "I thought I'd come prepared in case I needed to go upside somebody's head. I'm sure glad there wasn't nothing jumping off up in here, cause I sho' nuf didn't feel like going upside somebody's head today," he laughed. "I'll be right back. I don't smell nothing on the stove, Alice," he added.

"I'm making smothered pork chops with rice. That don't take no time to whip up. It'll be simmering in onions once you get back," she assured.

"That's what I'm talking about," he winked. "And make some of those crescent rolls too," he added. "Or skillet corn bread," he suggested on his way out. "Either one is fine by me."

"I like that guy," Ian grinned. "He reminds me of my grandfather."

"How far along are you, Shanda?" Tiffany asked. "No wonder you looked fat to me," she smiled. "I should have guessed."

"We're almost twelve weeks," Rashanda announced. "So that's why I wanted to come home now. I wanted to let you know before I came home for Christmas next month, because I'm already starting to show," she confessed.

Ian's hand in hers, Rashanda rubbed her belly and walked toward the sofa. Ian sat next to his wife, his arm draped across her shoulders.

"We told my parents last week," Ian added. "We wanted to

tell them before Thanksgiving since we're spending Thanksgiving with them. We thought we'd spend Thanksgiving with my family and Christmas with you," he paused. "I know this is a lot of information, but I hope you're happy for us."

"Where will you live? How are you going to finish school with a baby?" Mr. Jordan growled.

"Well, as the Resident Hall Coordinator, I get to live in a one bedroom apartment, so there'll be plenty of space for the baby," he explained. "And Rashanda and I will work out a system so that one of us is available to watch the baby when the other one has class. And if we can't avoid taking a class at the same time, the students in my dorm and the resident assistants have all agreed to pitch in to watch the baby."

"There's also a lady who works in the cafeteria who said that her mother hires herself out as a childcare provider. We met her last week, and she reminds me of Big Momma," Rashanda added. "And once the baby is six months old, I can take her to the on site daycare center that the university has for students and faculty," she continued. "It's really nice."

Mrs. Jordan smiled at her daughter. "It looks like you guys have this all worked out," she smiled. "I'm going to be a grandmother," she grinned. "I'm going to be a grandmother!" Alice rose to her feet, a grin plastered across her face. "You're definitely staying for dinner," she stated. "I won't take no for an answer. Tiffany come and help me get dinner going. And you are welcome to spend the night here if you don't want to drive back tonight," she added. "It'll take me five minutes to put fresh sheets on Rashanda's bed."

"I don't know about that, Mom," Rashanda said. "We'll stay for dinner, but I think we'll just head back." Her eyes cut to her father. Mr. Jordan stared blankly at Ian.

"Why are you looking at Dad?" Tiffany laughed. "You're married, and Ian already knocked you up so Dad should be cool," she laughed loudly walking into the kitchen. Her mother smacked her backside as she walked through the doorway. "Ouch! What'd you do that for?" Tiffany whined.

"You just don't know when to keep that simple trap of yours shut, do you?" Mrs. Jordan asked. "Slice that onion and close your mouth!"

Like a solar eclipse, the blank stare and slight crescent moon smile that was fighting for control of Mr. Jordan's face was now replaced by a stern frown.

Chapter 10

The Road Trip

"What do you mean that you just knew?" Justine asked. "How can you just know something like that? How did you know? Did you see something?"

Kendal smiled mischievously. "I only met her that one time," he reminded. But I just knew, chile," he shrugged. "It's an intuitive thing. Chapter members can always spot other chapter members," he offered casually. He used the term casually now. Like membership in a secret organization, Justine learned from Kendal that the term applied to gay men or women. They were chapter members.

"But how?" she pleaded. "I've known her my entire life and I didn't have a clue," Justine admitted. "That's because you're not a chapter member," he yawned.

Kendal turned the volume up on the stereo, and the mellow sounds of Diane Schur pulsed softly through the car's speakers. "It's been a long weekend, fish," he yawned. "I'm going to take a quick snooze. I can't believe I have to punch in tonight," he groaned. "I'm going to kill Ms. Cornet for making me work today. She knows that I don't like to do a half shift on Sunday. If I'm going to work Sunday, I prefer the banker's hour shift. Nine to five. How many times do I have to remind her of this? Cecelia and I are going to have a sit down when I see her Chanel – St. John draped tail tomorrow," he yawned again. "You just keep your eyes on the road and don't drive my car into a ditch, Miss Thang," Kendal instructed. "I don't want to hear my father's mouth if I send him another bill. I just need to listen to my girl Diane Schur until I fall asleep, and then you can listen to whatever you want."

Justine raised her hand to stroke the stress spot in her head, but thought better of it, and instead squeezed the stress ball in the cup holder as her friend settled into the passenger seat, his car blanket tucked neatly under his chin. Only a male chapter member would travel with a special car blanket.

"Don't kill me," Kendal giggled softly.

"How did I miss that my best friend is gay?" she whispered softly. "But how can she be gay? She went on a few dates with that cute guy, Dell Curry from River North. Did she know that she was gay then? Maybe she's just test driving gay," she continued.

"Look, fish," Kendal blurted. "I know you're trying to whisper to yourself, but I can still hear you! I need to get a nap so that I don't fall asleep at work tonight. If you don't let me catch a few winks, I'm going to make you work my shift," he threatened. "And for the record, yes, Grace was gay when she went on a date with that guy. You don't just become gay. It's not a virus. You don't catch it," yawned Kendal. "Some of my gayest friends are married with children. Puh-lease! Now, shush!"

"Ok, crabby," Justine giggled. "Go to sleep!"

⇚⇛

Like donning a new pair of prescription lenses after a lifetime of blurry vision, you don't realize what you've been unable to see clearly until your vision is improved.   Embracing her new truth had been as eye opening as her first pair of eyeglasses. She remembered her visit to the optometrist, an appointment made after her high school math teacher suggested to her parents that her grades might improve if she could see the chalkboard without squinting. At first, Grace had whined like a small child about having to wear glasses, but once she put them on her face, the world immediately became crisper and sharper. Colors were brighter and she saw definition and depth in objects for the very first time. Her overall appreciation for the world had improved. Grace had ceased squinting at street signs, amazed that her corrected vision allowed her to read a street sign from as far away as twenty feet. She'd ordered contact lenses, but found herself donning her glasses out of sheer expedience and haste in her rush to get to school on time. Learning that her mother, Lydia Moore, wore glasses had given her comfort. And later, when she was introduced to her birth father, one of the first things that she admired about him was the distinguished eyeglasses that he wore. She had a genetic predisposition for nearsightedness.

Grace hadn't considered how transformative her discovery had become, impacting almost every aspect of her college experience. Her sudden announcement at the Kappa Gamma Mu pledge meeting was met with stunned gasps. Muffin adjourned the meeting and scurried through the house to find members of the executive board. Grace was required to sign a pre-typed document acknowledging that she was voluntarily choosing to abandon the pledge process so that she could further explore a personal identity issue. The carefully crafted statement was read to her from the Kappa Gamma Mu Membership Intake Guidelines. As instructed, she signed on the line, hugged Muffin and left the house. Once outside, Muffin ran behind her and thanked her for being brave enough to craft a story that would not reflect poorly on Muffin as pledge mom. Grace smiled and repeated Muffin's hollow promise to keep in touch. "Definitely, let's stay in touch, Muffin."

The sea of students felt like family to Grace. An only child, and a natural loaner, she thrived on the activity and action at the student union, preferring to study in the noisy student union instead of the library. She loved living on campus and was glad that her fattened net worth provided her an opportunity to live in an expensive on-campus student apartment that offered meal services. When Grace desired company, she could wander into the student television lounge or study room. But when she wanted privacy, she could retreat to her unit. The furnished unit had a sofa and two chairs along one wall, and a twin sized bed on the opposite wall. A walk-in closet attached to a small bathroom shared a wall with the small kitchen. She'd decided to buy the full meal plan and seldom used the small galley kitchen in her apartment. On a whim, she'd purchased cereal, milk and a few snack rations, but she'd yet to turn on the stove. The unit lacked a dishwasher, so she'd stocked up on paper plates, bowls, cups and plastic cutlery. As she purchased the disposable paper products, Teenie's voice rang through her head. "Reduce, Reuse, Recycle. Save the environment! Only use paper and plastic when you absolutely have to," Teenie preached to anyone who would listen. Grace was glad that her friend had embraced a new paper and aluminum recycling initiative that was sweeping the nation's college campuses.

Her parents had tried to encourage Grace to get a roommate, but as an only child, she didn't have the experience of sharing a sleeping space with someone else. She was glad that she'd held firm and had her own apartment. It was her sanctuary.

Grace was still growing accustomed to the freedom that her

inheritance afforded her. In a sea of forty thousand students, her inflated net worth was unrecognizable. The financial aid dependent students roamed campus with the same freedom and confidence as the offspring of corporate tycoons, trust fund babies, the children of second or third generation doctors and lawyers and blue collar small business owners who'd parlayed a skilled trade or craft into a multi-million dollar family business. With her bronzed skin, no one expected her to be a member of the golden gentry. She was just another black girl on the University of Illinois' vast campus.

A few times, she'd noticed her former pledge mom, Olive Jean "Muffin" Crown holding court like royalty as she paraded around the yard wearing her father's college football jacket with CROWN boldly emblazoned across her back. As best she could tell, none of the students on campus knew that Grace was a member of the wealthy Moore family, with the exception of the girls who were in her pledge class. Occasionally, she recognized girls from her brief pledge experience, the plaid or pastel colored Kappa Gamma Mu letters emblazoned on sweat pants adorning their small derrieres. Each time, the girls pretended that they didn't see Grace. She relished her decision to abort her pledge mission.

Grace preferred to keep her wealth private, but her trust fund administrator had insisted on notifying the university administration of her arrival on campus. This news garnered an invite to a private reception hosted by the president of the university where she learned that the University of Illinois was yet another of a long list of charitable establishments that benefited from the in perpetuity endowment established by her grandparents.

The pupils of the university chancellor had dilated slightly when she was introduced as Grace Dudley, granddaughter of Amelia & Michael Moore of Wilmette, Illinois. At the president's reception, she felt like a debutante being presented to society. No one introduced her as simply Grace Dudley, an entering freshman. Each introduction included the tag line 'the only grandchild of Amelia & Michael Moore of Wilmette, Illinois.' She began to brace herself for 'the look' that she received from the stunned guests, the slight tilt of the head and wrinkled brow that represented the universal body language for confusion. "My mother was Lydia Moore," Grace would offer quickly. "She was the only child of Amelia & Michael Moore." The guest would then swallow and smile knowingly as they admired her blonde, textured hair and olive skin. Grace wasn't sure if the smile was shock at her obvious biracial heritage or a realization that she was the sole heir to the Moore family's considerable wealth. "Your grandparents were lovely people," one silver haired woman gushed. "Your grandmother and I rushed Kappa Gamma Mu together," she smiled. Grace returned her smile before being led away to meet others.

As she exchanged casual banter with the university chancellor, Grace shared that she'd recently purchased a new car. She briefly mentioned that she was disappointed to learn that freshman students were not allowed to register cars on campus. She complained that the walk from her apartment was longer than she anticipated and she wasn't looking forward to trudging through the Champaign snow. The following morning, half awake as she stumbled into the kitchen for a glass of juice, she noticed a large brown envelope peeking beneath her front door. She tore into the package with her short nails and pulled out a gold vehicle sticker paper clipped to a campus map. The sticker bore the university's crest which granted her parking privileges at on-campus lots reserved for executive level university personnel and tenured professors. She'd noticed the sticker on cars parked in reserved spots on campus. Grace grinned.

She pulled out a slip of paper that read. Welcome to U of I! I trust that you will use your special privilege with discretion. The note was not signed. Grace shook her head from side to side. So this is what it's like to have real money!

The following weekend, she took Amtrak home and drove her new BMW back to campus.

She loved her new car. All of her friends had weighed in on the type of car that she should buy. Maria had suggested that she buy a convertible. Teenie had recommended that she buy a BMW or a Saab. Grace had never seen a Saab so she had her father take her to test drive one. She liked it but thought that the interior would be too small to squeeze all of her friends inside. Justine and Rashanda didn't have an opinion on the type of car that she should purchase but agreed that she should buy a black car because all cars look good in black. Teenie agreed. Grace decided to buy a champagne gold BMW with honey colored leather seats. She wanted to get a convertible, but she didn't want to wait eight weeks for it to be delivered so she settled on the hard top. She bought the model from the showroom floor. Her dad had accompanied her and thought the car was too small, but in the end he decided that it was her choice to make.

Checkbook in hand, her trust fund administrator had accompanied them to the dealership, a large, black binder that looked more like a school notebook than a checkbook, tucked under his arm. Kent Hebert was his name, and he had come along to facilitate the transaction. When Grace told him that she wanted to buy a car, he cleared his calendar and drove to Newberry East. A short man with a small build, Kent observed quietly until Grace made her choice. Her requests that he call her Grace instead of Miss Dudley were politely ignored. "I handle all of Miss Dudley's financial affairs," explained Kent. "When we have agreed upon the purchase price, please let me know," he finished. Kent sat in a chair by the window, gripping his black binder to his chest, his feet barely skimming the floor. Grace placed him at just barely five feet tall.

When she'd met with the attorneys to understand her inheritance, they'd explained that as a minor, she would be appointed a trust fund administrator who would be involved in all large purchase decisions until she turned twenty one. The trust fund administrator was paid through the law firm and had complete discretion to honor all reasonable purchase requests. Any purchases deemed unreasonable by the trust fund administrator would be funneled through the law firm for a second opinion. The law firm explained that this was a longstanding wealth preservation practice that the firm used to ensure that clients demonstrated prudent fiscal judgment.

Kent wrote a check for the entire amount of the car. The stunned sales person retreated to the general manager's office to caucus. Grace watched as he pointed through the glass window. Soon, other men wearing suits entered the small office. After a few moments they invited Kent into the closed door session. Just as quickly as he'd entered, Kent returned to his post by the window.

"What was that about?" Grace asked.

"Everything is all taken care of, Miss Dudley. They needed to call the bank to verify the availability of funds," Kent explained in his matter-of- fact tone. "I anticipated that they might, since it's fairly standard practice in a cash transaction of this magnitude, and of course, if you pardon my frankness, they're not accustomed to someone who looks like you paying cash for a car, Miss Dudley," he stated blandly. "I fully anticipated this, so I made sure that the bank president himself was available to receive the call," he finished before resuming his perch on the chair, the large binder checkbook clinging to his tiny frame. "We should be on our way in no time now," Kent assured.

Her father had been surprised that Grace was paying cash for the car, but Kent had explained that with Grace's considerable net worth, there was no need to pay finance charges on a depreciating item when she could afford to pay for it outright. Grace and her father were called into the office to sign a few papers as the car was moved from the showroom floor into a covered garage area where the car's functionality would be explained. Grace giggled like a child, as the nervous sales person handed her the key. Kent stood like a tin soldier near the car.

"So who are you exactly?" the sales person asked sheepishly. "That is of no concern to you," Kent stated, his tone crisp and monotone. "Please just explain to my client how to operate her vehicle so that we may be on our way," he finished robotically. Grace drove the car off the lot that day.

₞₡

Riding down Interstate 57 heading back to the university, she drummed her fingers along the leather trim of her new toy. She'd activated the heated steering wheel just to see if it really worked. It did. Her palms were sweaty. Turning off the heated wheel, Grace flipped a switch and opened the sunroof to cool off.

In the cafeteria and on campus, spiked purple hair, pierced lips and visible tattoos paraded unceremoniously beside the starched preppy duds of the conservative students. Her first week on campus, she noticed students of the same gender freely holding hands. The sight made her slightly uncomfortable. She'd returned to her apartment and pulled out the Bible that she'd brought with her. Flipping through its pages, she couldn't remember where she'd seen the scripture on homosexuality, her biblical navigation skills still novice in nature.

After Lori's funeral, Grace encouraged her mom to buy her a Bible.

"Mom, why don't you and Dad go to church or read the Bible," she blurted one morning while her mom washed the breakfast dishes.

"Just not something that we ever got into I guess," Mrs. Dudley shrugged. "We were raised Catholic, but we stopped practicing our faith before your mama came to live with us. We just felt there was too much hypocrisy in the church. White folks looking at us like we weren't supposed to be Catholic," she huffed. "I was just tired of explaining myself and trying to fit in so we stopped attending Mass. We still have faith in God, but we just stopped going to church."

"Do you have a Bible I can read?" Grace continued.

"I don't have one. We never took a Bible to Mass," she explained. "But I can take you to get a Bible, Grace," her mother offered. "Reading the Bible might help you make sense out of Lori's death," she comforted.

They'd gone to the book store and purchased a small Bible. Grace remembered what Lori had suggested when they talked about the Bible. "The Bible is the one book that you keep reading forever. There's no right or wrong way to read God's word," Lori coached. Grace tried to read a passage from the Bible in the morning before school, and again at night before bed. Sometimes, the language and names frustrated her, but she continued. She learned that there were sixty-six books in the Bible and it was written in two parts: the Old Testament and the New Testament. While reading the chapter introductions, she learned that Jewish people only believed in the Old Testament while Christians believed in both the Old Testament and the New Testament. She remembered that Lori often referred to herself as born again or saved. She flipped to the back of the Bible and looked up every verse that referenced Saved. Grace read in Romans chapter 10 verse 9 that to be saved only meant that if you believe in your heart that Jesus died for your sins and rose from the dead you will be saved from sin.

One night during her nightly Bible review, Mrs. Dudley knocked on Grace's door.

"Come in," Grace sang. Her father entered the room first, carrying a small cedar chest that he placed at the foot of her bed.

"I completely forgot to give you this chest of your mother's belongings," Mrs. Dudley grinned. "You know your daddy and I are getting up in years," she giggled.

"Speak for yourself, woman!" Mr. Dudley barked. "I thought you gave the child her mother's things when you gave her the letter that you wrote to explain that she was adopted," Mr. Dudley interrupted.

"How could I give her the trunk when the trunk was up in the attic?" she asked. "You know I can't bring down that trunk by myself, you old fool!" Mrs. Dudley barked.

"Well, why didn't you tell me to get it for you?" her husband asked.

"Because I forgot it was up there, Mr. Dudley. Did you go up there and get the trunk? You're the one who hauled it up there," she barked.

"Woman! I hauled that trunk up there over fifteen years ago. I can't keep track of all the hauling that I do around here," he shouted. "Up and down, up and down. Sometimes I feel like a mule!"

Mrs. Dudley cut her eyes at her husband before smiling softly at Grace. "Your daddy just asked me what you were doing, and when I told him that you were reading the Bible he asked me if you were reading your mama's Bible. And that's when I remembered that your mama had a Bible that she used to read all the time." Mrs. Dudley flipped up the lid on the small trunk.

"Your mama didn't have that many personal things, but we saved the few things that she had that we thought you might want. There are a few pieces of jewelry in here and a comb and brush set that she used to brush her long hair," she explained reaching into the trunk and pulling out the meager contents one by one and spreading them on the bedspread: a watch that had stopped ticking, a string of pearls and a hair adornment that resembled a small comb. "She always thought that she'd be back home with her parents once you were born, so we never sent for her things," her mother continued. "We didn't keep any of her clothes or anything," she finished.

"We don't believe in that, Grace. When someone has made their transition, no need holding on to their clothes when folks here could use them. We gave her clothes to charity," Mr. Dudley explained.

"But she did have this Bible that she read all the time," her mother continued, stroking the small book. She handed Grace a small red, leather Bible. The Bible was care worn. Grace flipped through the Bible's pages. Inside, there were markings throughout. At the top of most of the pages, the page number had been circled.

"Do you know why some of the page numbers are circled?" Grace asked hopefully.

"I do actually. Your mama circled the page after she read it so she could track how many pages in the Bible she'd read," Mrs. Dudley chuckled. "Never made sense to me how she would flip through the book reading random pages."

Grace glanced at her new Bible with its pristine pages. She'd been afraid to write in her Bible, fearing somehow that it was sacrilegious to mar God's word. Her mother's Bible had pen marks and underlines in red, blue, black and even purple ink along with highlight markings in pink, yellow and green, a rainbow assurance from God that it was okay to write in her Bible.

When her parents left the room, Grace fingered her mother's things. She pulled a few strands of blonde hair from the hairbrush and stared at them before inhaling the brushes' bristles and running the brush through her long hair. She placed her mother's strands of hair back into the hairbrush and next fingered the black velvet bag tied with a gold chord. She unfastened the chord and a string of pearls spilled onto her bedspread. Remembering a PBS special that she'd seen, she rubbed the pearls across her front teeth and felt a slight abrasion. The pearls were real! On the PBS special, the host had shared that a simple way to test if pearls were real was to rub them along your teeth. A cultured pearl would feel abrasive whereas a synthetic or freshwater pearl would feel smooth. Of course my mother's pearls would be real, silly. Her parents were wealthy! Grace picked up the hair adornment and placed it in her hair. She smiled at her reflection, glad to have a few personal items that had once belonged to her mother. I wish I could remember anything about you, Mom. I don't remember the way you smelled or the way your skin felt. I really need to talk to you. Mom and Dad are great, but they're so old, I don't know if they would understand what I'm feeling. I don't know if you would either, for that matter.

Grace gripped the red, leather Bible and flipped through its pages, admiring the rainbow assortment of pen and highlight markings on its worn pages. Her mother's name was engraved on the front cover in gold lettering: Lydia Caroline Moore. On the first page, the name was written in long hand, a heart dotted the letter I in Caroline. She smiled at her mother's signature and wondered how old she'd been when she received the Bible. Her question was answered by the next page. The Bible had been presented to her by her parents for her twelfth birthday. Grace placed the Bible on her nightstand on top of her new Bible before carefully placing her mother's belongings back in the small chest. She decided to clear space on her large bureau to place the chest on top, causing a few papers to scatter to the floor, the miniature golf score card glided through the air like a sky diver in flight. Grace studied the score card and bit her lip, wondering if she should go on another test date.

The date with Dell Curry had been fun. He'd taken her to play miniature golf. She liked miniature golf. The distraction of playing a sport that she enjoyed relieved some of the pressure that she felt about being on a date. Grace found herself stealing quick glances at Dell. He was cute, and she was nervous. She remembered to flip her hair incessantly as Maria instructed. She laughed at his jokes and waited for the heart racing adrenaline rush that her friends promised her would happen with a boy that she liked. Her prom date with Doug had been her last dating experience. There'd been no adrenaline rush with Doug. But the prom date wasn't a "real" date, she reminded herself. It was a publicity stunt crafted by the well meaning Teenie as part of the Lori's Angels production. She'd been nervous on her prom date with Doug, but she knew that he wasn't interested in her. And besides, her friends had been with her as buffers, and he'd been pressured to go to prom with her. It was a charity date. This time, she was all alone. As she and Dell walked the small eighteen hole miniature golf course, she wondered if there was any chemistry between them. She'd beaten Dell at miniature golf and wondered if that had impacted the chemistry formula.

Even with her limited dating experience, Grace considered herself an expert on chemistry, due to years spent listening to her friends' lunchtime boy banter. When Dell reached for her hand to walk to the car, she felt nothing. Once inside Sanfratellos for pizza, when his knee rested against hers at the booth, again she felt nothing. She wanted chemistry.

She'd heard Teenie gush about chemistry with all of the boys in her stable: Glen Horton, Brian Kraft and David Barton. Teenie shared that even though she and David were just friends, she'd felt instant chemistry with him when she met him which made it all the more challenging to maintain a platonic friendship. Maria had described the chemistry withTodd as an electric current. And Rashanda shared that she felt a jolt of electricity when Ian's knee bumped into hers during one of their first tutoring sessions. Even Justine had used the word chemistry to describe how she felt when AM held her hand for the first time. Grace also remembered Lori explaining that she broke up with CJ because of a lack of chemistry and how she felt giddy in Doug's presence. Chemistry. Grace wanted to experience that feeling.

She felt tense and willed herself to relax and enjoy his company. It wasn't working. He was a likable guy, but as the date wore on, she found him dull and uninteresting. A sports fanatic, he bored her with his incessant chatter about the Bears, Bulls, Sox and Cubs. He was determined to know all of the statistics for all of the Chicago sporting teams so that he could compare them against the Texas teams. Grace's school girl giggles were now replaced with yawns and blank stares. The silences became awkward. By the end of the night, her heart hadn't fluttered once. She suspected that Dell felt the same way. As he walked her to the car, she'd stopped flipping her long hair, and he wasn't reaching for her hand. A perfect gentleman, he escorted her to the door, but didn't try to kiss her goodnight as her friends suspected that he might. After their third date, she knew that there was no chemistry between them.

Her encounter with Claire had been different. Her eyes closed, and her body hunched over the table at the student union, Grace slowly rolled her neck in a counter clockwise motion several times before reversing and rotating her neck clockwise.

The soft hands on her shoulder caused the hairs on the back of her neck to stand up. Grace's eyes jolted open. "Let me help you," the voice said. "These chairs are ergonomically the worst chairs for studying. The tables are too low, so your neck cranes at an awkward position if you've been sitting for too long." Her boney fingers kneaded into Grace's neck in a slow, rhythmic pattern.

"I'm Claire, by the way. They should offer free massage services in the student union during midterms. Either that or invest in proper seating. What's your name?"

"I'm Grace," she mumbled softly. "Grace Dudley."

"Hello, Grace Dudley," Claire smiled. "Are you a freshman?"

"I am," Grace said.

"My boyfriend, George, is a freshman," Claire offered. "He's in his twenties, but he served in the military for four years, so he's one of the oldest freshman on campus. I'm studying to be a physical therapist and I work as a part-time masseuse on the weekends, so whenever I see a potential client I swoop in like a vulture attacking road kill," she teased. "That's a pretty gross analogy, but you know what I mean. I'll give you one of my cards. Your neck is really tight. Have you ever had a full body massage?" Claire asked as her fingers worked Grace's neck muscles and shoulders.

"No, I haven't," Grace stammered.

"You should check out the spa where I work. We're on campus next to the Burrito Buggy. Here's my card."

"Thanks, Claire."

"George is ready to go, so I'd better scoot. We offer student rates during the week," Claire explained. "I only work weekends, so if you come during the week, you won't get me, but we have some pretty buffed guys, most of them ex-jocks who work during the week," she winked. "They will flirt with you to get a bigger tip, but they're harmless. It's pretty affordable. Of course, I'm biased, but I think students should get a massage at least once a month."

Grace could hardly speak. Her entire body tingled. She wondered if this was the chemistry feeling that her friends described.

She scheduled a massage for the following day. During the telephone registration, the receptionist asked if she preferred a male or female masseuse. She requested a male masseuse. His name was Toby. The towering Toby was waiting for her outside when she pulled into the salon parking lot. He stood at least six feet six inches tall. As she climbed out of her new BMW, she noticed Toby grinning at her like she was an ATM with an unlimited withdrawal limit.

"I'm sorry that I'm late," Grace panted. "My professor kept us after class."

"It's fine. You're my last client. You're a tall one, pretty lady," Toby grinned. "Do you play ball for Illinois?"

"No. I'm just tall," Grace smiled. "You're pretty tall yourself," she shot back.

"I played ball for Illinois until I tore my ACL," he offered. "I'm going to play ball in Italy or Greece next year, but I have a kid who lives down here, so I wanted to stay near campus until his mother and I can firm up the custody arrangement," he continued. "Follow me. I saw on your sheet that this is your first massage. I'll take good care of you," he winked. "And don't worry, I won't talk during your massage," he assured. "If I'm doing my job properly, you should fall asleep. Before we get started, do you have any trouble spots that you'd like me to focus on?" he asked eying her chart. "You didn't indicate any when you registered over the phone, but I always like to double check."

"My shoulders and neck are tight from studying in the chairs at the student union," Grace added.

"Those chairs are what keep me in business," Toby grinned. "I'm going to step out so you can change. We'll start face up. I'll turn on the table warmer. I can always adjust the temperature if it gets too warm. Strip down to whatever layer you're most comfortable in. Just so you know, most female clients remove their bras but keep their undies on, but that's up to you. Climb on to the table lying on your back and cover with this sheet," Toby patted the massage table. "Lastly, is there any area that you want me to avoid?" Toby asked.

"Huh, what do you mean?" Grace asked.

"Do you want me to massage your hair and glutes?" Toby asked.

"My hair and glutes?" Grace giggled.

"Some of the black women don't like to get their scalp massaged because they don't want the massage oils in their hair. Do you want your scalp massaged? You are black aren't you?" he asked.

"I'm biracial," Grace replied, using her new racial identifier.

'That's what I thought," Toby smiled. "I could tell by the texture of your hair. I'm famous for my scalp massages, so I'll hook you up. You can just wash the oils out without a whole lot of drama. What about your glutes or your buttocks? Want me to knead those out for you?"

"Sure, why not," Grace giggled.

"I'll be back in five minutes. Like I mentioned, once I start working on a client, I don't talk. It alters the ambience and tone of the experience. But if you need me to adjust the pressure, just say so," he whispered. Grace noticed that his voice was now much softer than it had been earlier.

Grace disrobed down to her undies, glad that Toby had explained the standard practice and climbed on to the warm massage table. Moments later she heard a rap at the door.

"Come in," she replied.

He entered the room without a word. She watched as Toby lowered a dimmer switch on the wall and pushed the play button on a boom box. Instinctively, she closed her eyes as soft music pulsated through the speakers. She could hear Toby's raspy breathing and wondered if he was a smoker. Grace heard the familiar sound of a match being lit. The scent of lavender filled the room. Her foot kicked involuntarily when Toby surprised her by gently running his fingers through her hair. She inhaled the lavender aroma as his fingers kneaded her scalp and her neck. Feeling his warm, spearmint breath on her face, she was glad that she'd popped a mint in her mouth after class. Toby's strong fingers worked her arm muscles in a rhythmic pattern. She suppressed a giggle when he massaged her toes. Her skin felt like putty and she felt herself getting sleepy. Every muscle in her body relaxed and she wondered why she'd never before been introduced to the art of massage therapy. She felt herself drifting in and out of consciousness. Off in the distance, she heard a deep voice.

"I'm going to lift the sheet so you have privacy and I want you to flip on to your stomach and place your head in the cradle, Grace," Toby's voice instructed.

Still in a dreamlike state, Grace obeyed his command and settled on her stomach, snuggling into the intense heat of the massage table. Toby expertly massaged her neck, arms, legs, back and shoulders. She didn't even giggle when his fingers kneaded her buttocks through the sheet.

Once again, she felt her body drifting away. A parade of prisms danced beneath her eyelids, purple, red and yellow triangles and circles, the geometric shapes that always ushered her into dreamland. The deep voice beckoned softly.

"You're all set, Grace," Toby whispered, gently nudging her shoulders. "You must have enjoyed that because you feel asleep," he commented. "Take your time getting dressed and I'll meet you outside with some water. It's important that you hydrate after a massage."

Toby stopped the music and turned up the lights slightly before leaving the room. Beneath the sheet, Grace stretched her body and yawned. Sitting upright, she stared at her reflection in the floor length mirror on the wall. That felt amazing. My shoulders feel less tense and more relaxed. Grace ran her fingers through her long hair. But when Toby massaged me, I didn't feel the electric charge that I felt when Claire massaged my neck. What does that mean? She gave Toby a generous twenty five percent tip for the massage service.

Chapter 11

The One You're With

The yawn was lion-like and loud, all that was missing was a roar. She looked around self consciously, embarrassed that her boorish behavior might have been witnessed. Wiping the night's sleep from her eyes, and half awake, she sauntered into the cafeteria, her growling stomach leading the way. She paused at her new best friend, the salad bar, and frowned disapprovingly. This is a hospital! You'd think that they would have a more appealing selection on the salad bar. They don't even have romaine lettuce! And the carrot slices look pathetic and mushy. Gross! Tempted by the smell of burgers sizzling, she allowed her nose to guide her eyes to the grill station and watched as a silver basket of onion rings was pulled from a vat of hot grease. A few of the tasty treats dangled from the side of the basket. She felt her jaw drop and licked her lips longingly. Don't do it, girl! Fried food is strictly forbidden. You've already gained ten of the freshman fifteen!

Her weight gain was courtesy of the carbohydrate loaded food served in the cafeteria, plus a newfound penchant for daily milkshakes from McDonald's. She alternated between vanilla, chocolate or strawberry, each holding the same special place on her palate. Since beginning her new fitness regimen, she'd cut back her habit to one milkshake per week. Everyone had warned her that new college co-eds usually gained the dreaded freshman fifteen from eating cafeteria food and late night, snack filled study sessions. She patted her thicker mid-section. As a fresh basket of golden crinkle fries was salted, she almost caved in, but instead decided to buy a bag of popcorn and a cup of coffee. She'd always enjoyed the smell of coffee brewing, but never really cared for the taste. Now, she couldn't start her day without a warm cup of java with two packs of Equal sprinkled in. Drinking coffee had been her mother's idea. She'd described it as her secret appetite suppressant. So far, her coffee diet was working. The scale in her dorm bathroom registered two pounds less than the prior week. Her mother warned her against using artificial sweeteners. "Just use sugar. God made sugar. You don't know what types of chemicals are in that artificial stuff, Sweetie." Her mother's voice cautioned. But sweetening her coffee with sugar didn't taste the same. Plus, she didn't want the extra calories. Vowing to limit her fake sugar intake and slowly wean herself from the blue packet habit, she'd disciplined herself to only use one packet in each cup of coffee, down from her usual two. She added more half and half to make up the difference. Her coffee was so laden with cream that the color was as light as her skin.

Her popcorn and coffee in hand, she speed walked back to the room and hoped that the baby was awake. She wanted her baby sister to recognize her face. Hours earlier, when she held the baby for the first time, she'd trembled with fear. She'd never really given it much thought, but she'd never held a baby. She'd held infants as young as six months, and picked up toddlers, but never a newborn baby, fresh from the oven. Her heart filled with joy when she saw the baby sleeping peacefully in her square, plastic bassinet, swaddled like a pink burrito in the hospital issued baby blanket. Squinting at the sun beaming through the open drapes, she glanced at the hospital bed and was greeted with soft snores.

It marveled Maria that Liz could sleep soundly in a room bathed in sunshine. She glanced at the corner, expecting to see Richard dozing in the room's lone chair. And then she remembered that Richard had said he was going to run a quick errand and would be back before lunch. Mom's been in labor for over twelve hours. She's exhausted. And Richard was up all night with her. He probably went home to shower and get clean clothes. Smiling at her sleeping mother, Maria quietly moved the telephone away from the bed and turned the ringer to vibrate. She remembered hearing the nurse explain to her mother that with the phone on vibrate, she could rest, but a red light would blink to notify anyone in the room to an incoming call. Sipping her coffee, Maria stared lovingly at her baby sister and then at her mother. She read the nametag on the bassinet, the wording written in large block letters: Mother: Elizabeth Jeanine Dawson. Baby: Girl Dawson. She thought back to when she learned that her mother was expecting.

છી૭જી

"You're too old to have a baby, Mom," she spat. "You're almost forty!"

"I'm only thirty eight, Maria," Liz reminded her. "But I'm in great shape so the doctor said there's no reason why I can't have more children."

"But you're so old now," Maria whined. "And you said more. You're going to have more than one?"

"Who knows? We'll see how this one goes! Besides, I won't even be thirty nine when the baby is born," Liz beamed. "I'm so excited. I think I'm going to find out if it's a boy or a girl. No, I want to be surprised. Richard doesn't care if it's a boy or a girl. I don't think I do either," she finished. "What do you think I should do?"

"I'm going to have a sibling that's eighteen years younger than I am," Maria frowned, ignoring her mother's question. "People are going to think that I'm the baby's mother! Why didn't you tell me that you and Richard were planning to have a baby, Mom? You just can't spring news like this on me. How does Neal feel about it? And Daddy, have you told, Daddy?"

Liz laughed. "You know how your brother is," she paused. "When I told him he just said 'Congratulations! That's pretty cool, I guess,'" Liz shared. "I don't think he's concerned one way or the other. And since Neal lives with your father now, I'm sure he told your dad."

"What did Dad have to say, Mom?" Maria asked.

"I couldn't care less what your dad thinks about my life now," Liz shrugged dismissively. "I don't need his approval nor do I care about his opinion. Now that you're in college and Neal lives with him, I haven't spoken to him in months. There's no reason to talk to him."

"Are you surprised that he broke up with his secretary?" Maria tested.

"Not at all. I didn't expect that to last," Liz offered. "When you fool around with a man who was cheating on someone to be with you, what makes you think that he won't cheat on you to be with someone else?" she stated. "Always remember that, sweetie."

Maria considered her mother's comment. "Good point, Mom. Wait! Did Dad cheat on her too?" she asked.

Her mother's look was distant and far off. She slowly lifted her left eyebrow, smirked and shrugged. "No comment! New topic! Should I find out if I'm having a boy or a girl?" her mother asked.

"When I was pregnant with you and your brother, they didn't have the high tech ultrasound equipment that they have today, so you couldn't find out the sex. I know I can find out now, but I'm not sure if I want to know or not."

⇗⇘

Before Maria left for the University of Pennsylvania, she watched as her mother's lithe frame filled out. From behind, Liz looked as thin as ever, her large cotton tunics draped over slim capris or shorts. Her legs and arms were tan and toned while her midsection appeared to house a small soccer ball. By the end of the summer, her face was fuller and her hands and feet were retaining water from the humidity and heat. But Liz never complained. She just eliminated salt from her diet to help combat the sodium induced swelling. Even on the most sweltering days, while everyone complained about the miserable heat, Liz grinned and rubbed her belly with delight as she munched on cold watermelon and sipped ice water. Determined to preserve her athletic frame during her pregnancy, Liz and Richard walked every night when the sun went down.

Munching on her popcorn and sipping her lukewarm coffee, cooled by the high amount of cream that she'd added, Maria lifted her eyes toward the slowly creaking door. Expecting to see Richard's tall frame, she grinned widely as Mama Kaye walked in draped in one of her signature hats and a bright red, wool cape. She waved animatedly at Maria and blew her a kiss. Maria placed her popcorn on the night stand and walked toward Mama Kaye.

"Hi there, sweetie pie! You look adorable," she cooed embracing Maria in a tight hug. "Still as rail thin as ever I see.

You've gained a little weight, but you could use to gain a little more," she whispered.

"I'm trying to lose the weight that I gained, Mama Kaye," Maria whined.

"Rubbish! Don't you do no such thing, you hear me? You look perfect and healthy. Don't lose another nair pound," she cautioned squeezing Maria's frame gently and smoothing her long hair. "Now let me take a look at that beautiful baby sister of yours," she squealed softly. "I couldn't wait to get down here to lay my eyes on her." Her left hand clutching the brooch that was affixed to her cape, she looked like an academy award winning actress poised to accept her Oscar. Tears welled in Mama Kaye's eyes. "Oh, my goodness, if she doesn't look like the spitting image of you and your mama when you were babies," she said. "Just the spitting image."

"You knew my mom when she was born, Mama Kaye?"

"Chile, I knew your Mama before she was born. I was friends with your grandmother when she found out she was expecting, little Miss Lizzie Busy," she smiled. "And this little darling looks just like her. And you too. I came to the hospital when your mama had you, so I know what you looked like on your first day on earth too. She's gonna be just as pretty as you are. Your grandmother was a looker just like you and your mama. It's good genes. I tell the pretty, young girls at the church all the time, 'don't mess up your gene pool, now. If God gave you good genes, don't waste them,'" she chuckled. "Do you know what she's planning to name her?"

"You know Mom always uses family names," Maria smiled. "I think she's naming her Jeanine Mary after her mother and grandmother," she offered.

"Actually," Liz yawned. "That's close, but Richard and

I discussed it and decided to name her Jeanine MaryKaye," Liz smiled. "MaryKaye will be one word," she explained.

Maria and Mama Kaye turned toward the bed.

"You're naming your baby after me?" Mama Kaye blushed.

"You know I believe in family names, and you're family," Liz beamed. "It just felt right."

Mama Kaye walked toward the bed with both arms outstretched. Liz leaned forward and nuzzled her head in Mama Kaye's ample bosom.

"My stars. I don't know what to say," she blushed. "Jeanine Mary Kaye. Are you going to spell Kaye with an "e" on the end too?"

"Of course, that's how you spell it," Liz smiled. "We plan to call her Jeni Kaye for short."

"I wasn't expecting this," Mama Kaye smiled. "This is such an honor."

"Well, you're the reason Richard and I got together in the first place, Mama Kaye. You're the one who told me to live and be happy, so it's only fitting that we name our daughter after you."

The hospital door creaked again and Richard appeared. Carrying a bottle of champagne, he quickly hid something behind his back before walking into the room.

"Hi beautiful! I thought you'd still be sleeping," he beamed leaning over and kissing Liz on the lips, bending slightly at the knee, he placed something under the bed.

"What are you hiding?" Liz asked.

"I bought a bottle of champagne!" he shrugged.

"But you had something else in your hand too," Liz drilled.

"Hi, Mama Kaye! You look as fly as ever. You are wearing that cape!" Richard grinned. "Maria, thanks for holding it down while I ran out for a minute," he winked.

Maria noticed that Richard still wore the same clothes he had on when he left the hospital, along with facial stubble. He clearly didn't go home to shower and shave.

"That daughter of yours is quite a looker, Richard. You're going to need a double barrel shotgun to keep the boys away from her when she turns of age," Mama Kaye whistled.

"Any knucklehead who tries to come near my little Jeni Kaye will need FBI clearance," Richard grinned, his word directed toward his sleeping daughter. "In fact, I think I'm going to start a security fund along with her college fund so I can pay guys with guns to follow her every move when she becomes a teenager."

"You're still wearing the same clothes, I thought you were going home to shower and shave?" Liz noticed. "My dad and Neal are on their way down to see the baby."

"I thought I'd shower later. I bought some champagne so we can have a toast when they get here."

"What's in the bag that you put on the floor? Is it something for the baby?" Liz asked.

"Nothing gets by you does it? You just have to know everything don't you?" he smiled. "Now I see why your nickname was Lizzie Busy when you were little."

"She was into everything. You couldn't put anything past her. She had to know everything. And would snoop to find out what she wanted to know if you didn't give her the information she sought," Mama Kaye concurred.

Richard bent down to pick up the bag that he'd placed under the bed. "I was trying to wait until we were alone to give you this," he explained. "But since you insist on knowing everything, this is for you."

Liz stared at the bright, red Cartier bag dangling from Richard's fingers.

"Richard! Is this what I think it is?"

"I don't know. Why don't you open it and see."

Sitting at the edge of the bed, he rubbed Liz's leg beneath the thin hospital blanket.

Reaching inside, Liz pulled out a bright red box with gold embroidery along the border. The box was tied with a white silk ribbon. Liz gently pulled the ribbon apart and opened the box.

"Oh, Richard!" Liz squealed. "You shouldn't have! I thought we were going to wait and do this for my fortieth birthday."

"No time like the present! I wanted you to have it now," Richard explained. "I'll do something else special for your fortieth. When I told the Cartier salesperson that you'd just had a baby, he called it a "push" present," he laughed. "He said that he sells a lot of "push" presents since the Cartier store is so close to Northwestern Hospital."

"A push present, because I pushed a baby out?"

"I guess," Richard shrugged.

"Gross!" Maria squirmed. "That's a bit too much information for me."

"When I walked through the hospital, I saw a couple of black nurses and a few nursing assistants who smiled when they saw me dangling the red bag. I was in the elevator alone with one of them who told me that the white husbands always come back with push presents from Cartier or Tiffany, or they pull up with expensive foreign cars with large red bows on the roof," he chuckled. "The nurse said she was just glad to see a black husband toting a push present to the hospital," he laughed.

"The nurse probably thought you had a white wife," Mama

Kaye mumbled.

"Mama Kaye! Not in front of Maria," Liz admonished. "Let's be nice today."

"I'm not a child, Mother," Maria protested.

Liz pulled the watch from the case. The thin, brown leather band framed the rectangular face of the watch. "I've always wanted a Cartier watch," Liz sighed. "You're the most thoughtful husband in the world, Mr. Dawson," she purred, tears rolling down her cheek. "I will treasure this always."

"I will treasure you always, Mrs. Dawson. I love you, Liz," Richard smiled.

"I love you too, Richard," she cried.

Mama Kaye and Maria watched the scene as though they were watching a Broadway production. Tears welled in Mama Kaye's eyes. As if on cue, Jeni Kaye cooed softly and squirmed in her pink cocoon.

"Okay love birds, it looks like the real star of the show is either hungry or wet," Mama Kaye shared. She reached into the bassinet and picked up her namesake. "That's a hunger cry," Mama Kaye confirmed.

"How can you tell?" Maria asked.

"You really can't tell yet, but she's too fresh to be complaining about being wet. But I always say you should check the SOPs. Do you remember the SOPs, Liz?" Mama Kaye quizzed.

"Of course I remember my standard operating procedures, Mama Kaye. Check and change her diaper first. If she's still fussy, then play with her a little bit, she might just be bored or want some stimulation. If that doesn't work, put her on the tap," Liz giggled. "She's probably hungry."

"That's right. In that order. Don't just feed her. She might just want to be held or might want to play on the floor for a little bit. Try stimulation first and then whip out the chocolate milk tap. Or in your case, the strawberry milk tap since you're so high yellow, your milk is probably strawberry or vanilla," she teased.

"Okay, you two are grossing me out! Are you going to breast feed her, Mom?" Maria asked.

"Uh, huh. I breast fed you and Neal for at least six months. I plan to do the same with Jeni Kaye."

"I just peeked, and her diaper is bone dry, so she's probably hungry, Liz." Mama Kaye handed the baby to Liz. "Mama Kaye needs something to eat, sugar. Show me where the cafeteria is," she suggested to Maria. "Can I bring something back for you, Liz? How about you, Richard?" She folded her cape and placed it on the window seat before perching her hat on top.

"I'd like some French fries, and a strawberry-banana, yogurt shake, please," Liz squealed like a ten year old. "Nursing burns an extra five hundred calories a day, so I have room in my diet for an occasional indulgence."

"You got it," Mama Kaye smiled. "Richard, what can I get for you?"

"I think I'll just nibble on some of my wife's fries."

"Sounds good. We'll be back in a bit. Feed my namesake!" she yelled over her shoulder as they walked into the hallway.

As they made their way to the elevator, two nurses were chatting at the nurse's station, their backs to the hallway.

"Yeah, I'm sure his wife is black," the older black nurse said. "I saw her. She's light skinned, and has green eyes, but she's black! She's really pretty too," she squealed. "And he had a Cartier bag!"

"Are you sure it was a Cartier bag?" the younger nurse said.

"Positive! I've been working as a nurse in this hospital for over fifteen years, girl, I know that bag when I see it!"

"I'm so glad to finally see one of us getting a push present," the other nurse giggled. "I wonder what he does for a living."

"Who cares?" the older black nurse replied. "I'm just glad that his wife is black. I can't wait to see what her push present was."

Mama Kaye grinned knowingly at Maria as they silently walked past the nurse's station. The nurses scribbled on clipboard charts, their eyes downcast, seemingly oblivious to passersby in the hallway.

In the elevator, Maria stared at Mama Kaye. "You were right! How did you know that the nurse assumed Richard's wife was white, Mama Kaye?"

"Chile, you don't get this many gray hairs in your head without knowing a little something about what people are thinking," she chuckled.

"But how'd you know?" pleaded Maria.

"First of all, there aren't that many black folks in this hospital. And the whole idea of getting a push present sounds like something that some spoiled white woman made up," she spat. "I've never heard of a push present."

"Teenie said that her aunt got a new car when she had a baby, but her aunt called it a 'thank you for having my baby' gift," Maria shared. "You've met Teenie a few times. She's black and so are her aunt and uncle. Her uncle said that the baby was a gift from God and he wanted to give his wife a gift to show that he appreciated all that her body went through to bring God's gift into the world."

"Well, it's a good idea. After having a baby, I think a woman deserves a nice gift," Mama Kaye admitted. "Having a baby is the closest that a woman comes to death without dying. Remember that, Maria. Don't just agree to carry any knucklehead's seed," she cautioned. "Speaking of knuckleheads, how are things with Thing One and Thing Two? You know I can't keep their names straight," she chuckled. "But I see you're wearing someone's big ring on your finger. That ring is bigger than your mama's sparkler!"

Blushing, Maria glanced at the large diamond on her right ring finger.

"It's complicated, Mama Kaye," Maria sighed.

"No it isn't, sugar. It's only complicated because you make it complicated. I can look at you and see what it is. Thing Two gave you a big ring, but you still like Thing One, and now you're confused."

"How'd you know?"

"Do you want me to count all of the wisdom gray hairs on my head? I told you I know what I know. I got these gray hairs honest, chile," Mama Kaye grinned. "Oooh, those onion rings smell too good to pass up. I need those like I need a hole in my head, but I'm going to get a batch of those and a cranberry ice tea. Get a large cup and we can share it. You know how I make it. You want anything?" she asked.

"No, I'm fine. I'll just share your onion rings," Maria grinned.

"Now don't get the cran-apple or the cran-grape mix. It won't taste right. If they don't have plain cranberry juice, just get me a lemonade, please. And don't put too much ice in the iced tea."

"Got it," Maria assured. Walking to the refrigerator section, Maria picked up a bottle of cranberry juice. At the fountain station, she grabbed a large cup and filled it half way with ice. She grabbed another large cup and filled it with iced tea. She met Mama Kaye at the register.

"Now this cup only has ice in it," Mama Kaye smiled at the cashier.

"Actually, I'm supposed to charge you for the cup," the cashier whispered. "But I won't."

"Why thank you, sweetie pie," Mama Kaye winked. "Now I know I don't look like it, but I'm a senior citizen. Do seniors get a break in the cafeteria? And my daughter just gave birth to my third grandchild. And she named it after me," she boasted. "Jeanine MaryKaye is her name. My name is Kaye. But everyone calls me Mama Kaye. And this is my granddaughter, Maria." Maria beamed that Mama Kaye referred to her as her granddaughter. "Does Mama Kaye get a discount for having another granddaughter today?" she smiled.

"Congratulations, Mama Kaye!" the cashier laughed. "Tell you what, I'll just charge you for the cranberry juice and the onion rings, and I'll give you the iced tea on the house," she winked.

Maria watched in awe as Mama Kaye's presence worked its magic. She seemed to have a special effect on everyone that she encountered. Her aura exuded love, warmth and kindness. She made people feel at ease. Strangers were drawn to her and wanted to do special things for her. Mama Kaye called it the pretty girl plan B.

♊♂

"I didn't always look like this," she explained to Maria one day. "I was a looker like you and your mama. I used to turn many a head back in my day. And I worked it too," she reminisced. "I didn't abuse it, but I knew how to use my physical attributes to get my way when I needed to," she explained. "But I was a nice, pretty girl. I was never mean to people or conceited. You never know who has the ability to be a blessing in your life. I knew some women who were mean pretty girls. But not me," she paused. "I called people by their name. And I tried to be nice to everyone. No matter who they were or what they did. I had a smile and kind word for everyone. Even the girls who weren't blessed with beauty, I was always nice to them. And that always shocked them. I think unattractive girls expect attractive girls to be mean and arrogant. I was never that way. My mama would have peeled my head if I walked around acting like some stuck up beauty queen," she chuckled. "To tell you the truth, I didn't realize that I was a looker until I became a teenager. My parents never fawned over me. Don't get me wrong, I got my fair share of compliments from the fellas, but I never paid it no never mind. I just thought it was part of the courting ritual," she ranted. "But beauty does fade," she cautioned. "My grandmother and my mother were lookers too. And they stayed lookers well into their golden years. They always took care of themselves and made sure that they were put together when they left the house. Hair, make-up, clothes. They were always sharp when they went into the street. My mother and my grandmother wore pearls and heels like women today wear sneakers and sweats. So early on, I decided to be just as nice as I was pretty. I knew that eventually my looks wouldn't be able to work their magic forever, so I had better have a plan B," she explained. "So I called it my 'pretty girl plan B'- Girl, plan to be just as nice as you are pretty. It's worked well for me. And now that I don't turn heads the way that I once did, people still respond to my kindness the same way that they responded to my physical beauty. Inner beauty lasts, Maria. Outer beauty will fade. And when you have inner beauty, you're beautiful on the outside."

"That's what my mom always says," Maria shared.

"And where do you think she learned that little gem?" Mama Kaye smiled.

"From you, Mama Kaye," she smiled

କ୍ଷର

"Get some ketchup packets and napkins, Maria. And I'll go mix up our beverage."

Maria did as instructed as Mama Kaye found a table near the window. Like a chemist, Mama Kaye poured the bottle of cranberry juice into the cup of ice. She then poured the iced tea over the cranberry juice and alternated back and forth between the cups. "There!" she exclaimed. "It should be evenly mixed now. Did you get straws like I asked?"

"Yes," Maria said, ignoring the fact that the retrieval of straws had not been part of Mama Kaye's ketchup and napkin instruction. She handed Mama Kaye a straw and watched as she took a sip.

"Perfect! I should have been a bartender!"

Maria lined three ketchup packets in her hand and managed to open them simultaneously. She squeezed ketchup into the corner of the onion ring boat. She'd shared enough meals with Mama Kaye and knew that she did not like condiments poured over her food, preferring to dip her food into the condiment as needed.

"We'll get your mama's food on our way back to the room, so it's nice and hot for her," Mama Kaye explained. "She'll be nursing Jeni Kaye for a minute anyway and won't be able to eat. Now what are you going to do about your heart, Miss Maria?"

Never one to mince words, Mama Kaye always jumped right to the point.

"And let me take a look at that ice skating rink on your hand, young lady!"

Maria let Mama Kaye grab her hand. "That thing is so big it looks fake!" she squealed. "But I know it's not, because your mama told me that she had to add it to her homeowner's insurance. All of the rings I collected combined aren't as big as that one," she shared.

"What do you mean all of the rings that you collected?" Maria repeated.

"I received five or six engagement rings," Mama Kaye offered casually. "I told you that."

"Uh, no you didn't! You were engaged to five or six different men?" Maria asked.

"Not really, but I had about five or six of them vying for my affection at one time," she grinned. "I told you I was quite the looker. They would give me a ring to try to keep the other ones away. Now I would tell each one that I wasn't ready to settle down. And each one gave me a bigger ring. I just wore the rings for fun."

"Were they diamond rings?"

"Uh huh. But they were small little diamonds. I never let any of them actually propose to me, but I accepted the rings," she chuckled. "They knew I was being courted. I was quite a catch," she grinned. "It made the other ones work harder."

Maria watched as Mama Kaye dipped an onion ring in ketchup and sipped her beverage. There was no pattern to Mama Kaye's onion ring ketchup dipping. She didn't dip each onion ring in ketchup and never double dipped. Maria preferred to eat her onion rings plain. She enjoyed Mama Kaye's signature cranberry juice iced tea concoction.

"How did you decide which one to marry?"

"I married the one that I thought would be the best for me in the long run," Mama Kaye replied matter-of-factly.

"You didn't marry the one that you loved?" Maria asked incredulously.

"Of course I loved him, but I loved two or three of them,"

Mama Kaye confessed.

"At the same time?"

"At the same time. It's possible for your heart to love more than one person at the same time. They were all different. I was young. I was being courted. They all offered me different things."

"What did you do with the rings that you collected?"

"I threw them in a drawer. I think I still have them. But this isn't about me. My time has come and gone. This is about you. Why did you let Thing Two give you a ring?"

"His name is Dante, Mama Kaye," Maria sighed.

"Chile, I am not going to remember that boy's name. So let's just call him Thing Two. Do you love Thing Two? I know you're still in love with Thing One, that's obvious. But do you love Thing Two?"

Maria shrugged. "I don't know. He's so different from Thing One. See, now you have me calling them Thing One and Thing Two. Dante is so different from Todd."

"But Todd doesn't love you, honey," Mama Kaye whispered. "He doesn't love you," she repeated. "Has he seen the sparkler on your finger?"

"No. But he knows that I'm dating Dante. He saw a picture of us together in the paper when Dante got drafted to the NFL."

"What did he do?"

"Nothing."

"Move on, sugar," Mama Kaye offered gently. "Todd doesn't want you. If he did, he would have come for you."

"But, he could just be…"

"But nothing, girl. If the boy wanted you, he would have come back to claim you. Now move on and love the one you're with. Sometimes you just gotta love the one you're with! I told you to rip off that Todd band-aid several months ago. Listen to Mama Kay, I know what I'm saying. Todd isn't the one for you. Move on or you'll be no good to the next man. I can't believe that you haven't met any boys at college that like you. As pretty as you are? But I guess that beacon on your finger is like a repellent," she chuckled. "Now, why are you wearing it on your right hand, again?"

Stunned by Mama Kaye's brazenness, Maria stared out the window at traffic below, an onion ring dangling from her finger.

"Did you hear me?"

"Uh, huh," Maria stammered. "It's not an engagement ring, Mama Kaye. It's a friendship ring," Maria explained.

"Well, haven't you met someone at college that you like and that likes you back?"

"Well, there is this one guy," she paused.

"Go ahead. What's his name?" Mama Kaye asked.

"His name is John."

"What's his last name?" she asked.

Maria stared at Mama Kaye as though she were seeing her for the first time.

"Does the boy have a last name?" Mama Kaye repeated.

"I don't know his last name. I've only met him once, and I've seen him in the cafeteria a few times. But he seems interesting."

"Interesting? Well, at least that's a start. Does he like you?" she asked.

"I don't know," Maria shrugged staring at her large diamond. "I don't know."

Chapter 12

30 Rockefeller Center

The crowded terminal smelled like heat, warning the patrons that an old boiler had recently been cranked up to warm the terminal. The heat smell mixed with the scent of wet wool and popcorn from a small vending machine nestled in the corner next to a dilapidated water fountain or "bubbler." She crinkled her sensitive nose and joined the long ticket line, greeted by a large Rockettes' banner, the dancers' long legs performing their signature kick. Turning her head slightly, she watched a girl approaching wearing a Howard University sweatshirt. She couldn't tell, but at first glance, the girl looked white. Tanisha glanced to the heavens and contorted her face into a sarcastic smirk. "You have quite the sense of humor, big guy!" she mumbled under her breath.

"Excuse me, did you say something?" the elderly gentleman asked softly, his position in line just ahead of hers.

Tanisha shook her head from side to side. "No. I was just mumbling to myself," she smiled. "I didn't realize I spoke out loud."

"Aloud," he corrected gently. "You didn't realize that you spoke aloud," he smiled. "It sounds better than saying 'out loud' if you don't mind my saying. It's grammatically correct to say out loud," he repeated. The words slipped out of his mouth dripping in vinegar. "But aloud just sounds more erudite. I'm a Yale graduate myself.

An English major actually," he offered noticing her sweatshirt. "Class of 1962. My wife is also a Yale grad. She went to Yale Law and Harvard for undergrad. I went to Harvard Law. We met at a homecoming event at Yale. She died last year," he shared. "So I guess I should say that my wife was a Yale grad," he sighed, his eyes misty and distant, as though his pupils paused to glance at a photo of his wife catalogued in his memory. "It was a car accident. Just one of those things that happens to people, but when it happens to you, it turns your life upside down. Very tragic," he sighed. "I'm traveling to meet my kids in Florida. Thought we'd do something different this year since it's our first Thanksgiving without their mom. You look like a freshman," Class of 1962 smiled. His thick head of hair was silvery white. His eyebrows were the same shade. She wondered if he had been a blonde or a brunette. His eyes were a deep blue, almost hypnotic. "You know what erudite means don't you?" he asked. She was surprised that he wasn't gasping for breath after his lengthy soliloquy.

"Excuse me, what did you say?" Teenie asked. Stunned by his rapid fire questions, she was unsure which question deserved the courtesy of her first reply.

"Erudite. What does erudite mean?"

"Intellectual?" Teenie replied.

"Lucky guess, freshman. But by the way I used it in a sentence I would have been very disappointed had you not been able to define it. I expected you to say smart."

"Actually, I know the word from playing Scrabble with my dad," she corrected. "And I used to read the dictionary all the time."

"Then why did you respond in the form of a question?"

Bad habit," she shrugged. Her eyes panned the train station

wondering why the line hadn't budged at all.

"You are a freshman aren't you?" he asked.

She decided to express her condolences. "Yes, I'm a freshman. And I'm so sorry to hear about your wife," Tanisha offered. "I plan to go to law school also," she acknowledged, hoping that she could change the subject away from death and grief. It saddened her. "How could you tell that I'm a freshman?"

"Just a lucky guess," he winked. "You just look like a freshman. Heading home for Thanksgiving, huh? Where's home for you?"

As the check-in line slowly inched forward by one, Tanisha pushed her new weekend bag with her foot, wondering why she hadn't paid twenty dollars more for the bag with wheels. Penny wise and pound foolish. "I'm from Newberry East, Illinois, which is just outside of Chicago," she smiled.

"Chicago is my second favorite city. New York is my favorite, of course. I still live in Greenwich, Connecticut, but now that my bride is gone, I'm thinking about selling the house and moving into a condo. It's too much space and too many memories. We were married over thirty years and I still refer to her as my bride. But now it's time for a fresh start," he offered. "I have another friend whose wife died of cancer, and he said that it's harder to watch your loved one die slowly. That at least with a car accident there was no long, drawn out suffering," he sighed. "I suppose he's right. But it just happened so fast. One minute she was going to the mall and the next I'm planning her funeral. It happened that fast. The kids and I didn't get to say goodbye. At least with a terminal illness, you get to say goodbye," Class of 1962 sighed. Teenie noticed his eyes staring at a gold wedding band.

Grateful that his comment was not framed in the form of a question, Teenie was unsure how to reply. "I can only imagine,"

Teenie said, hoping that her soft comment didn't elicit more criticisms from the English major. "How many children do you have?"

"We have two. They look just like their mother, thank God. My sisters were fat and funny looking, so I'm glad that they don't look like my side of the family. That would have been tragic," he laughed. "My wife was a beauty. She was pretty enough to be Miss Connecticut, but she didn't believe in beauty pageants. She wanted to be taken seriously as a lawyer. But one of our daughters was Miss Teen Connecticut, and now she's a lawyer, so it's possible to be a beauty queen and be taken seriously. I'm glad that my wife lived to see her graduate from law school and pass the bar."

Teenie toed her bag again with the moving line. "That's nice," she offered.

"I thought that it would be fun to be in a warm place for Thanksgiving. I wanted to go to Hawaii, but my girls can't take off that much time from their jobs. So we decided to meet in Florida. My wife loved Thanksgiving. We always hosted the Thanksgiving dinner at our house with a houseful of people. She came from a large family," he sighed. "She was a great cook too. But now that she's gone, it's not going to be the same."

Her eyes soft, Teenie smiled and remembered her Grandma Bootsy's advice. "Sometimes folks just need you to listen. They don't need you to fix anything or add your two cents. They just want to be heard. Especially old folks, and people who are grieving, sometimes they just want someone to talk to," Grandma Bootsy explained one day. Tanisha decided that this was such a time. He wore penny loafers with no socks. In the middle of November, the tops of his feet were exposed, pale and veiny. His black wool slacks bore a freshly laundered crease. His leather jacket was unzipped layered above a light blue oxford, his gray chest hairs peeking through the top of his shirt. She wondered why he didn't wear a tee-shirt beneath his oxford. Her dad, Jackie always wore a tee-shirt, even in the summer. Isn't he cold? He's going to Florida, Teenie. It's in the eighties in Florida. Teenie wondered again if Class of 1962 had been a blonde or a brunette before his hair turned silver.

"We are going to do something completely different and have crab legs for Thanksgiving dinner. We might even go to Disney World," he continued.

"That sounds like fun," Teenie offered. She wondered what she'd missed while she was zoned out critiquing his appearance. "I've never been to Disney World."

"You haven't? It's a magical place," Yale Class of '62 offered. "If you don't mind waiting in the long lines, it's a lot of fun. My daughters love it. I think they're going to make me take them to the Cinderella breakfast," he chuckled. "I don't mind though. I just want all of us to have a good time. My daughters are both engaged, but their fiancées aren't coming along. It'll just be us this time."

"That'll be nice. I'm Tanisha Carlson, by the way," she introduced.

"Look at me. I've forgotten my manners. I'm talking your head off and didn't introduce myself. I'm Kip Hampton," he smiled.

Tanisha counted four more people ahead of her in line. "I've never met anyone named Kip before. What a fun name. Is Kip your real name?" she asked. "I hope you don't mind my asking." She imagined that his name was John, Thomas or Robert. With his mop of thick, silver hair, he didn't look like a Kip.

"I don't mind at all. In fact, Kip is my nickname. My God given name is Kilpatrick. Kilpatrick William Hampton, IV," he stated. "It's a family name and it's a mouthful. I've gone by Kip since I was knee high to a grasshopper." I knew his name would be something formal.

"I have a nickname too," Tanisha smiled. "My friends call me Teenie."

"Teenie? As in you are so teenie?" he teased.

"Yes," she smiled.

"But you're not teenie, Teenie. You're paper thin, but you've got to be at least five feet eight or nine. Am I right?" Kip asked.

"I'm just under five nine," she clarified. "I got the nickname in camp when I was in middle school. Some friends thought that Teenie would be a cute nickname for Tanisha," she shrugged. "And it stuck. In fact, two of the girls who gave me the nickname are my classmates at Yale now. Anyway, my parents don't call me, Teenie. They still call me, Tanisha," she explained.

"It's a fine nickname to have, Teenie," he winked. "And Tanisha is a fine name too. Tanisha passes the lawyer-blind date test," he smiled.

Tilting her head to the side, she lifted one eyebrow and smiled. "What's the lawyer-blind date test?"

"A name tells a lot about a person. If you were an associate in my law firm, and you were handling a multi-million dollar case for one of my most important clients, I couldn't introduce you to the client as Teenie. It's a cute nickname, but the client probably wouldn't take you or me very seriously. It doesn't engender much confidence," he continued. "But if I introduced you as Tanisha Carlson, most clients would be fine with that. What's your middle name?"

"Denise," she stated.

"I would probably have you use Denise Carlson professionally or maybe Tanisha Denise Carlson or T. Denise Carlson. Or if I wanted to set you up on a blind date and told the young man that your name was Teenie or Tanisha, he'd be okay with that because both of those names are cute," he continued. "But if I told him that your name was Beulah or Ethel, he would probably think that you had a nice personality, but were hard on the eyes," he laughed. "Beulah or Ethel would be fine as a lawyer name, but it would fail the blind date test. You have a name that passes both," he stated.

"Oh, I get it," Teenie giggled.

"Kip Hampton sounds like a quarterback's name, not the name of a Harvard educated lawyer. My business cards have my proper name Kilpatrick W. Hampton, IV, but once I meet the client, I invite them to call me Kip," he explained. "Kilpatrick gets them in the door, and Kip keeps them there. I'm the rain maker at the firm, so I'm always concerned with making more rain."

"The rain maker?" Teenie repeated. "What does that mean?"

"I'm the guy who makes it rain money," Kip chuckled. "I manage most of our biggest client relationships. And most of my client relations are forged at five star restaurants, exclusive golf clubs and on the slopes of Aspen. I haven't seen the inside of a courtroom in years," he laughed. "When we have big cases with our major clients I usually join the attorneys at the table as a show of force so the client can see me, but I don't get involved in the day-to-day litigation matters any longer. The partner who's running the file makes sure that I get high level updates so that I know what's going on," he paused.

Feeling another filibuster, Teenie decided to interrupt. "Kip, if I worked at your firm, why would you have me use my middle name?" asked Teenie, her head tilted to the side again.

"Tanisha is a nice name, but it sounds a bit too ethnic, if I'm being honest. It's pretty, but I've never met any white girls named, Tanisha. You don't want your name to scream your ethnicity, Teenie. If you were handling a legal matter for an ethnic client, it wouldn't matter. But some of my blue chip clients wouldn't want you working on their file just based on your name. So when you start practicing law, you should plan to use your middle name or Teenie," he suggested casually. "Are you flying out of LaGuardia or JFK?" Kip asked. "They have better flights to Chicago out of New York City. And they're cheaper too. It's a small fortune to fly out of Connecticut. I usually make my family take Amtrak into the city to get a good flight. Every now and then I'll hire a car service to get them to the airport. I can easily afford to fly out of Connecticut, but I only fly out of Connecticut if it's an emergency," he paused. "If you're heading to JFK I can tell you how to take the subway. It's a straight shot. My daughters tease me that I'm a cheapskate. But I'm just frugal. There's a difference. Millionaire next door! You have to think like a millionaire and save your money, Teenie. Don't spend money on cabs in New York City when the subway system is so good. And at this time of day, it's safe. I'd let my daughters ride the subway at this time of day. Now at night, I always hire a car service so we don't have to rely on taxis. Are you heading to LaGuardia or JFK, Teenie?" rattled Kip.

Her jaw slightly ajar, Teenie stared at him as though seeing him for the first time.

"Neither. I'm not catching a flight," she felt her lips moving.

"Oh, I thought you said that you lived outside of Chicago," he said.

"I do. But I'm not going home for Thanksgiving. I'm meeting

my boyfriend and his family at their place in New York City for the weekend," she said dryly. Although replying politely, she felt like a marionette, the words coming out of her mouth controlled by a puppet master. She wondered if she were in a state of shock. Your name sounds too ethnic for the blue chip clients.

"I'm meeting one of my daughters at 30 Rockefeller Center so we can see the big Christmas tree and ice skate," Kip rambled. "It's a family tradition. When my wife was alive we sometimes stayed at the Waldorf Astoria, but this time, we're staying in Midtown at the Plaza Hotel. I'm looking at condominiums in Central Park West. My friends think that I'm a fool for even thinking about buying a place on the West side of Central Park, but I like that area. It's interesting. We own an apartment in a Co-Op building on the East side of the park, but we're renting it now. I want to try living on the west side. If I like being a west sider, I'll just hold the east side place for my daughters to use. It's been in my family for generations, so I'll never sell it."

Only three more customers stood between Tanisha and the ticket counter.

"Does your boyfriend's family live in Harlem?" Kip asked.

She imagined that her caramel face turned the color of a vine ripened tomato, her eyes flames of fire. "No," she replied slowly. "Why would you assume that my boyfriend's family lived in Harlem, Kip?" she asked sternly.

"You said New York City and not Brooklyn or the Bronx so I figured that they must live in Harlem," he replied. "They are really updating that area nicely. Some of the senior associates at my firm are buying places in parts of Harlem where a few years ago there were no whites at all."

"My boyfriend's parents own a place on Riverside Drive," she stated. Tanisha was unsure whether Riverside Drive was east or west of Central Park, but she remembered Brian telling her that it was very near Central Park.

Now Kip's face turned bright red. "That's a very nice street. My realtor is taking me to look at a few properties on that street," he offered. "What do his parents do for a living?"

"You know what, Kip," Tanisha said boldly, no longer feeling like a marionette. "I don't think that's any of your business." She leaned her body into his and with her index finger motioned for him to lean into her face. "And for the record, my boyfriend is white," she whispered. "By the way, suggesting to someone that they use a different name because their name sounds too ethnic is a tad ignorant. I'm sure you meant well, and I know you're grieving the death of your wife, but grief shouldn't make you say stupid things, Kip. From one Yale student to another, you really shouldn't say things like that to people, it makes you sound like a bigot!" she whispered.

"Next in line, please," the clerk bellowed.

Straightening at the waist, Kip stared at Tanisha. Now his face was the color of a vine ripened tomato, his frozen expression one of shock and disbelief. The hue of his complexion grew deeper as though her words had been inked with red dye and stained his cheeks as she spoke. The babbler had been silenced. Without a word, Tanisha lifted her duffel bag with one arm and gently patted Kip on the back with her free hand.

"And yes, I meant to say that out loud!" she grinned. "While you marinate on that for a minute, I'm going to leap frog in front of you so we can keep this line moving," she smirked as she jumped ahead of him. "It was nice to meet you, Kip. Happy Thanksgiving and enjoy your trip!" she smiled as she walked toward the Amtrak ticket counter.

Her ticket firmly in hand, she meandered thru the thick holiday crowd, which had grown more massive during her wait in line. Glancing over her shoulder, she saw Kip's eyes searching the crowd for her as he tucked his ticket in his carry on. She paused to use the restroom, lingering at the sink wondering if she should seek him out and provide him with an avenue to apologize. He's a lawyer. He's not going to apologize. He'll try to argue and convince me that he's right about my name. He'll insist that we sit together on the train which will get on my nerves.

Like a spy, she stuck her head outside the restroom door to see if the coast was clear. There was no sign of Kilpatrick "Kip" Hampton. In the lobby, she joined a throng of families with young children, their ice skates slung casually over one shoulder, obviously headed to 30 Rockefeller Center for the day. The platform was filled with people. She listened as the ticket agent announced that extra cars had been added to accommodate the additional holiday passengers, reminding the passengers that there would be no need to push and shove. Once on the train, the seats filled quickly. Teenie plopped into the first open seat that she saw which was next to an elderly woman who adjusted a tan sleep mask and covered her shoulders with a blanket. Her head positioned against the cold glass of the window, she was clearly prepared to nap during the brief train ride into Manhattan. Teenie was glad for this, she didn't want to talk to anyone.

As a final distraction, Tanisha took out her homework. She had a paper to finish writing. She'd written most of the paper and only had to summarize her findings and write the conclusion. Staring at the notebook in her hand, she found herself reading the same paragraph for the third time, the words appearing like

Yiddish on the page. She didn't understand Yiddish. Kip's words consuming her thoughts, she forced herself to concentrate. It wasn't working. As the conductor bellowed "All Aboard!" Teenie slipped the notebook in her backpack, thinking she might take a quick nap. As though taunting her like a hangnail, the girl wearing the Howard sweatshirt raced through the crowded train car. The girl was definitely white.

₨)ℓℒ

"What do you mean you're not coming home for Thanksgiving, Teenie?" David asked.

"I'm seeing someone, David," Teenie blurted. "And he wants me to go to New York with him and his family."

The silence on the other end of the phone was deafening.

"David?" Teenie stated. "Are you still there?"

"You've only been in school for two months, Teenie. It couldn't be that serious," he said. "You're already that serious about a guy that you just met?"

"I didn't just meet him, David," she said softly. "We've known each other for a few years and started dating about a year ago."

"Are you talking about the guy that was stalking you?" asked David.

"It's the guy that I met at camp a few years ago," Teenie said.

"The guy from camp? The guy that gave you the hickey?"

Teenie was suddenly embarrassed to have to admit this to David. "Uh, huh," she mumbled softly.

"How did he resurface?" David asked.

"It's a long story, but I bumped into him at my senior prom of all places. We started talking again, and hanging out. He's really a nice guy."

"And he's white, right?" David asked.

"Yeah. He's white," Teenie confirmed.

David's exhale sounded like the exhale of a smoker blowing smoke rings into the air.

"You never cease to amaze me, Tanisha," David said.

"What? Don't be mad at me," she pleaded.

"How did you decide to spend Thanksgiving with him and his family?"

"It just seems like it would be fun," she said. "We're going to see the Rockettes and ice skate at Rockefeller Center," she listed.

"You're choosing to see the Rockettes over me?" David stated coldly.

"He's a really nice guy, David. I want you to meet him."

His laugh was guttural. It was more like a cackle than a laugh. "Why would I want to meet him?" asked David.

She didn't want to bite her lip again. The last time she'd drawn blood. "Because I told him all about you, and he wants to meet you," Teenie explained.

"If you've been seeing him since prom, that means that you were seeing him when we made the New Year's Eve deadline, weren't you? Don't answer that. I don't want to give you another opportunity to lie to me."

Her brow creased into a frown. "I didn't lie to you, David," she reasoned.

"When I told you that I would wait until New Year's Eve of your freshman year, but no longer, that was your opportunity to tell me that you were already seeing someone."

He was right and she knew it. Teenie wished she knew how to crack her knuckles. She wanted to do something to relieve the tension that she was feeling. "But technically, I didn't lie. It was more like an omission," she corrected.

"Whatever you want to call it, you could have told me about him, Tanisha."

He's mad. He only calls me, Tanisha, when he's mad. "But you know what? At least it's out in the open. At least I know where I stand with you. It's over. Our friendship or whatever we had is now over. Goodbye."

"But David," she pleaded. "I'm only eighteen. Just give me more time. I'm just so confused." The click was soft and gentle. "Hello? Hello?" she repeated. "David, are you still there?"

ℬℭ

"Tanisha! I know you're in there. I can see your shoes under the door, and I can hear you talking on the phone. Open the door, girlfriend," Monica yelled.

Teenie walked to the door, her eyeliner smudged like coal under a football player's eyes.

"You look like a burnt mess," Monica groaned.

"I look like a burnt hot mess," Teenie corrected. "If you're going to borrow my slang, at least get it right," she yawned. "The saying is 'a burnt hot mess.' What time is it?"

The sky had a purple haze. She guessed that it was after six.

"It's almost five thirty," Monica confirmed. "Your cat nap should have been over an hour ago. Laura told me to come down and make sure you were awake so we can get to dinner. For once, she's starving. And you know how she gets when she's hungry. Growl!" Monica snarled, her hand swiping like a tiger. "Who were you talking to on the phone?"

Confused, Teenie furrowed her brow and stared at Monica. "I wasn't on the phone. I just woke up when you knocked on my door."

"Well, you must have been talking in your sleep, because I heard you and it sounded like you were on the phone. I couldn't hear what you were saying, but I heard your voice."

"I must have been talking in my sleep then. I didn't know that I did that. I had this freaky, crazy nightmare," Teenie shared.

"Is that why you look so scary?" Monica teased. "It looks like your eye liner is racing to your nose."

Teenie grabbed the tissue that Monica waved in her face and proceeded to wipe under her eyes, folding the pink tissue into triangles, she wiped away the smudged eye liner. "I dreamed that I met this crazy man at the train station on my way to meet Brian and his parents in New York for Thanksgiving. His name was Kip and he kept talking about his dead wife and correcting my grammar and then he said that my name was too ethnic to practice law. And then I kept seeing this white girl in the terminal and on the train wearing a Howard sweatshirt, and right before I woke up, David Barton hung up on me because I told him that I was dating Brian Kraft and not coming home for Thanksgiving but was going to New York to ice skate in Rockefeller Center with Brian."

"But you are still going home for Thanksgiving, right? That's what you decided to do. We're all on the same flight."

"Exactly," Teenie agreed. "That's why the dream is so odd."

"Well, Sigmund Freud would say that our dreams are our subconscious talking to us. Deep down you might be feeling like you should go to the Big Apple. Maybe you're feeling guilty and should rethink your travel plans," winked Monica. "Or maybe the white girl wearing the Howard sweatshirt is your subconscious fearing that David is seeing someone seriously. How did Brian take the news that you wouldn't be going to New York with him and his family?" she asked.

Squinting into the mirror attached to the inside of her closet door, Teenie reapplied a line of the liquid eye liner that she now favored. She tossed the eye liner on her desk and brushed her hair, pleased that her mane now grazed her shoulders. "He totally understood. Said he didn't expect that I'd be able to dodge my family for the holidays my freshman year. His family goes to their place in Aspen for Christmas break. He works as a ski instructor, so he'll be there until school starts again in January. He invited me to come for a few days, but I don't think that's gonna work."

"Why not?" Monica asked. "You ski don't you?" she asked like a mother asking her child if she brushed her teeth in the morning, the answer so obvious that anything but a yes would appear absurd.

"I ski a little, but I can't imagine skiing in Aspen, Colorado," she whistled. "I'd probably kill myself doing my little snow plow down a big mountain. I skied down a small hill in Wisconsin a few times, and I didn't do that with much confidence," she finished.

"But skiing out west is so different. It's powder so it's easier. The hills are steeper, but the snow conditions are friendlier, especially to beginners. Wisconsin is icy. I hate skiing in Wisconsin. I do it, because it's close and better than nothing, but I hate it. I have to dig too hard into the mountain," Monica explained. Tanisha thought about David. That's exactly what he said. "Clearly Brian is a good skier if he's an instructor, so let him teach you. For free. Ski lessons in Aspen are expensive. I skied there last spring. My family rents a condo there every spring. My dad used to be a ski racer so he had us all in ski school when we were two. I was skiing black diamond runs before I learned to read. Well, I was reading, but I wasn't in school yet."

Am I the only person who hasn't skied in Aspen? "I'll have to think about that one. I told Save Mart that I'd work over the

Christmas break holiday, and I need the money. But back to my dream, before I forget the details, what do you think it means? It was so vivid and real," she explained.

"Was it in color?" asked Monica.

"I think so, but I'm not sure," Teenie paused. "I normally don't remember my dreams, but this one was so detailed. It felt like I could smell things and everything. It just felt so real. But I don't remember if it was in color or not.   I think it was in color. I remember Kip's eyes being blue. His hair was silver. Or maybe I just imagined that his eyes were blue. Is it possible to imagine something when you're in a dream state? Isn't a dream state an imagined state?"

"That sounds like a philosophy question," Monica said in falsetto. "You must go to Yale."

"But I don't remember any other colors. Why do you ask? Does it mean something if the dream was in color?"

"How do I know? I just wondered if you dreamed in color. I usually dream in black and white," she squealed abruptly. "I'm so mad at you, Teenie Carlson!" Monica grabbed a large duffel bag nestled between Teenie's bed and her movable closet. "I saw this duffel bag too, but the one that I saw didn't have wheels. The sales lady said that she'd just sold the last wheeled duffel, and it was probably to you."

"You snooze you lose," she grinned. "I'll be right back. I need to brush my teeth," Teenie announced gripping her bathroom toiletries bucket.

"But we're going to dinner, Teenie. Brush them after we eat. Laura will be tapping her foot if we're late."

"Laura will be fine. I need to brush the sleep grime from my teeth. It'll take one minute," Teenie assured slipping past Monica with her toothbrush in hand. As she stepped through the door, the phone rang. "Just let the answering machine get that."

"I'm going to answer it because I'm sure it will be Laura calling from the lobby, wondering why it's taking us so long to come down. You know how evil skinny people who don't eat get when they are finally ready to eat," Monica laughed. "Hello. This is Teenie's room."

Not bothering to close the door on the single bathroom, Teenie quickly brushed her teeth in the mirror. She could hear Monica explaining that she was brushing her teeth. "That's what I told her," Monica agreed. "But you know how she is about her dental hygiene," Monica explained. "We'll be down in two minutes, promise!"

Staring at her reflection, the image of the girl on the train wearing the Howard sweatshirt returned. Teenie squinted. The girl looked like Monica.

Chapter 13

People are People

The woman wore an oversized sweatshirt emblazoned with the batman logo, the gold yellow bat mocking the navy blue pinstripe skirt suit that Justine wore. She was clearly over dressed. Kendal had personally selected the expensive ensemble. He'd had a friend in the couture section call him when the suit was on final markdown. Even at final markdown, the purchase was more than Justine had ever spent on an article of clothing, but on Kendal's nod, she dutifully handed over her already inflated Field's credit card. One hundred hours of toil. That's how long it would take her to pay off the suit. She was glad that associates weren't charged finance charges on purchases that they made. It was one of the few perks that carried real weight now that the employee store discount had been reduced to a mere ten percent.

Kendal's friend, Helga, in the alterations department had been summoned and ordered to hustle down to tailor the suit for her. Like a soldier armed for battle, her weapons a spongy red pin cushion and tattered, brown tape measure, Helga appeared to have sprinted from the alterations department. Her labored breath reeked of stale coffee. She seemed to grunt and mumble under her breath as she poked and prodded her way around the suit moving Justine's arms and turning her as though she were a lifeless mannequin. Justine had never had anything tailored.

"I don't want it taken in too much," Justine offered softly. "I've never had anything tailored before," she added, her comments seemingly ignored by Helga who pulled and pinned in a rhythmic fashion.

"Fish," Kendal sighed. "Don't tell anyone that you've never had your clothing altered. You are almost twenty-one years old," he stated slowly, over emphasizing each syllable. "You are a grown up, so it's time that you started building your wardrobe," he snickered. "It's long over due. You work in retail for goodness sake. We have some of the best tailors in the world at our disposal so it's time that you stopped wearing things straight off the rack," he grunted, appearing to shiver at the mere mention of wearing something off the rack. The other associates hadn't even reacted when Kendal marched boldly into the ladies fitting room after Justine announced that she had on the suit.

"View your clothing as an investment." he articulated slowly, the word investment exaggerated and stretched out like he was speaking to someone trying to read his lips. "Clothing is an investment," he repeated slowly once again. "Always have alterations do a special nip and tuck to customize the garment to your frame, darling, especially if you buy the item on sale, and we know you know better than to pay full price for retail, fish! Take a fraction of the money that you're saving and have the item tailored. Chile, why you think I always look so pieced and pulled together?" he twirled. The small dressing room was not large enough to accommodate a flamboyant dancer's twirl. Kendal bumped Helga. Justine feared that she might choke on the pins dangling on her lips.

"Helga, honey, take it in an extra eighth of an inch at the

waist," he ordered gently. "That'll make Ms. Thang think twice about eating a chocolate donut for breakfast," he winked. "Cause when you spend good money for your clothing, you work extra hard at the gym to make sure that you can look good in your investment," he snarled. "So fish, no more chocolate donuts or muffins for you; you cannot have a muffin top poofing out your Ellen Tracy suit. This is a classic. You will keep this suit forever. Trust me, girlfriend, as long as you stay off the donuts." He patted Justine's expanding mid section knowingly. "Now, the darlings in alterations always take care of Kendal when Kendal has over indulged at the buffet," he chuckled. "Helga has probably altered Kendal's Hugo Boss slacks at least three times. Helga takes good care of Kendal because he sends all of his clients to her." Justine smiled at the way Kendal referred to himself in the third person, calling it the royal plural.

Helga seemed to smile through a mouth full of straight pins. A red velvet pin cushion adorned her wrist like a puffy bracelet, the tape measure necklace that all alterations personnel wore draped around her neck. "Even stuff that fits can always be made to fit a little better, isn't that right, Helga?" he cooed. "I'm putting Helga's kids through college with my clients alone," he continued without waiting for Helga's reply. "My clients worship me, fish. I'm their fashion god. If I tell them that something should be altered, they trust me and have it altered. No questions asked," he snapped. The snap was firm and confident. Kendal filed his nail, the emery board appearing out of thin air. Justine wondered if it had been tucked up his sleeve. Manicures had become his favorite obsession, the emery board never too far from his grasp, often tucked in his sock if his trousers lacked a deep enough pocket to conceal his grooming accessory.

Justine wondered what her name would sound like coming from Kendal's mouth. Around clients he referred to her as JW, pronounced Jay Dub or Miss Wellington, but never Justine. But in private, it was always, fish or Miss Thang. She wondered if he called his other female friends, fish. She would soon find out.

She'd finally been invited to one of Kendal's infamous Chapter Member parties. Justine was nervous, fearing that the party would be filled with women dressed like men and men dressed like women. She was embarrassed to think that way, but she didn't know what to expect. Her friends had never attended a Chapter Member party, so they couldn't give her any tips. At the risk of offending her new best friend, she tap danced around the question.

"What should I wear to the party?" she asked, careful not to say your party for fear that Helga might be offended if she had not received an invitation. "Should I dress up?"

"The theme is denim and diamonds, so wear denim and diamonds, dingbat," Kendal frowned. Dingbat? She'd been christened with a new nickname.

"So that's it. Just denim and diamonds?"

"Just denim and diamonds, fish," Kendal said. "It's not that complicated. It really isn't. And if you don't come dressed in the party's theme, you won't get in."

Justine knew that Kendal was serious. He took his theme parties very seriously: Hats and heels, Ties and tiaras, Sailors and sarongs. Kendal was known for his theme parties. This was the first time that he'd invited Justine.

"After observing you closely for over two years, you have officially passed my non-crazy test, fish," Kendal had explained one day. "I'm having a party next Friday. Come. The theme is denim and diamonds. Don't embarrass me," Kendal rattled.

All of Chicago's elite Chapter Members knew that Kendal hosted a Chapter Member party on the first Friday of every month, unless he was scheduled to work, which was rare. Even the department manager who controlled the schedule knew that Kendal was always scheduled off on the first Friday of every month. If absolutely necessary, he would work a morning shift as long as he clocked out by one o'clock. His parties were known in the Chapter Member circle as two degrees of separation. If he didn't know you directly from the person who had received the invite, then you were not welcome in his home. His motto was simple. "I am not trying to meet new people at my home while I'm hosting a party. If Kendal has never met them before the party, they are not welcome at Kendal's party. Kendal Franklin works in retail. It's easy to meet Kendal."

The two degrees of separation strategy always helped his sales numbers too. People pining for an invite to one of his Chapter Member parties would have Kendal's motto explained by a mutual friend. The hopeful would eventually wander into Field's.

"I'm Clay. I'm Jorey's friend. Jorey told me to stop by so that you could help me pick out a sweater," Clay would announce boldly. Kendal would remain stoic and unfriendly. "And I also need a new pair of slacks and possibly a new sport coat," Clay would add. Kendal's attention piqued, he would spring into action. After the obligatory visit from alterations to have at least one of the items tailored, if Kendal was comfortable that Clay had spent enough money in his department, he would end the sale with, "I'll have to tell Jorey that you stopped by. I'll see Jorey at my Chapter Member party," he'd mention subtly. Kendal wouldn't directly invite Clay. But Clay knew that he was now welcome to come as Jorey's guest, and only as Jorey's guest. This was as good as an invite. Kendal wouldn't consider Clay a client until Clay visited his department for at least six months. He dubbed it the probationary period. He knew that people paid at least one visit to him at Field's in order to get an invitation to the Chapter Member party. Justine had watched Kendal work his magic on more than one occasion, and she'd always wondered what was so special about Kendal's parties. She could only imagine, but she knew that when Kendal dragged in on the first Saturday of the month, Friday night's party was branded across his forehead, his oversized Jackie Onassis sunglasses hiding his bloodshot eyes. She wondered if the bloodshot eyes were from being over served at the bar, a lack of sleep or a combination of both. But Kendal never requested a day off after his Chapter Member parties. He'd worked retail long enough to know that requesting time off on a Saturday after being scheduled off on a Friday was a retail taboo. Besides, the Saturday shopping traffic was full of tourists and suburbanites excited to be shopping in downtown Chicago. It was the easiest day to make your monthly quota if you were good, and Kendal was very good.

Justine wondered how long the alterations process would take. Helga had now chalk marked the seat of her pants. Justine wondered where Helga had stashed the chalk. To Helga, Justine was nonexistent, she marked and pinned at Kendal's command.

"Will there be dancing at the party? Should I bring something?" she quizzed.

"It's a party, fish. There will be music, dancing, fun, games. Clearly, you don't get out much. And of course you should bring something. Never go to someone's house empty handed. You know that. It's rude. Bring a bottle of wine, a pie, a candle, a bag of ice, Jay's potato chips. Something," he groaned. "I know your mama raised you better than that. I met Andrea, and I know she taught you to bring something for the hostess." Justine laughed at Kendal's reference to himself as the hostess and not the host.

Kendal reminded her of Teenie with his long list of commandments. He referred to them as his 'Thou Shall Nots:' Thou shall not pay full price for retail. Thou shall not finance a car, unless it's at zero percent interest. Thou shall not finance depreciating assets. Thou shall not wear white shoes and black hosiery. Ever! Thou shall not ask a woman if she's pregnant, she might just be fat. Instead ask her how many children she has. Thou shall not drive around in a dirty car for more than two days. Thou shall not wear red to a wedding or funeral. It's tacky. And on and on.

She wished that one of her friends could come to the party with her. But she knew that was not possible. They didn't know Kendal and they were busy with college. Teenie was away at Yale and Maria at the University of Pennsylvania. Rashanda lived close enough to come, but now that she was married, a full time student at Northwestern and pregnant, Justine knew that attending a party did not fit into Rashanda's new life. The only one of her friends who might be able to make it was Grace. She passed the two degrees of separation test, and the University of Illinois – Champaign was only a two hour drive from Chicago. She wondered if Grace would come after their last fight.

Kendal knew that Justine was nervous about attending her first Chapter Member party. Earlier in the week, she had peppered him with questions trying to get him to describe what his parties were like. "Fish, people are people. I'm inviting you into my world, so you can either hang or not. I know you're trying to get me to give you a roadmap of what you should expect, but I ain't gonna do that," he said. "There will be people, music, food and libations. You need to just come with an open mind and have a good time. Free of expectations and inhibitions."

Inhibitions? What does he mean inhibitions? I know what inhibitions are. Does he think that I will be inhibited in some way? Will this be like some scene out of a bad movie? After receiving her verbal invitation from Kendal, and unable to reach any of her friends, she solicited her mother's advice.

"Have I ever been to a Chapter Member party?" Andrea repeated. "A chapter of what?" her mother asked. Andrea was making corn bread for dinner, a pot of collard greens simmered on the stove. Justine hoped her mother had cooked a shank of ham with the collard greens and not a smoked turkey leg. Since dating Bob, the realtor, Andrea had stopped eating pork.

Realizing that her mother was unfamiliar with the term of art, Justine rephrased the question. "Have you ever been to a party given by a gay person, Mom?" Justine walked toward the stove and lifted the lid. She grinned as a large ham bone bobbed in the murky, green water.

"No. I can't say that I have. Why, is Kendal having a party? And put the lid back on, Justine. The greens need to simmer undisturbed for at least another hour."

"How'd you know that I was referring to Kendal?" Ham? Did Mom and Bob break-up?

"Because any fool can see that Kendal is a sissy," Mrs. Wellington stated blandly.

"Mom! No one uses that word any more! I can't believe that you just said that."

"Well, that's the word we used when I was growing up. I didn't mean any harm. I like Kendal. He's very nice, and I'm glad that you're friends," Andrea added. "I'm glad that you had him to lean on during your AM break up."

"Mom, let's not even go there. I don't want to talk about that. Have you ever been to a gay party?"

"I said I hadn't, Justine. There's a doctor at the hospital that I believe is light in his loafers, but he keeps to himself. He's handsome as all get out, and all of the silly, young nurses always flirt with him and chase after him like sixteen year olds. They're too stupid to see that he's not interested in them," she giggled. "Set the table for five, Justine. Bob is joining us for dinner tonight."

That answers that question. I guess they didn't break up. "Well, how do you know for sure that he's gay, Mom? Maybe he's just not interested in them."

"I don't know for sure. But I've been around the block enough times, and my spider senses tell me that he is. It's just a woman's intuition. Go to the party, Justine. You need to get out. I'm sure it'll be fine. People are people, Justine."

That's the same thing that Kendal said! "I noticed that you're cooking the greens with ham, Mom. I thought you said that Bob didn't eat pork," Justine challenged.

"He doesn't, but I know that you and your brothers prefer ham in the greens instead of the smoked turkey. And so do I, actually," Andrea said. "The smoked turkey was fine, but I've cooked collard greens with ham for so long that I just prefer that taste." Andrea gingerly poured the cornbread into the muffin pan. "I tried the no pork thing for a while, but it just didn't work for me. I enjoy an occasional pork chop and you know I love bacon. I don't eat pork that often, but when I want it, I want it."

"And Bob's okay with that?" Justine asked. She grabbed five plates and set them on the small kitchen table. She reached into the utensil drawer and counted out five forks and knives and added them to her stack along with five napkins.

Mrs. Wellington just laughed. "What choice does he have? I'm a grown woman, Justine. I can eat or drink whatever I want whenever I want," she said boldly. "I'm still the same me. If he can't deal with me enjoying what I like to eat every now and then, that's his problem. But he's okay with it. I had a bacon, lettuce and tomato club when we had lunch on Monday. Use the large dinner napkins, Justine," Andrea corrected. "I like to use the larger dinner napkins when we have company," she added as she placed the corn muffins on the stove. "Don't let me forget to put the corn muffins in thirty minutes before we sit down to eat," she ordered. "Should we use the linen napkins and eat in the dining room today?" Andrea asked. "No. It's just Bob. And I don't feel like ironing those things," she answered for herself.

"I didn't realize that you were even eating pork again," Justine acknowledged.

"Yup. I didn't eat pork that much to begin with, but I'm officially back on the swine," she giggled. Without lifting the lid, Andrea turned the burner down to a low simmer. She cracked an egg into her macaroni and cheese mixture. Through the glass oven door, Justine stared at the large roast chicken swaddling a can of beer. She loved her mother's beer roasted chicken. "It's okay to try new things when you're in a relationship, but don't lose yourself to become what the other person wants you to be," Andrea said. "Be yourself. I know you don't want to talk about AM, but I'm proud of you for not letting him pressure you to enroll in a college in Boston. If you're happier working at Field and going to school part-time, then that's what you should do. You're a grown woman now, Justine. Go to Kendal's party. If you feel uncomfortable, just leave. Who knows, you might meet someone at the party."

"But it's a Chapter Member, I mean gay party, Mom," Justine said.

"Honey, who says that everyone at the party will be gay? You're not gay and you're going. People are people."

Everyone at the party may not be gay? People are people. Everyone at the party may not be gay?

૭〇ભ

She turned her attention back to Batgirl. That's what she'd nicknamed the adult student that interviewed her. "DePaul is very casual," Batgirl commented, smiling uncomfortably at Justine's expensive suit. "Many of the professors dress in jeans for lectures. Some wear suits," she stammered, her eyes roaming every seam of Justine's perfectly tailored jacket. "But none of the students dress up for class," she said. "Do you have to wear a suit to work every day?" Batgirl asked.

Feeling self conscious, Justine fumbled a reply. "I thought that I'd be meeting the department head today," she lied quickly. "And a friend suggested that I dress up to make a good impression. I'm going to strangle Kendal when I see him! I feel pretty silly now," she admitted. "Especially since you so clearly don't have to dress up for your job," she sneered. I'm going to have to work over one hundred hours to pay for this suit!

"Don't feel silly," Batgirl smiled, ignoring Justine's sarcasm. "It's a beautiful suit. A classic, actually, and it fits you like a glove. It's just rare that students come to the peer interview dressed in a suit," she smiled rising to her feet. "You'll meet the dean at your next visit.   By the way, I am recommending that you meet with the dean," she added. "Anyone who comes dressed in a tailored suit deserves to meet with the dean of admissions," she winked.

Justine felt bad for mocking her batman sweatshirt. "Feel free to dress more casual when you meet the dean, Justine," Batgirl added.

"Will do. How casual do you mean? Should I wear jeans and a DePaul sweatshirt?" Justine asked. She struggled to remember the girl's name.

"I wouldn't wear jeans, but khakis and a button down shirt or a sweater set would be more than appropriate," she coached. Justine wondered how long it would take before she'd be allowed to conduct peer interviews wearing an oversized Batman sweatshirt. Sophie! Her name is Sophie!

"Sophie, if you don't mind my asking, are you a huge Batman fan?" Justine asked. "Or is Batman making a comeback?" Before she repeated this story to Kendal, and strangled him for outfitting her in the most expensive piece of clothing she'd ever purchased, she wanted to gather all of her facts.

"Not really," Sophie explained. She folded Justine's student application back into the brown folder and walked around to the front of the desk. "My roommate loves Batman so he bought me this shirt. He said that Batman and Robin were the first men who made it acceptable for men to wear tights in public, so he worships them," Sophie giggled.

Justine frowned at her reflection. Denim and diamonds. She fingered the diamond necklace and tiara that her mother had worn to a costume party with Bob. The theme was "Diamonds are Forever." Andrea had gone as a Bond girl to Bob's James Bond. Justine thought it was corny but was glad that her mother had loaned her the fake bling. She piled on the diamond bangles and glanced at her derriere in the mirror. "Better. The jeans are fitting better now that I've cut out the donuts," she said aloud.

"Should I have bought a denim shirt? Who owns a denim

shirt?" Justine groaned. "I wonder if Kendal will kick me out for not having on enough denim or diamonds. Maybe I'll wear this black cashmere sweater in case it's chilly. She tossed the tiara on the bed and unbuttoned the white blouse, laying it carefully across her bed. Pulling the black sweater over her head, she placed the diamond necklace on top. "Much better. The black makes the diamonds pop, and since the sweater is short sleeved, you can see the bracelets. Perfect!" She placed the tiara on her head and smoothed down her hair. "Denim and diamonds. I have on denim and I have on diamonds. He didn't say that I had to be covered head to toe in either," she continued. She dialed a taxi and grabbed her inside ballet flats, as instructed by Kendal. Accustomed to waiting at least twenty minutes for a taxi, she was stunned when the dispatcher told her that a car could be there in five minutes. She was grateful that she'd applied her make-up after taking her shower. She brushed her hair again and raced into the hallway slipping on her boots and ski jacket. In Chicago, the taxi blew twice and gave you two minutes to appear before driving away in search of another fare. She dropped her ballet flats into her large purse on the foyer table and grabbed her keys. A final mirror check, she pulled the tiara from her head and tossed it into her bag. With one hand on the knob, the phone rang. She remembered another one of Kendal's thou shall nots. "Never answer the phone when you have one foot out the door, it will only delay you, fish."

The ringing phone now muffled by the large wooden door, Justine locked the door, zipped her new ski jacket and skipped down the stairs, hoping that the taxi would be there waiting. She didn't want to stand alone on the street in the cold and dark for too long. Besides, it wasn't safe. It was nine o'clock at night. As she raced down the stairs she wished that she'd invited Grace to come to the party. She missed her friends. "Chin up, Justine. This is a first. You're going to your first Chapter Member party, and this is the first time you've gone to any party by yourself!"

Chapter 14

Paper Dolls

There were eighty ceiling tiles, if you counted the tiles that were cut in half, forty-eight if you only counted the perfectly square tiles. She'd counted them several times. The fluorescent lighting was dim and dull, casting an ugly gray haze over the room. At least two of the four fluorescent bulbs were burned out. The dim lighting was giving her a headache.

The television suspended in the corner of the ceiling showed the Miss America pageant. She wondered if Vanessa Williams watched the pageant. Probably not. Too painful. "Well, at least in your lifetime, you won't think it odd that a black woman is in the Miss America pageant. Until 1984, a black woman had never won the Miss America pageant, and rarely won the state pageants. But now there are eight or nine black contestants!" Miss Nebraska, a chocolate brown contestant with long black hair finished her monologue to a standing ovation. She performed a monologue taken from the novel <u>A Raisin in the Sun</u> by Lorraine Hansberry that was later adapted into a play and a movie.

Miss Nebraska had tears streaming down her cheeks when she finished. Oddly, she'd chosen to perform the "I Am a Man" speech made famous by Sidney Poitier where his character assumes his role as head of the household and confronts the bigoted neighbor. Seeing Miss Nebraska approach the microphone, Rashanda had turned up the volume as high as it would go, glad that she didn't have a roommate to disturb. "I love that book! She was really good. I bet she is a theatre major. I didn't realize there were that many black people in Nebraska. Who knew?" Rashanda had taken to speaking aloud. She was told that it was good for the baby to hear her voice. "Thanks to Rev. Dr. Martin Luther King, Jr., there are people like us everywhere, baby. You can live anywhere you want. Get in where you fit in." A contestant approached the microphone to perform her talent, a song from Les Miserables. Rashanda turned the volume down for the Les Miserables performance. "No more musical show tunes! I hope Miss Nebraska gets extra points for performing a speech that was originally made famous by a man. The beauty contestants always sing or dance. Just once I'd like to see one of them tell jokes as her talent."

Please God! Let everything be okay with the baby! Hospitals still frightened her. Bad things happened at hospitals. Death and cancer treatment. Well, technically, cancer treatment had been a good thing; at least for her mother. Her mother's cancer had been in remission for several months. Although it was too soon to deem her cancer free, the doctors were cautiously optimistic that she'd beaten it. Her hair had grown back almost to its original length, and she'd gained some of her weight back. Mrs. Jordan was pleased with her new leaner look, but Mr. Jordan wanted her to put on a few more pounds. Rashanda discouraged this and encouraged her mother to maintain her newly trim frame and stay on the healthier diet that she'd embraced during her cancer battle. But her mother explained that men from the south liked women with meat on their bones. So she buttered her bread on both sides and dipped it in gravy as she'd done her entire life, her face slowly beginning to fill out like a chocolate crème pie. Rashanda prayed that her mother would at least limit her meat consumption.

The side effects had been the worst. Vomiting, nausea, night sweats and tremors. She hated going to the chemotherapy treatments with her mother. Waif like patients wearing thin hospital gowns floated through the oncology unit like zombies, their flimsy wisps of hair framing their faces like peach fuzz. Some wore clothes that appeared two or three sizes too large. They looked like bald paper dolls. As a child, Rashanda loved playing with paper dolls, fastening the colorful, paper outfits to the dolls and performing skits. When her sister, Tiffany, was born, she couldn't wait to play paper dolls with her. Tiffany didn't appreciate the magic of the paper dolls. Her chubby toddler fingers were unable to demonstrate the appropriate level of care necessary to keep the delicate paper dolls from tearing. Tiffany preferred the sturdy hard plastic baby dolls that could be dragged through the house by their hair or tossed down a flight of stairs unscathed. Skin and bones, the patients in the oncology ward seemed as fragile as the paper dolls from her youth. She wanted her mother to be tough like Tiffany's hard plastic baby dolls.

The chemotherapy sessions seemed to last forever. The radiation left burn marks on her mother's chest, a forever tattoo of her battle with cancer. There were eight chemotherapy stations in each large room. There were two televisions angled to be shared by four beds. Both stations aired the same channel. As best as Rashanda could tell, none of the patients watched either television. Many read Bibles or casually flipped through magazines, making idle chatter with the person who'd driven them that day.

"Do you need anything? Do you want me to change the

channel? I'm sure the other patients won't mind. You should try to get some rest, you look tired." At any given point, one of these phrases or questions was always being uttered. None of the patients ever napped. She wondered if it were possible to take a nap while receiving chemotherapy. Probably not. The patients probably fear that if they doze during the session, it could be the sleep of death. The chemotherapy stations were always full. Rashanda had never considered how many people had cancer.

Mrs. Jordan refused to shave her head, choosing instead to let it fall out in clumps. She shopped and bought a wig that she wore all the time. Even to bed. The female patients didn't wear wigs for their chemotherapy sessions. Their bald heads displayed proudly around the room. She understood. Why fake it? Everyone there had lost their hair. No need for pretense in the chemotherapy session. But not Alice Jordan, she sat with her wig and make-up, frail, yet poised and stoic as though the tubes running through her body were not shooting painful toxins sent to battle the invasive cells attacking her system. Her painted on eyebrows sat like two thin caterpillars atop her false eyelashes. Rashanda hadn't realized that her mother would lose her eyelashes and eyebrows. "At least I don't have to get my moustache waxed for awhile," her mother had joked. Not all patients lost all of their hair. Each patient was different. Rashanda wondered if her mother had lost her pubic hair. If she lost her eyelashes and eyebrows, she probably lost that hair too.

Rashanda watched as her mother wiped her forehead with a towel, the sweat sliding from beneath her wig like a slow moving waterfall. Rashanda knew better than to suggest that she remove the hot wig.

"What does it feel like, Mom?" Rashanda asked. The other

patients seemed to be moaning in despair.

"It feels like I'm getting better."

"But does it hurt, Mom?"

"Sometimes things have to hurt to get better."

It wasn't the answer that Rashanda sought, but she knew her mother well enough to know that it was the only answer that she was going to receive. Alice Jordan was not a complainer. After almost twenty five years of marriage, Rashanda had never heard her mother complain about her father or about the endless amount of chores and laundry she managed. Day after day, Mrs. Jordan cleaned, shopped and prepared three meals a day, never mumbling a complaint about her role as homemaker.

"Aren't you tired of picking up after Daddy?" Rashanda asked one day. "He always leaves his socks on the floor and his newspaper scattered everywhere. He comes in and plops on the sofa while you come in from your part-time job at Sears and cook and clean. When do you ever get a break from your job?"

Mrs. Jordan smiled and shrugged. "I get my rest. Your dad's work is outside of the home, and my work is inside the home, so when he comes home, he needs a break. I don't consider it work taking care of him or our home. When I was a little girl, I prayed for God to give me a good man, a nice family and a beautiful home, and I have all that I asked for. Your daddy is a good man, Rashanda. I'm not going to curse my blessing."

Rashanda remembered frowning and thinking that her mother was a new fool. Actually, she remembered thinking that her mother was an idiot. She regretted that thought now. But she was a teenager at the time, barely thirteen. And teenagers are wired to view their parents' behavior as idiotic. It's part of the teenage rite of passage. She wondered if her child would feel the same about some of her decisions. She adjusted her position in the hospital bed. *God, please give me strength. Please protect my baby.*

They decided that they didn't want to find out the baby's gender. "It's a baby! Let's be surprised." They'd both said almost in unison. Her sister, Tiffany, thought she was stupid for not finding out. But Tiffany was still a teenager. Technically, Rashanda was still a teenager. Even though she was a married woman, she was still a teenager. *Lord, please let everything be okay.*

"You have dilated one centimeter," the nurse explained as she approached the bed, a clipboard resting on her enlarged abdomen and wide hips. "But the doctor is releasing you to go home and rest. Many women walk around one centimeter dilated for the entire last trimester. The baby's heart rate is fine and your contractions have subsided. Pre-term labor contractions are very common. So you can put on your clothes. The doctor signed the discharge paperwork so I'll have you sign as soon as I complete your chart. Where's your boyfriend?"

"My boyfriend? He's my husband, and he went to the cafeteria to get me a milkshake," Rashanda replied. *Thank you, Lord!* "Why'd you think he was my boyfriend?"

"You're married?"

"I took off my wedding ring because my fingers are so swollen." Rashanda waved her fingers in the air to demonstrate. "See?"

"Once you have your baby, your fingers will go back to normal. Glad you got him to marry you. Most girls your age who visit labor and delivery aren't married yet. At least you got him to marry you before the baby was born."

"I wasn't pregnant when we got married," Rashanda added.

"Oh, of course you weren't," the nurse smiled. "Like I said, once you have your baby, your fingers will go back to normal. You're just retaining water."

"I know that," she replied harshly. "My husband is a pre-med student."

"Well, good for you. You nabbed yourself one with ambition," the chubby nurse added. "But a baby changes things. I hope he sticks with it and finishes medical school, that way you might be able to afford to stay home and take care of your children." She scribbled on Rashanda's chart and removed the baby monitor cords connected to her abdomen.

"We're not going to add to our family right away. And I'm going to law school," Rashanda continued. "I plan to become a judge."

But she could tell that the jolly nurse was no longer listening. Ian burst through the door carrying two milkshakes. "Sorry it took so long, Shanda. I ran into a couple of my professors in the cafeteria and they were asking me questions about the upcoming final exam that I'm helping them write." Ian placed the milkshakes on the nightstand. "Why are you removing the monitor? Is the baby okay? What's going on?" he panted.

Rashanda reached for her husband's hand and squeezed it tightly. "The doctor said that since my contractions have subsided, and I'm only one centimeter dilated, they're discharging me."

"Not to worry, Dr. Ian, pre-term labor contractions are very common," the doctor added, walking in behind Ian. "I thought I'd pop in to say goodnight to my favorite patient and see if you had any questions before I scrub in to perform a C-Section. Hello there, Mrs. Hall."

"Hi, Dr. McKnight."

"I'm sure Nurse Betty explained that pre-term labor comes and goes. If it happens again, just limit your activity and it should subside. Try to stay away from spicy foods and things that normally give you indigestion. And since you only live ten minutes away from the hospital, you can get back quickly if anything changes. Nurse Betty, did you explain how they'll know that she's in active labor?"

"No. I was just completing Rashanda's chart and was going to explain that to her next," Nurse Betty stammered.

"You mean Mrs. Hall. We refer to the patients by their surname, Nurse Betty," Dr. McKnight corrected gently. "I'll let you explain that then. Don't let her forget, Dr. Ian."

Rashanda noticed Nurse Betty's jaw clench.

"How are you feeling, young lady?" he asked.

"I'm fine, Dr. McKnight," she smiled. "I'm a little tired. But I haven't had a contraction for over two hours. I can feel the baby kicking a lot though."

"That's good. You should go home and get some rest. If you still haven't had any contractions within twenty-four hours, just go about your regular routine, but take it easy for the next two or three days. You can go to your classes, but drive instead of walk," he winked. "I'm on call all night, so just call me if you have any questions or something doesn't feel quite right."

"Will do," Ian assured. "Is there anything that she can't eat or drink, Dr. McKnight?"

"Not really. I'd limit the spicy stuff, but your bride is eating for two, so she can eat whatever she wants. That big head son of yours needs all the nutrients he can get. You're having a boy, right?"

"We don't know. We wanted to be surprised, remember? We've only had one ultrasound and I don't think they were able to see anything yet."

"That's right. It was just a guess. I haven't peeked at the

ultrasound photo myself, and it's too early to really tell, so don't think I spoiled your surprise," he winked. "We'll all find out together. One thing we do know, it's a baby!" He patted Rashanda's foot lightly, his salt and pepper gray hair looked distinguished and interesting next to his olive skin. "I'm off to increase the world population. I'll see you at your next appointment, Mrs. Hall. Or should I say Judge Hall? And Dr. Ian, you page me if you need to, I don't care what time it is," Dr. McKnight ordered as he walked swiftly toward the door. "You're in good hands with Nurse Betty." Rashanda grinned at Dr. McKnight's reference to and embrace of their career aspirations.

"Yes sir, Dr. McKnight." Rashanda thought Ian might salute the exiting doctor like a five star general, the admiration and respect for his esteemed medical mentor radiated from his pores.

Dr. McKnight had delivered Ian. Like Ian, Dr. McKnight and his wife had their first child when he was still in college. He and his young wife moved in with her family so that her parents could care for their baby while she worked as a teacher to support her husband through medical school. Their first born son had been Ian's pediatrician, both McKnight doctors serving as the inspiration for Ian to pursue a career in medicine.

As Nurse Betty silently scribbled on the chart, and held out the clipboard for Rashanda to sign, Rashanda prayed that she didn't have to have a C-Section. She wanted to deliver her baby. She feared being cut in the abdomen, and knew that a C-Section required a longer recovery period.

"As the doctor stated, you should take it easy for the next twenty-four hours. Limit your activity and walking. If you aren't having any more contractions, slowly get back into your regular routine. Try not to lift anything heavier than your backpack."

"Please tell her not to lift the heavy laundry basket, Nurse Betty."

"Let your husband do the laundry. This shouldn't happen, but if your water breaks or your contractions are five minutes apart, you need to return to the hospital immediately. In active labor, sometimes the mother may experience nausea or an extreme pressure in the abdominal area that may feel like a need to relieve her bowels."

Rashanda giggled. Nurse Betty stared somberly at Rashanda before continuing.

"If you experience intense pressure in the abdominal area, and your contractions have been timed at within five minutes apart, you must resist the urge to bear down or push as though you are having a bowel movement. Do not push. For most first time deliveries, the active phase may last for a few hours, but each pregnancy is different. The other things that define active labor are listed on the back of this sheet."

"Thank you, Nurse Betty," Ian said. "You've been very helpful."

Nurse Betty smiled. "Vaya con Dios. That means Go with God."

"I know. I speak Spanish too," Rashanda winked.

"What was that about? Why do you have Rashanda-tude in your voice?"

"Never mind. Let's get out of here. I really don't like hospitals."

Rashanda tossed her swollen legs over the bed and kicked her mules to one side. Her normally thin feet and ankles were so swollen that she was unable to squeeze her feet into loafers or sneakers. She wore a pair of suede Birkenstock mules, one size larger than her regular shoe size, grateful that the Evanston sidewalks were shoveled regularly. She couldn't imagine bending down to squeeze her fat calves into winter boots.

Without prompting, Ian walked over and helped steady Rashanda as she slipped on her oversized sweats. He knew the drill. She slipped her left leg into one side and then her right and pulled the elastic waistband over her bulging abdomen. The baby kicked as the elastic encircled her stomach. Ian had teased her that she always put on her sweat pants with the left leg first. She'd never paid attention to the order in which she put on her pants. At first, she wondered if it had anything to do with her being a lefty. But Ian was also a lefty, and he put on his pants by inserting his right leg in first. It was just a preference, an odd quirk that most people never noticed or paid attention to in the ritual of getting dressed, but something that her beloved husband had observed.

Ian studied his young wife like a textbook. He nicknamed her his favorite subject. On their first month anniversary as husband and wife, besides knowing all of the important dates in her life, her favorite foods and colors, he could recite her favorite movies, books and television programs. By their second month anniversary, Ian knew exactly how she liked her coffee and the consistency and thickness of how she preferred her grits and cream of wheat to be prepared. He knew which nail she painted first when giving herself a manicure, and which side of her teeth she brushed first. His commitment to knowing every detail about her unnerved her at first. She thought his devotion a bit odd and feared that he might have a secret toenail collection stashed somewhere. She snooped through his things one day and was relieved when she came up toenail free. They talked about it that night at dinner. "I love you, Rashanda. I want to know everything about you. I want to know what makes you tick so that I am prepared to care for you for the rest of your life."

"But I feel like you're studying me like there's going to be a test, Ian. It's freaking me out."

"I just want to know everything about you so that I can make you happy. You're my favorite subject and I want to get an A as your husband. I know once I'm in medical school and the baby comes my husband grade may slip to a B, but I won't ever let it slip lower than that. I want to be an exceptional husband to you, Rashanda, because that's what you deserve. I want to anticipate your needs and meet them before you ask. And I'm afraid that when the baby comes we'll be so focused on the baby that we won't have time to get to know each other as well as we should. So I'm trying to learn everything about you so I can master the subject matter."

She couldn't argue with his logic. "But Ian, I feel like I'm a class that you're cramming for. I appreciate your devotion, but you could tone it down just a tad."

"I tend to get a bit neurotic when I'm mastering anything new. It's how I've always approached my school studies, but I'll back off a little bit."

And he had. He still studied her like a textbook, but she hadn't felt the need to search for any more hidden toenail collections.

After slipping on her oversized Northwestern University sweatshirt, she wrapped the large, purple, wool poncho over her shoulders, a much appreciated surprise gift from Justine. The gift had come in handy as her expanding belly didn't allow her to zip her winter jacket, and their limited student budget did not have surplus to purchase a new winter jacket. Rashanda had been wearing one of Ian's old jackets around campus, feeling like a fashion mistake. Justine had stopped by for a quick visit last week and teased her about looking like ten miles of bad road.

"If Teenie and Maria saw you in that old jacket, they would peel your head!" Justine screamed. "You look like fashion road kill."

"Not everyone works at Fields and has access to a store discount," Rashanda defended. "Plus, I'm pregnant."

"Pregnant or not, I cannot have you dressing like that. Not when I work in retail! We are Lori's Angels, remember? We have a reputation to maintain."

"I know, but we are saving all of our extra money for the baby. We will have to pay for childcare, diapers, clothes. There's no money for fashion."

"Let me see what I can do," Justine smiled warmly.

A large box arrived three days later. She squealed when she saw the purple, wool poncho. The suede Birkenstocks were one size larger than her normal shoe size. The box also included three pair of expensive yoga pants and matching tops. The card on the top read, "No more fashion roadkill! Love, Lori's Angels." Rashanda smiled, wondering if Justine had contacted Grace, Teenie and Maria and taken a collection for her gifts. They'd talked about giving her a baby shower over their Thanksgiving vacations, but Rashanda told them that she felt superstitious about having a shower so early in her pregnancy. She wasn't ready for a shower for two reasons. One, she didn't want her friends to incur any additional expenses. With her trust fund, she knew that Grace could easily afford to host the shower and buy gifts, but she worried about Teenie and Maria, both had recently complained how expensive airfare was for the short Thanksgiving break and shared that they weren't sure if they'd be able to fly home or have to wait until Christmas. She missed her friends.

But more importantly, she wasn't ready to announce to all of her friends and family that she and Ian were married and expecting. She didn't want people to think that she'd been pregnant when they married. That it was a shotgun wedding. Her friends told her that she was being silly. But her pride was involved. They knew they wanted children, but she still couldn't believe that she'd gotten pregnant so early in their marriage. It hadn't been their intent. But they'd gotten married so quickly that they hadn't had time to agree on a contraceptive that felt right for them both. "You weren't doing anything to prevent getting pregnant, so now you're pregnant. That's how this works," Dr. McKnight had chuckled.

Her mother could hardly contain her enthusiasm and had already pulled Rashanda's crib from the attic and placed it in her bedroom. Her father was slowly getting used to the idea of Rashanda being married and pregnant. His scowls toward Ian were slightly less menacing. He still wasn't friendly toward Ian, but he wasn't hostile either.

Ian rubbed Rashanda's small belly. "I can't believe that you're showing already, Rashanda."

"Dr. McKnight said that since I was so thin and underweight that it's natural for me to show quickly. I've already gained twenty pounds, and he said that I'm probably going to gain around forty pounds, which I find hard to imagine."

"And you're staying off the sodium, right?"

"Of course, Ian. If my hands and feet swell any more I'm going to look like a sumo wrestler." Rashanda slid into her Birkenstock mules. "I'm guessing that five or ten of these pounds are the freshman fifteen. I've been eating dessert for lunch and dinner and I don't even really have a sweet tooth, and I've been chugging milkshakes like water. As soon as this baby comes, I'm going to hit the gym every day."

"Or not. We both have a full class load and we'll have a baby to take care of," Ian reminded. "Pushing the baby in the stroller around campus might be as close as we both get to exercise for a while."

Rashanda smiled at her handsome husband as he helped her stand to her feet.

"Let's go, Mrs. Hall. I'm going to get you settled at home and then I can make it to the library to tutor my chemistry students. We need the extra income now more than ever."

Rashanda reached for the two milkshakes nestled in the drink holder on the bedside table before looping her arm through her husband's.

Chapter 15

I Know You Are, But What Am I?

The brown paper bags tumbled out of the pantry, courtesy of her twice weekly trips to the grocery store. She stuffed them back inside. Cooking on the weekends had become her new favorite pastime. So far, her culinary skills included a pot of chili, angel hair spaghetti with turkey meat sauce and cornbread. Grace loved cornbread. She prepared it in a round cake pan. Hot and fresh from the oven, she sliced the delicate bread and smeared liberal helpings of sweet butter on its tummy and savored it like a dessert. Sliced like pie, she usually ate three slices of cornbread before stopping herself. The goal was to learn to cook something new each week. "Cook one meal from a cookbook each week!" That was her personal goal, scrawled on a slip of paper and mounted on her refrigerator with a small orange and blue Illini magnet. So far, she'd only cooked three things, but it was a start. She'd watched her mother prepare enough meals, so she knew the mechanics of cooking, but she'd never actually done it herself.

"Mom, show me how to cook," Grace pleaded.

"I don't mind cooking for you. I've cooked my entire life. I cooked for your mama her entire life. Let me do for you while I can, Gracie. I'm getting older and won't be able to do for you and your daddy soon, so let me take care of you while I can. You keep your nose buried in your books."

Grace knew that her aging mother's sense of usefulness was intricately linked to her role as homemaker and caregiver. She understood that. But now Grace felt like a small child in the kitchen. In the required home economics class that she took her sophomore year at River North, she learned how to measure ingredients and made snickerdoodle cookies, grilled cheese sandwiches and pancakes, but she didn't know how to season a steak or sauté vegetables. As instructed, she'd purchased a cookbook and told herself that she'd teach herself how to cook.

Chip laughed when she told him that she was reading a cookbook to learn how to cook.

"Grace, you sound just like your mother. I remember when Lydia came to my office once and told me the same thing. That Ethel refused to teach her how to cook."

"I think my mom thinks that if she teaches me how to do it, I won't need her to do it for me."

"It's very common. Older people need to feel useful and needed. And you know I know that Ethel is also your mother," he added. "So forgive me if I don't always refer to Lydia as your birth mother. But you know that you can easily afford to hire someone to cook for you. That's what your grandparents did. Your mother, Lydia, used to always talk about how Ethel would let her sit in the kitchen with her to keep her company, but she never taught her how to cook anything."

"But I don't want to hire someone to cook for me, Chip. I want to be able to cook for myself."

"Well, I'm proud of you. You're a young adult now, so you should learn how to cook. If she were alive, your mother would probably be doing the same thing, reading some cookbook and teaching herself how to do for herself. Instead of spending money on a cook, she'd be sending that money to some charity or another. Your mother had a heart of gold and a passion for helping the poor. You come from good stock, Miss Grace Ann Moore Dudley, daughter of Lydia, the love of my life."

She smiled at the gentle reference to her birth mother. She wondered if Chip ever wished that Lydia had given her his last name too. She wondered why her mother hadn't. After learning of her adoption, her parents had shown Grace her birth certificate for the first time. Grace Ann Moore. After her mother died and her adoption was finalized, her parents had made Moore part of her middle name.

Chip and Grace talked on the phone every weekend when the rates were their lowest. When Chip called her, she made him hang up and dialed him back so that she paid for the call. Sometimes he would remind her of her vast wealth and tease her for being so concerned about the long distance rates. "Grace, you do realize that one of your portfolios owns a substantial share in the telecommunications industry so you own part of the phone company, my dear. You can afford to talk as long as you want, whenever you want." Grace ignored Chip and still insisted on Sunday only phone calls. Grace had been raised by people who were children of the Great Depression and World War II. It was natural for Grace to mimic the frugality of her parents. Her entire life, she had watched Ethel and Greg Dudley live frugal lives which included only calling their relatives down south on Sunday when the rates were at their lowest.

Excited by the upcoming Thanksgiving break, she wanted to surprise her parents and cook a meal for them. She hoped that her mother would be proud of her for learning to cook and not take offense at her new skill. The brown paper bags now neatly stacked on the floor of the near empty pantry, she moved to the refrigerator and opened it. The smell of spoiled food seeped out like a genie in a bottle. Frowning, Grace's eyes scanned the shelves for the culprit. The sparse refrigerator was home to a half gallon of unopened chocolate milk and three vanilla yogurt containers that also hadn't been opened and neighbored a quart of orange juice. A square box of shrimp fried rice (her dinner from the night before) was the only item on the middle shelf, directly above a container of bologna. A box of unsalted butter sat on the bottom shelf, the butter an indulgence that she'd treated herself to like the BMW.

Raised in the south, her parents adored butter, and swore that it was one of the things that they missed most about working for the Moore family, the liberal purchase and use of sweet cream butter. Now that they lived on a modest, fixed income, Ethel bought the less expensive margarine or vegetable oil spread instead of butter. She splurged and bought sweet cream butter for Thanksgiving baking and Christmas cookies. Grace loved butter and was almost as excited to spread sweet cream butter on her toast during the weeks between Thanksgiving and Christmas as she was to receive her gifts from Santa. Grace had purchased six four stick boxes of butter for her parents' freezer and tossed the margarine into the trash. Her mother had gasped and scolded her for being so wasteful. "Mom, I can afford to buy you butter anytime now, and I want you to have the best. Please let me buy you butter."

"I don't want you wasting your money on me and your daddy, Grace. We get along just fine."

"I know you do, Mom. But let this be my gift to you. I want you to be able to eat butter anytime you want. And see, I even bought you a new butter dish to match the canisters. Look!"

Ethel covered her hand to her mouth. "How'd you find the exact style? This is perfect! You know I like to let my butter sit on the counter room temperature so that it's nice and soft. There ain't nothing worse than trying to spread cold, hard butter on your food. As long as it's covered, butter will keep on your counter for a week or better. Most folks don't know that. You don't have to refrigerate butter so long as you eat it within a week or so." After she left, Grace suspected that her frugal mother retrieved the wrapped sticks of margarine from the trash and used them.

Grace pulled open the vegetable drawer and the sour smell intensified. Spoiled produce. She slid the metal garbage can nearer the refrigerator, feeling ashamed of her next task. She knew that Ethel Dudley would have a conniption if she saw the amount of food that her daughter discarded regularly. She could hear her mother's voice. "Waste not, want not!"

With her toe on the lever to keep the trash can open, Grace stared at the wilted lettuce and limp celery in her hand. "I can't think of any recipe that calls for wilted lettuce and limp celery. Sorry, Mom." She heaved the produce into the trash. The fruit drawer was next. She'd only eaten three of the red strawberries from the large container. The others were now covered in mold. She stared at the green plastic basket filled with strawberries. It looks like a science project, like I'm trying to grow mold cultures to find the cure for strawberry disease. Why'd I buy a pint of strawberries? I don't really like strawberries. Because they were on sale. You know why you bought those strawberries, Grace, don't even try it.

She picked up the broccoli and wondered if the tips were supposed to be golden yellow. She thought about tossing the broccoli florets into the trash but decided to make a cream of broccoli soup instead. Grace lifted the broccoli to her nose and inhaled. The broccoli was odorless. She'd remembered seeing her mom cook broccoli with yellow tips so she put the broccoli on the counter and decided to make a soup. Reaching into the back of the vegetable drawer, she located the source of the smell. Tucked in the corner sat a large baking potato. The once brown potato was now soft and oozed mucus the color of eggplant from its wound. The eggplant mucus appeared to serve as an adhesive that had managed to attach the potato securely to the plastic drawer. Gripping her bare hands around the bad potato, Grace pulled it from the drawer and tossed it in the trash.   Grace decided to bury the potato in plastic and escort the smelly culprit to the garbage shoot. Once back inside her apartment, she cracked a window and washed the plastic drawer in warm soapy, lemon scented water.

The cookbook on the counter was open to soups and casseroles. She flipped through a few pages but didn't see a recipe for cream of broccoli soup. Grace looked through the index. Still no recipe for cream of broccoli soup.   She added sweat cream half and half and cheddar cheese to her grocery list. Cream of broccoli soup was her favorite soup and she remembered from the many bowls that she'd consumed that one of the main ingredients was thick, heavy cream and cheddar cheese. Since going to the grocery store had become one of her new favorite pastimes, she was glad that this time she had a legitimate reason to shop. Her name was Sarah.

Sarah had short black hair cropped at the neck and thin eyebrows that she thickened with eyebrow pencil. The strawberry purchase had been influenced by Sarah. Appearing out of nowhere, her voice had startled Grace. "The strawberries are a good deal." Grace smiled and picked up a pint. "Taste one," Sarah encouraged. "They're really sweet." Sarah lifted the lid of the pint in Grace's hand and waited for Grace to pick up a strawberry. "They're organic which means that they were not treated with any pesticides so it won't kill you to eat one straight from the pint. Try one." Grace bit into the juicy fruit and smiled. "Told you," Sarah grinned. "The tomatoes are on sale this week too. They're also organic and vine ripened, so they're really sweet too. Most stores pick the tomatoes when they're green so they don't spoil during shipping and then they spray them with CO_2 to make them turn red. Did you know that?"

"No, I didn't know that."

"You're in good company. Most people don't know that. But if you're buying tomatoes grown on a farm hundreds of miles away from the grocery store where they'll be sold, the produce would be damaged in shipping if they waited for them to ripen and then picked them. They wouldn't last very long on the shelf. But green tomatoes are still hard and sturdy so they make heartier travelers, and then they begin to ripen in transit. But these are grown fresh by a local farmer," she explained. "And they're not picked until they're ripe. Personally, I believe that you should know where your food comes from."

"I love fresh tomatoes," Grace stammered. "My mother always grows tomatoes in our garden at home."

"The tomatoes are right over there. Happy shopping," Sarah disappeared into the back of the store, behind the Employees Only sign.

Like a child waiting for her mother to take her hand and guide her through the parking lot, Grace stood frozen in the produce section. In a dream state, she managed to make her way to the tomatoes and picked up two large ones. Her reaction to the strawberry taste had been manufactured. The strawberry was sweet, but she was not a strawberry fan. Once home, she'd eaten two more strawberries as a test before burying the strawberries to be entombed in the fruit drawer of her refrigerator. But she loved tomatoes. Ethel Dudley grew the most beautiful tomatoes that Grace had ever seen, so Grace had been raised to appreciate the sweetness of a vine ripened tomato. Her taste buds could discern the difference between a vine ripened tomato and a tough restaurant slice. Grace enjoyed her mother's tomatoes on her sandwiches, burgers or alone on a slice of bread with mayonnaise. That afternoon, she'd made herself a toasted bread and tomato sandwich with a light coating of mayonnaise topped with a thin slice of Buffalo mozzarella cheese from the deli. She was glad that Sarah had encouraged her to buy the fresh produce. She'd gone into the store to buy orange juice and bread for toast, her breakfast staple when she awakened too late for breakfast in her dorm, which happened with a great sense of regularity. She'd only stopped at the strawberry display to bend down and tie her shoe.

Her newfound friend, Sarah, worked in the produce department, but she also sometimes worked at the checkouts on the weekends when the store was especially crowded. The wilted lettuce and celery purchases were also influenced by Sarah on a different trip to the produce section.

"Excuse me. How can I tell if the celery is fresh?" Grace asked, searching for a reason to ask Sarah a question.

"Well, it's fresh now. We only sell fresh produce," Sarah shot back.

"That's not what I mean. Once I get it home, if I don't use it right away, how can I tell if it's still fresh?"

"Oh. Well, you just break off a piece. If it snaps when you break it off, it's still fresh. If it's limp, then it's no good. Now, you can still cook with wilted celery if you're making a soup or a stew, but I wouldn't recommend it. It won't kill you. I just think produce should be bought and used while it's fresh. You should buy your produce the same day that you're going to use it or maybe the day before but no sooner. That's what the Europeans do. They stop by the store each evening on their way home to pick up fresh food and a fresh loaf of bread. Food tastes better when it's fresh."

"Oh. That's a good tip."

"I've noticed that you're in the store a lot. Are you a Culinary Arts major or something?" Sarah asked.

"No. I actually haven't declared a major yet. I'm trying to decide between communications and psychology. I'm just trying to teach myself how to cook."

"Why? Is the dorm food that bad? The food in my dorm is pretty good."

"You're a student at the University of Illinois too?"

"Uh, huh, most of the clerks that work here are. I'm Sarah."

"I'm Grace."

"So why are you trying to learn to cook, Grace?

"I just feel like I should know how to cook. My mother is a great cook, but she never taught me how to cook."

"Well, if you can read, you can cook."

"I don't get it," Grace shrugged.

"If you can read a cookbook, then you can follow a recipe and cook."

"Oh. I never thought of it that way, but I guess that makes sense."

Sarah continued to arrange the apples on her display in a pyramid pattern. Grace was glad that the produce section was empty and that Sarah wasn't being swarmed by other shoppers with questions. Sarah swatted at a pair of flies who swarmed above her apple display. "I so wish they'd let me swat these flies, they're such a nuisance. But the manager doesn't want dead flies lying around the food. So he'd rather let the little pests buzz around and land on the food." Sarah seemed to be talking to herself.

"Can you recommend a cookbook that I should buy, Sarah?" Grace liked saying her name.

"I would start with a basic American cookbook. But don't buy one, just check it out of the library and copy the recipes that you really like. Take advantage of your tax dollars and use the library, you're a poor college student."

"Good idea," Grace smiled.

"Good luck. Happy cooking."

Her eyes had a slight slant, but not enough of a slant to be full blown Asian. Grace knew that much. Several of Grace's dorm mates were Asian. She was now almost able to distinguish between someone from China, Japan and Korea thanks to the help of her dorm mate, Tomoko. One Sunday afternoon, a bout of cabin fever luring her from the solitude of her studio apartment and down to the student television lounge to study, Grace and Tomoko were the only students in the room. Julia Childs' The French Chef program hummed softly in the background while they studied.

"Tomoko, do you mind if I ask you something?"

"No. Go right ahead."

"I know you're from Japan because you told me that. But how can you tell if someone is from China, Japan, Korea or Vietnam for instance? I know that may sound ignorant to you, but I want to learn how to differentiate which country people are from when I meet them. Can you help me?"

Tomoko smiled softly. "It doesn't sound ignorant. I think

it's good that you want to learn and educate yourself. It sounds ignorant to me when people assume that all of us are 'oriental.' That's ignorant. Most of the time, I can tell people from my country by their name. Japanese names follow a consonant-vowel-consonant pattern."

"You can't tell just by looking at them?"

"Sometimes I can. But sometimes I can't, especially if the person has really assimilated into the American culture for instance. A lot of Asian women lighten their hair now and visit tanning salons, so it's not as obvious. I can usually tell someone from China because their eyes are very slanted, almost slits. And many have puffy slanted eyes. But the other Asian countries aren't as obvious even to me. But when I hear them speaking in their native tongue that helps me. Obviously, I speak Japanese, but I don't speak Cantonese or Mandarin. I understand a little of both, but I can't read either. I also speak a little Vietnamese."

Grace blushed. "I just assumed that you could understand all of the Asian languages.

"Nope. They're completely different. That's why so many of us speak three and four languages."

"Wow!"

"Americans are the only ones that I know who only speak English. People in my country think Americans are stupid for only speaking one language. No offense."

"None taken."

"I know that many American schools are now teaching Spanish, but it's not like it is in my country. You are expected to learn English like math. And then you learn Spanish, German or French as your foreign language."

"Really?"

"I'm fluent and literate in Japanese, English and French. And I understand a little mandarin and Vietnamese. And because French is one of the romance languages, I can get by in Spanish speaking countries. In the United States, they really should be teaching another language from birth when children's brains are like sponges. My parents only spoke Japanese in our home, so my siblings and I were bilingual before we started school. We could read in English and Japanese before kindergarten."

"Who taught you English?"

"My parents spoke and read English too, but we became fluent in English from the kids in our neighborhood and our classmates."

"Did you teach the kids in your neighborhood any Japanese?"

Tomoko smiled. "We tried. They wanted to learn it too, but some of their parents would yell at us and tell us that we were responsible for World War II, bombing Pearl Harbor and killing their relatives. They'd shout other stuff at us that we didn't understand at the time."

Grace's jaw was ajar.

"Hard to believe, huh? I remember this couple coming to our house saying that they couldn't do anything about us living on their street, but they did not want their children learning Japanese words and phrases. So our parents made us stop teaching them our language. We still played with their kids, we just stopped our little language lessons. Now that I think about it, we were never invited into their house. We always played with them outside. And you thought blacks were the only ones discriminated against by whites in the old US of A, huh?" Tomoko grinned. "And this was only fifteen years ago."

⁊

Sarah was working the express lane at the checkouts. Grace stood in her line, glad that her shopping list included a cucumber and an onion for her weekly pot of spaghetti. In her mind, she and Sarah were friends.

"Hello, how are you today?" Sarah smiled.

"Fine, how are you, Sarah?"

Hearing her name, Sarah looked up from her register and smiled. "Did you cook your celery? I remember you asked me about celery freshness the last time you were here."

Her head down in search of her wallet, Grace's eyes darted upward, shocked that Sarah remembered their celery freshness discussion from a week before.

"Well, uh, not exactly. No actually, I didn't. I thought I was going to make this recipe, but then I didn't have time."

"It's no good now so you may as well toss it out. Try to buy your produce no more than a day in advance of when you plan to cook with it, otherwise you're wasting your money." Sarah typed in the price lookup code on the onion. "These onions aren't bad, but next time you should buy the Vidalia onions, they're sweeter."

"I will remember that."

"Your name is Grace, right?"

Grace thought she was going to melt. "Yes, my name is Grace. Good memory."

"I didn't remember it at first, but I word associated it when I met you a few weeks ago. 'The world would be a better place if we all showed each other more grace.' Sounds silly, but that's how I remember names. I word associate them."

So far, Grace had seen Sarah every time she'd visited the grocery store. She wondered when Sarah had time to study. Grace felt like she was floating back to the parking lot.

While she was shopping, the sun had begun its nightly setting routine; the baby blue sky now splattered with an orange purple haze like a Monet watercolor. Grace loved this time of the evening, especially in the fall when the air was crisp and smelled of burning leaves most nights. Sweater weather. Grace opened her sunroof and tilted her head to admire God's sky. A chill wind ran through her thick hair. As a child, she imagined that God sat at a canvas each day and painted a different watercolor sky just for her enjoyment. She leaned her head against the headrest and exhaled deeply, her eyes staring through the sunroof.

"You forgot your onion, Grace," a voice said loudly. "I'm glad I caught you before you drove off."

She stared through the window and smiled.

"Are you going to open the window or should I drop it through your sunroof?"

Grace hit the center console button to lower the window.

"I put it to the side and forgot to toss it into your bag. Sorry about that." Sarah handed Grace the onion. "Are you okay? It looked like you were sleeping for a second. You're not sick or anything are you?" Sarah's look was one of concern and worry.

She thought about lying. "No. I was just admiring the sky. This is my favorite part of the evening, so I was just taking it all in before I go back and hit the books. I'm going to cook with my fresh onion and then study," she corrected.

Sarah smiled. "Well, happy cooking. I better get inside and tend my register before I get fired. Nice car by the way."

Feeling caught, Grace shifted her car in gear and drove home wanting to talk with someone about Sarah. That evening, she called Justine as she put her groceries away.

"You think she's Asian and black?" Justine asked.

"No, I don't think she has any black in her, but I know she's not one hundred percent Asian either. I think she's Asian and white. Her skin isn't dark enough to be mixed with black. She's very pale."

"Look who's talking, little miss half white girl. In the winter, you're almost translucent."

"Shut up, Justine. Well, that's true. But Sarah's hair is really straight and jet black. My hair has texture, so people can usually tell that I'm mixed with something. They don't usually guess black right away, because my hair is so blonde." Grace ran her fingers through her thick mane, her hand gripping her head in response to Justine's next question.

"Do you think she's gay?"

The question startled her. She was taken aback that her best friend had so quickly cut to the chase. But that was Justine's way and always had been. Justine was unable to beat around the bush. She lacked the beat around the bush gene.

"You mean, Sarah? Do I think Sarah is gay?"

"No, I mean the man on the moon. Isn't that who we've been talking about? Of course I mean Sarah."

"How would I know?"

"I don't know. You tell me. How would you know? Is there a gay high sign that gays give each other so that you know the other person is gay? Exactly how does it work, Grace?"

Grace stared at the telephone in her hand and paced. "Are you being funny?"

"I'm dead freaking serious. How can you tell if someone is gay?"

"What's with the tone in your voice, Justine?"

There was silence on the other end of the telephone. The

seconds ticked away like minutes, thick and long.

"Justine, are you still there?" Grace sat on the kitchen floor. Wearing thin, unlined sweat pants, the tiles were instantly cold against her legs. She wanted to walk over to the thermostat and adjust the temperature, but she sat frozen, awaiting her friend's response, fearful that if she were to move, she'd miss her reply.

Grace could hear Justine moving around. "I knew eventually we'd have to talk about this, Justine, so let's talk. Does it bother you that I'm gay?" The question felt unfamiliar leaving her tongue, just like her counselor warned her that it would.

This time, Justine responded quickly. "I thought I was cool with it. I'm cool with Kendal's gayness, but I guess I still can't believe that you're gay. We've been friends since grade school, Grace. Were you gay in grade school?"

"I guess." Grace stretched her fingers in and out. She wanted to run and find her counselor's notes, the tips on how to guide the "coming out" discussion. She stood to her feet and remembered that they were in her car. She'd left them in her trunk. Her back against the cabinet, she slid back to the cold floor, her long legs cramped in the small galley kitchen.

"You guess? But you went on a few dates with Dell Curry, that cute waiter from the pizza restaurant in Newberry East. You liked him, he liked you. Why'd you go on a date with him if you knew you were gay?"

"I don't think I realized that I was gay then," Grace shared softly, her words choppy and tense, barely above a whisper. She forced herself to breathe.

"So one day you just woke up and said, 'I think I'm gay today.' I guess I just don't get it."

"It's hard to explain, Justine. I wish I could explain it to you in a way that makes sense to you." Grace knew that this conversation was long overdue. Justine's visit with Kendal had been her official coming out to her friend, but she and Justine had never talked in depth about it.

"Well, did you know that you were gay when we were younger?"

The counselor's voice rang through Grace's head. "You must be able to tell your story, Grace. Your friends and family will want to hear it from you. If you're uncomfortable telling your story, they will be uncomfortable hearing your story. But if you tell your story without shame or regret, they will receive it as the truth that it is and begin to accept it. You must be comfortable with it before you can expect others to be comfortable with it. Being gay is outside of the societal norm, so most people won't accept this news well initially. It will take some time for them to digest it." At Kendal's suggestion, Grace had visited the student health center and availed herself of the free counseling services. The counselor had been very kind. Not shocked at all by Grace's admission. Grace felt as though she were just one in a long line of co-eds who came to her that day to discuss how best to talk about their newfound gayness with family and friends.

"I think I did. But I was so self conscious about so many different things back then, Justine. I was almost six feet tall in middle school. I got teased for my height and for being light bright and damn near white. Oh, and then hearing that I was adopted and my mother was white was pretty heavy duty. And then Lori died. And right after that I found out that my birth father was biracial and married and my grandparents ruined his career. And let's not forget learning that I'm a Moore heiress. My life has been one made for television sequel after another. You know the story.

You lived it with me step by step. So with all of that going on, I never really paused long enough to think about my sexuality," she finished.

"I guess I never thought about it like that," Justine replied.

Grace now felt empowered. "At Battle Creek Junior High when Lori, Tanisha and Maria were always talking about boys I thought I was just a late bloomer. And since you and Rashanda never talked about boys then, I wasn't really too worried about it. I just figured that my boy crush gene would kick in eventually. I had fun at prom with Doug, but he was Lori's boyfriend, so I wasn't attracted to him. And I thought Dell Curry was cute, but there was no chemistry on my part. When I kissed him I felt nothing."

"You kissed him?"

"I thought I told you that. On our third date, he kissed me at the door. It lasted about one minute and I told him that I was worried that my parents would catch us."

"I remember that. You did tell me that. Well, maybe you just didn't have any chemistry with Dell or he was just a bad kisser. That doesn't mean that you're gay."

Denial and disbelief. Her counselor had prepared her that this would be the most common initial responses. Her eyes closed, Grace ignored Justine's comment and mentally focused on the notes that she'd taken in the counselor's office to help script her coming out story. "And since that completes my dating experience, I thought I just needed to get more boy experience. Like you said, maybe I just didn't have chemistry with Dell. But once I got on campus, and I saw other same gendered couples holding hands, it didn't make me uncomfortable. It confirmed what I already suspected about myself. I'm gay, Justine." Grace was glad that she'd remembered the term that her counselor had taught her for describing who she was. She really wanted to put Justine on hold and race to the car to get her notes.

"But what about all the Bible studying that you've been doing? Doesn't it say in the Bible that homosexuality is wrong?"

"But it also says that all have sinned and fall short of the glory of God and are justified by his grace. That's in Romans 3:23. Justine, there are a lot of things in the Bible that are not condoned now. Things like slavery, women being required to wear head coverings in church, women not being allowed to be leaders in the church or men being allowed to have more than one wife and people being stoned and killed for committing adultery. I'm no biblical scholar, but I believe that the God that I serve is compassionate, caring and forgiving. I think he made all of us different to teach the world tolerance and love for one another. I'm not naïve; I know how difficult it's going to be for me in the world. I know that many people will shun me and some will want to stone me," Grace paused. "It makes me think about the injustice that my parents suffered because of their love back in the sixties. Because my mother was white and my father was black, their love was wrong in the eyes of many. It was illegal in some states. She lost her family because of it. But now things are different. You're dating a white guy, and so is Teenie."

"I was dating a white guy. We broke up, remember?" Justine corrected.

"But you still have feelings for him don't you?"

"Of course I do. But we're not together right now."

"But you get my point. It's now more acceptable for you to date a white guy, but my white mother was ostracized and disowned by her family for loving a black man. Times have changed."

There was another awkward silence on the phone. "I'm

scared, Justine. But I also know that I know who I am, and this is who I am."

"Have you told the other girls?"

"Not yet. You're my best friend, so I've only told you. I want to make sure that you're comfortable with it first. Have you told them yet?" Grace braced herself for her friend's remark.

"You asked me not to tell anyone, so I didn't, chucklehead."

"I know you are, but what am I?" Grace teased.

"I am the world's best secret keeper," Justine rattled. Grace could almost see the grin on her best friend's face as she recited their childhood oath.

"I was thinking that I'd tell them over Christmas break. At first I was going to do it over Thanksgiving break, but with it being such a short weekend, I don't know if we'll all have that much time to spend together. Is Teenie coming home for Thanksgiving or going to New York with Brian?"

"She's coming home. I think she's planning to finally introduce David to her parents."

"Get outta here! Well, that should be interesting."

"At least that's what she said, but you know that girl is as fickle as the wind."

"What about Maria?" Grace asked.

"She's definitely coming home. Teenie is blowing off her Wednesday morning class to catch an earlier flight that lands in the afternoon. I think Maria's flight lands around the same time as Teenie's does so David is picking them both up from the airport. Teenie said that her father was not too happy about her being picked up at the airport by a boy that he's never met. Anyway, Rashanda and Ian will be at his parents for Thanksgiving, but I'm sure we'll see her."

"We'd better see her. I still can't believe that she's pregnant. I bet her skinny tail is showing already."

"She is. I saw her a few weeks ago. I didn't tell you that? She was looking like maternity road kill, so I used my discount to get her some cute clothes from Fields. By the way, I signed all of our names on the card so feel free to chip in on the gift, little miss trust fund."

"I got you. I'll just write you a check for the full amount. Don't hit Teenie and Maria up for any money. Let me just take care of it. In fact, I'll pay for the baby shower too. Hell, I'll buy their baby furniture as a gift from all of us. My trust fund administrator called and encouraged me to spend more money. Those weren't his exact words, but he told me that since my living expenses are so low, I might want to think about starting my own foundation, separate from the ones my grandparents established. Can you believe that?"

"I totally can't. But it's a good problem to have, little miss rich girl."

"It's a blessing. If I can help you out in any way, Justine, please let me. You guys are my sisters, so if you need anything at all, please don't think twice about coming to me. I want to use my money to help the people that I love."

"I think your BMW needs a twin sister."

"You're a comedian. I meant helping with school tuition or something like that."

"I knew that. I was just teasing," Justine laughed.

"Maybe when you realize that you're a student and stop playing personal shopper, I'll hook you up with a little something-something."

"Here we go with the college talk again. You sound like Andrea Wellington now. I'm working on my college plan, it's all good, but I must admit that the enticement of a new ride might get me to hit the books again a lot sooner."

Her body heat had warmed the tiles on the floor, either that, or she'd just become numb to the coolness. Grace crossed her legs in the yoga position. "What are you doing?" She looked forward to her upcoming session with her counselor so she could share how her first in depth coming out discussion had gone.

"I was just ironing my clothes for work tomorrow. By the way, you didn't answer my question?"

"What question?" Grace asked.

"Do you think Sarah is gay?

Chapter 16

Pumpkin Pie

The loud, bass filled music, acoustic piano and the beat of a drum were foreign to her. She was raised Catholic. The hymnal songs that she remembered singing on her holy day visits to Mass were pious and quite forgettable, not soulful and rhythmic like the gospel songs that filled the old sanctuary. Foreign as it was, she found herself trying to sing along, stumbling through the catchy lyrics.

"We've come this far by faith, leaning on to Jesus. Trusting in the Lord. He's never failed us yet. Oh, oh, oh, oh, oh, oh, oh, can't turn a-rou-ound, we've come this fa-aar, by faith." She mouthed the words with her head down, as though whisper singing into a microphone hidden beneath her sweater. Maria was a first soprano. The choir director at Battle Creek Junior High had actually encouraged her to try out for the school's award winning swing choir group known as Sir Camelot. "You have a beautiful voice, Maria. Perfect pitch and tone in fact. Within a year, I'm sure you could become a featured soloist," she'd encouraged. "Please try out for Sir Camelot, we could use your talent in the first soprano section." Maria wanted to do it and had shared her excitement with Todd.

"You're kidding, right? Your voice sounds like a squeaky child's voice," Todd scoffed without waiting for her reply. "That teacher is just saying that to flatter you so she can find more choir geeks to pad her program. Trust me, I know what I'm talking about. My dad's best friend is the superintendent of the Chicago Public Schools and he told my dad that the superintendent in your district will be doing major budget cuts. You know that means cutting out extra programs like music, art and any extracurricular programs that they can get away with. That choir program won't be around for too much longer. Besides, I've heard you sing in the car, and you sound aahight, you can carry a tune most of the time, but you don't sing well enough to be a soloist. Your voice is pitchy and squeaky like a child's voice. Your teacher is just looking for more warm bodies to justify keeping her music program. She's flat out lying to you. I'd tell you if you could sing."

Layers of enthusiasm fell to the floor with his every word. She thought she might cry. Todd rubbed her hair and gave her a kiss. She smiled, and believed him. Heeding his advice, she decided not to pursue the Sir Camelot audition. When the music teacher followed up, Maria lied and said that her parents didn't want her to participate in any additional extracurricular activities. And that was it.

The old sanctuary was warm, bordering on hot, but not nose bleed inducing hot. It felt warm and cozy like her grandmother's kitchen on Thanksgiving, with love streaming down the walls. Maria removed her bulky cable knit cardigan and placed it beside her on the pew. Dubbed a natural songbird as a child, her parents told her that she often sang herself to sleep when she learned to talk. By the time she was five years old she was making up lullabies that she would sing to her brother Neal. She remembered cradling him in her arms, the chubby fingers of one hand gripped firmly around a baby bottle, while the fingers from his other hand twirled her long hair, his eyes locked on hers. Her mother often sang Maria's catchy made-up lullabies to Neal when she rocked him to sleep. Maria loved music and unashamedly sang along to the radio. She sang loud and proud, even with her friends in the car, who always encouraged her to keep singing. But that was before. No one had ever suggested that she sang like a squeaky child before Todd. Lori and Maria had sung a duet as part of their seventh grade choir performance. They'd received a standing ovation and performed an encore. Self described tin eared Teenie had described Maria's voice as comforting and soothing, recordable even. But after Todd's comments, Maria seldom sang in public anymore, suddenly self conscious about the "squeaky child's voice" that no one told her she had. Her friends noticed that the songbird had stopped singing in the car. "Since Lori's death, I don't feel like singing," she lied. They believed her, just like she believed Todd.

Motivated by the spirit flowing through the church, Maria looked over her shoulder. Not seeing anyone within earshot, she decided to sing aloud. "We've come this faaar, by faith." Her ears perked at the sound of her own voice, almost unrecognizable to her absent the sound of running water, her background accompaniment. She always sang in the shower, glad that her dorm's bathrooms were single use bathrooms shared by three other students. The bathroom had a door that could be locked. Her morning and evening showers were her respite. With the steaming hot water running down her back, she sang loud and proud. Her repertoire included mostly ballads. Chaka Khan, Aretha Franklin, Angela Bofield, Phyllis Hyman and Whitney Houston, were her favorites.

She forced herself to sing louder, wishing the words were printed in the paper program that she'd received when she walked into church. She noticed a hymnal in the back of the pew and wondered if the song was in the back of the book. But she didn't know the name of the song. "'We've Come This Far, by Faith?'" she whispered softly. Everyone else sang along confidently. "How is it that everyone else knows this song?" she mumbled softly to herself.

Maria had stumbled into the church by accident. Walking back to campus, she'd been lured by the sound of gospel music and noticed a small, casually dressed group of University of Pennsylvania students walking into the old church. Upperclassmen, two of the girls wore sorority girl jackets. Maria thought she recognized the students' faces from campus. She noticed two boys each wearing a different fraternity jacket and knew that the event at the church must not be a private sorority event.

Curious, she decided to follow them. She stayed a comfortable distance behind the group. They were clearly on a date, holding hands as they strolled. Maria watched as the students paused to hug an older woman who stood in the vestibule. She waited until they walked inside the sanctuary before crossing the street and timidly walking inside. The vestibule smelled of chocolate chip cookies. An older woman and gentleman greeted her in the vestibule. She hadn't noticed the gentleman from her perch across the street.

"Welcome, my sister. Enjoy the service," the woman beamed.

"Service? Is this a church service?" Maria asked. She felt stupid for asking.

"Yes. It's our mid-week Praise the Lord Service. Some of the college students call it the 'Hour of Power,' because it's an hour of praise and worship intermixed with a few testimonies. Even Pastor Frank calls it the 'Hour of Power' now, so I should stop calling it the Praise the Lord Service, but that's what we've always called it.

We've been doing this service for over twenty years, and it's our most popular service for the University of Pennsylvania students. The Wednesday evening service was my idea. I thought the young people could use a mid-week prayer message to help them with their studies. And the smell of my famous chocolate chip cookies baking in the kitchen doesn't hurt either," she chuckled. "My husband was the pastor of this church until he passed. Everybody calls me Miss Lily."

"Oh, I'm sorry about your husband, Miss Lily."

"He's been gone for over nine years now, but I still miss him. Is this your first time here?"

"Yes, it is," Maria smiled softly.

"Well, welcome, honey. We're glad to have you. It's only an hour so you can get back to your books by seven o'clock. And Pastor Frank doesn't let the testimonies go longer than five minutes apiece, because we have Bible study after that, but most of the students only stay for the Hour of Power," Miss Lily winked. "See, I'm catching on. Enjoy the service." She handed Maria a one page paper program, which looked like it had been typed twenty years ago and recycled every Wednesday since. "At the end of service, please place your program in that basket over there so we can reuse it."

"Thank you." Maria chuckled, too embarrassed to ask Miss Lily what a testimony was. She wondered how Miss Lily knew that she was a student since she wasn't carrying her backpack.

The University of Pennsylvania was in Philadelphia, bordered by an underserved community with a heavy African American population. Many of the homes were in desperate need of repair, with trash littering the streets, and a handful of townies hanging on the corner outside of the package goods store at all hours of the day and night. As she walked to the drugstore, the men stopped their chatter and whistled as she passed. "How you doin' Miss Lady?" they called out. "You show is purty. Cute little red bone thing, you is. Are you Mexican?" the men called after her. As her mother had taught her, Maria smiled widely and kept walking. She'd watched her mother handle the unsolicited cat calls from men in Chicago her entire life. "Be flattered by the compliment, Maria. Smile and say thank you, and keep going about your business. They won't touch you. They're harmless. It's their way of paying a compliment to an attractive woman. It's just what they do." Liz Wesley had coached her daughter.

She'd walked to the outskirts of campus before, but never after dusk. This time, her walk was motivated by a need to pick up some Dr. Tichener's antiseptic mouthwash. Battling a slight tickle in her throat, she wanted the strong mouth rinse to gargle and knew that the on campus pharmacy didn't stock it. She'd already checked, plus, from past experience, she knew that it was only available in the black neighborhood pharmacies. Dr. Tichener's was Mama Kaye's secret cold remedy for a sore throat. "Just gargle with Dr. Tichener's for a few days, and it'll kill those germs in a hurry!" Mama Kaye always encouraged. Maria had grown up with a bottle of the powerful antiseptic mouthwash in her family's medicine cabinet. Sometimes on their regular visits into the city, she would accompany her mother to the inner city drugstore to pick up a bottle or two before heading back to Newberry East. The super strong mouthwash burned Maria's throat, but it always seemed to work, clearing up her sore throat after a couple of days. After dinner, with Mama Kaye's voice in her head, Maria stuffed her student identification and a twenty dollar bill into her pocket and walked the five blocks off campus to the mom and pop corner drug store to make her purchase. She timed her walk so that she could be back on campus before it got too late. The church was across the street from the drugstore.

The Greek letter adorned couples were sitting toward the front of the sanctuary in a girl-boy-girl-boy arrangement. She recognized the girls, both of whom were members of Alpha Kappa Alpha Sorority. Maria had met them at an informational rush tea. She thought they were nice but didn't want to interrupt their date. She decided to sit in the back of the sanctuary, in case she wanted to sneak out. She wondered how that would be perceived by Miss Lily, sneaking out before the hour of power was complete. She was also planning to pledge AKA, and didn't want an early departure to be held against her. Maria had been warned that girls interested in pledging were always being watched by others on campus to ensure that their behavior was appropriate at all times. She gripped her bag of medicine and sat in the back of the church, settling in for the remaining fifty two minutes of the Hour of Power.

Her foot tapped involuntarily. Though louder than she was accustomed, the music was tranquil and relaxing. She closed her eyes and listened to the singing all around her. With her eyes closed, she didn't feel self conscious about not knowing the lyrics. A loud voice startled her eyes open.

"Praise the Lord Saints. Praise the Lord again," the voice boomed over a silver microphone affixed to a brown, wooden podium. The owner of the voice was a short man with round glasses and faded blue jeans. He wore a bright orange New York Knicks tee shirt beneath a brown cardigan sweater. "This is the day that the Lord has made. Let us rejoice and be glad in it! Welcome to the Hour of Power at Shiloh Baptist. I'm Pastor Frank. Y'all know how we do it, but for those new to our mist," he pronounced "midst" as in the vapor "mist." "For those new to our mist," he repeated. "We sing two songs and then we have a testimony. And then we sing two songs and then we have another testimony or two. If we don't have any testimonies waiting in the wings, I'll give my testimony agin, or we'll sing an extra song," he chuckled. "And on and on until it's time to go. We wrap in one hour, and then you are welcome to enjoy some desserts in fellowship hall in the basement and then for those who can stay, we'll have Bible study back up here in the sanctuary. Amen?"

"Amen," the congregation replied.

"Amen. Now you all have no more than five minutes for your testimony, and I will have to stop you if it goes past that, so don't act out and forget y'all in church if I wave my card for you to stop. Folks sometimes want to get in front of a microphone and they forget they in church, be tryin' to act like they the preacher. Don't make me have to come up there and pull you down from that stage, cause you know I'll do it. I was a running back for Syracuse back in the day," he chuckled. "The old man's still got a few moves up his sleeves."

Maria guessed that Pastor Frank was in his early thirties. Her mother was thirty nine, and he looked younger than her mother.

Laughter and applause filled the sanctuary as Pastor Frank waved a young woman to the podium. He descended the stairs and sat in the front row as a stout young woman wearing a pink and green sorority sweater, walked toward the podium. Her eyes were soft and appeared blue or gray. Maria also recognized this girl from the sorority informational tea. She struggled to remember her name. Maria looked at the two girls on the date, expecting them to acknowledge their sorority sister with a wave or their sorority signal. She was surprised when they didn't. Instead, they leaned over the boy sitting between them and whispered.

As she approached the microphone, the girl removed her glasses and placed them on the podium. Maria noticed that she didn't have any papers in her hand, no notes or anything. She wondered if a testimony was a song.

She leaned in and spoke, her lips practically touching the silver microphone. "My name is Lucinda, but my friends all call me Lucy," she stated nervously. Her voice sounded loud and raspy against the microphone. Without prompting, the pastor swiftly walked up the two short steps to the stage and gently pulled her shoulders back, straightening her posture. "You can stand up straight, and we will be able to hear you just fine," he corrected softly. "We have a powerful new PA system now. Try it again."

The girl smiled sheepishly and gripped the podium like a life preserver.

"My name is Lucy," she said softly. "And I'd like to share my testimony."

Pastor Frank gave Lucy the thumbs up.

"It's all right, baby. God is listening and so are we." The woman in the pew ahead of Maria encouraged. Maria stared at the musicians, wondering when they would start playing.

Lucy took a deep breath before speaking. "When I was nine years old, I watched my mother's boyfriend shoot my mother." Gasps were heard throughout the sanctuary. "When the gun went off, my brother and sister ran into the kitchen to see what was going on, so I stood in front of them to block what they saw," she said slowly. A single tear ran down her face. "When I saw my mother on the floor, I just prayed to Jesus to save her and to protect us all. I thought I was going to die." Lucy took a deep breath. The sanctuary was silent. The only sound was that of Lucy's labored breathing. "Obviously, he didn't kill me, but I think he thought about it, though. He stared at me with this blank look on his face that I'll never forget." Lucy waved her hand across her face. "He looked like he was having an out of body experience, like he didn't know who I was. I remember it like it was yesterday. He had the gun pointed at me, but then he turned it on himself."

"Thank you, Jesus!" the woman in front of Maria yelled, her hands flailing above her head. "Thank you, Jesus!" Maria suddenly felt guilty, like she shouldn't be there. She felt like a voyeuristic stranger listening to Lucy's story.

Lucy continued un-phased by the woman's outburst. "When the police and the ambulance came, and I told them what happened, they said that I was probably in shock which is why I didn't run. But I wasn't in shock, I was afraid that if I ran, my brother and sister would see my mother lying there, and I didn't want them to see her hurt. I blocked their view. I was also scared that he might shoot them, so I stood in the doorway to shield them. I didn't want them to see our mother lying on the floor like that. He shot my mother in the chest, but thankfully, the bullet passed through her. She was hurt pretty bad, so she played dead and prayed for him to kill himself and not hurt us. She told me later that she knew she couldn't overpower him, and she was afraid that if she screamed out for us to run, he'd shoot her again. So we were both praying for the same thing."

"Hallelujah! Praise Jesus!" could be heard throughout the sanctuary.

Lucy's eyes were distant as though she were nine years old again and in her mother's kitchen. "But I didn't admit that to anyone for a long time, that I prayed for him to use the gun on himself," she shared softly, her voice almost a whisper. "I wanted him to kill himself, and he did." Lucy swallowed two or three times. "I know that God was with me during that incident. I could feel his presence. But I stayed away from church for a long time after that. I was grateful to God that my mother was okay, but I felt that my prayer killed someone. I still have that guilt on my heart. I feel like I should have been praying for him to run out of the house or drop the gun. But I wasn't. I was praying for him to die. I know now that it wasn't my fault, that he took his own life. When you're a child, you don't understand that. My counselor told me that I should share my testimony so that I can begin to forgive myself for what happened. I've been feeling guilty for praying for the man, who thought he had killed my mother, and probably thought about killing me and my brother and sister too, to die. It was nothing but God's grace and mercy that he didn't shoot us all. Or maybe he just didn't have enough bullets in his gun to kill us all. I don't know," Lucy paused as though considering this option for the first time. "Maybe that's what it was. I never asked the police." Lucy's voice was now raspy and hoarse. Maria leaned in closer to hear. "We moved after that. And my mother and I went through years of therapy. I had nightmares about what happened for a long time. I still do sometimes. The therapist calls it post traumatic stress disorder. She said that because it was such a traumatic event and because of my age that the memory will probably always be with me, but that it will fade over time. It has faded, but I still think about it every day. So does my mother. My brother and sister don't remember anything at all. I'm grateful for that. I was their shield," Lucy smiled.

"I truly thank God that they didn't see what I saw. The police were right. I was in shock. My mother's voice snapped me out of it because after he shot himself, my mother screamed. She was afraid he'd shot me. So when I heard her voice I knew that God had answered my prayer and she was still alive," Lucy managed to smile. "So today, I share my testimony and thank God for bearing the burden of my guilt, and I leave that guilt at the altar. Hallelujah. Thank you."

Everyone in the sanctuary rose to their feet in applause. Pastor Frank gave Lucy a hug. As Lucy descended the stairs to return to her pew, a white gloved usher, with one outward palmed hand positioned behind her back, pushed a box of tissue in Lucy's face. Lucy took three or four tissues before taking her seat, dabbing at the tears that streamed down her pink cheeks. Maria felt a tear on her own cheek.

"Thank you, Lucy. Scripture says that where two or more are gathered, I am there. Knock and he will answer. Seek and you will find. For I know the plans I have for you, declares the Lord, plans not to harm you, but to give you hope and a future. The Lord giveth and the Lord taketh away. Vengeance is mine sayeth the Lord!" Pastor Frank's voice boomed. "Saints, forgiveness begins within ourselves. We must forgive ourselves and release the burden of guilt. Leave it at the altar. Stop carrying your own personal cross. Jesus died on the cross so that you wouldn't have to carry that burden. He wants you to have abundant life. We share our testimonies as a living witness of God's grace and mercy. Testimonies lead others to Christ. If you have never been tested, you will not have a testimony. For my ways are not your ways, neither are your thoughts my thoughts, declares the Lord. Just as the heavens are higher than the earth, so are my ways higher than your ways and my thoughts higher than your thoughts. He is an on time God. God wants you to believe that his son, Jesus, died on a cross for you. For my yoke is easy and my burden is light. Let

Jesus carry your burdens. Leave them at the altar. Amen? Amen!" Pastor Frank walked back to his seat.

The musicians started playing another song that she didn't recognize, but everyone else seemed to know. Maria glanced at the couple on a date, both girls dabbed their eyes. Their boyfriend's draped their arms across their shoulders. "I had no idea," one girl mouthed to the other. "Me neither." Maria read their lips from her pew in the back. Her eyes still glued on the sorority girls, Maria reached when a somber faced, white gloved usher placed a box of tissue in her face.

The second testimony was brief. A man had surrendered his life to Christ after doing time in prison for selling narcotics. He wanted to share that God was a forgiving God and wanted to be in relationship with everyone no matter what sin or crime had been committed. To Maria, he looked like a townie, one of the men who had whistled at her on her way to the pharmacy, lured inside by the chocolate chip cookie aroma.

"Saints, God doesn't want you to be your own savior. That's why He sent His son. You can't fix yourself. He wants us to come to Him in our current state. Battered, broken and bruised. He's seen it all, and He still wants to be in relationship with us. Nothing's too hard for God. There is no sin that you can commit that is bigger than God's long arm of forgiveness and His love for you. He is omnipotent, omniscient. He's the alpha and the omega. The beginning and the end. God wants to meet you where you are today. He's knocking at your door. He wants to be in relationship with you. You and your neighbor, but he has his eye on you."

As if on cue, the band played a song entitled "Nothing's Too Hard For God." Maria was impressed at the pianist's singing voice. She always marveled at people who could play the piano and sing at the same time. She was enjoying herself. Sitting in the back pew, she felt like an anonymous movie critic. As the band prepared for the next song, she shifted when she noticed the sorority girls and their dates standing to leave. Nervous, she wondered how she should behave if they noticed her. Maria was unclear on the protocol for a girl who was interested in pledging a sorority when faced with two members of the sorority. Should she smile and wave? She didn't want to appear too eager, but she didn't want to be rude either. She slouched in her seat slightly and repositioned herself so that she was partially hidden by the large woman in the pew ahead of her. She pretended to read her program. She needn't have been bothered, the couples didn't glance her way as they exited. Both girls still seemed teary eyed and disturbed by Lucy's testimony. As the musicians played another gospel tune, Maria watched to see if Lucy was still in the sanctuary. She was.

The remaining testimonies were brief and delivered by elder members of the church. Maria glanced at her watch. It was almost seven o'clock. The smell of chocolate chip cookies wafted through the sanctuary like an expensive perfume. By eliminating junk food from her diet, increasing her salad consumption and daily exercise regimen, Maria had already lost most of the added weight that she'd gained as a freshman. But chocolate chip cookies were her weakness, especially chocolate chip cookies hot from the oven.

"Well, it's Wednesday, so you know the hospitality committee has baked an assortment of fresh desserts, so please join us for punch and coffee in fellowship hall. Ya'll need to come down and eat some of this stuff because if you don't eat it, then I'm eating it all week, and Lawd knows I don't need to get any chunkier," Pastor Frank chuckled.

She watched as Lucy stood. I really don't want to walk back to campus by myself this late. So if Lucy goes down for dessert, I'll go with her so we can walk back together."

Maria bundled her thick sweater and grabbed her pharmacy bag as Lucy approached her pew. "Hi, Lucy. I don't know if you remember me, but I'm Maria Wesley. I met you at the informational tea," Maria smiled.

"Oh, hi, Maria. I remember you. Do you go to church here?" Lucy asked.

Maria realized that Lucy's eyes were in fact a bluish green. She hadn't planned a response for this question. "Not exactly. I've heard other students talking about the hour of power and thought I'd come and check it out for myself. That was a powerful story you told," she said.

"Thanks. I'm glad you enjoyed my testimony," Lucy corrected with a smile. "I've been nervous about delivering that all week. But now I feel so much better. I feel like a giant weight has been lifted from my shoulders," she smiled.

"I meant testimony, not story," Maria mumbled softly.

"Are you going to fellowship hall for dessert?" Lucy asked. "They usually have the best desserts. Not that I need to eat any sweets," she smiled, patting her chubby mid-section.

"I was just telling myself that I would go down and have one chocolate chip cookie," Maria grinned. "I have a weakness for warm chocolate chip cookies."

"Me too. Follow me. I'll lead the way," Lucy smiled.

The fellowship hall was located in the basement of the church, accessed by descending a narrow flight of stairs in the corner of the vestibule. Middle age ladies scurried about placing desserts on a long banquet table adorned with a lavender tablecloth. A bouquet of plastic flowers served as the dessert centerpiece. Maria noticed

Miss Lily in the kitchen removing a cookie sheet from the oven.

"The pastor doesn't stand on formality on Wednesday. Normally we have to wait for someone to bless the food before we can eat, but he knows that the students have to get back on campus to study, plus he likes to start Bible study on time. Sometimes I stay for Bible study, but I'm not going to stay today. Do you wanna walk back to campus together? It's safe walking back at night, but I believe that there's safety in numbers."

"Sure. Good idea," Maria grinned.

"I'm going to have a slice of pumpkin pie," Lucy announced. "The chocolate chip cookies are right over there. They usually bake those last so they're hot and chewy."

Maria walked to the end of the rectangular buffet and smiled at the tray of cookies. She decided to enjoy two. "I'll work out and burn it off in the morning," she said aloud.

"It'll probably take at least an hour of intense cardio to burn off two cookies," the voice replied.

Maria turned toward the deep voice. Standing before her was John, from the Black House, leaning on a long handled broom.

She felt her face blush. "Hi, John. What are you doing here?" she stammered, suddenly losing her appetite for the warm cookies nestled in a napkin. She felt her heart skip a beat.

"I work here. Well, they don't pay me. But on Wednesdays I help out at the church before Bible study. I've never seen you here. Do you go to church here? And tell me your name again?" he asked.

"It's Maria. My name is Maria Wesley. You wrote that story about me and the incident in the cafeteria," she reminded.

"I remember the story," John smiled. "I just couldn't remember your name. I'm sorry about that. I interview so many people for the paper, that it's hard to keep all of the names straight. Do you go to church here?" he repeated.

"No. I had to pick up something from the pharmacy and I just…" Maria struggled.

"Let me guess. You smelled the cookies from the street and thought you'd wander in and help yourself?" he laughed. "They deliberately open the windows in the kitchen so that the guys loitering on the street will come in. I see that technique is still working. Did you hear any of the Hour of Power or are you just stealing cookies?" he teased.

"I heard the entire service actually, and I really enjoyed it. I was raised Catholic, so the music was a little louder than I'm accustomed to. But I really enjoyed the testimonies." Maria was glad that she remembered the proper word this time.

"Pastor Frank is really good. He makes you feel very comfortable. He's heard it all and he never seems phased by some of the stuff that people share. And some of the testimonies are pretty intense. And he's a stickler for time too. Looks like he ended the Hour of Power in under an hour today, but he will start that Bible study right at seven thirty. He knows that people have stuff to do, so he runs his church on time. I appreciate that."

"So do you go to church here?" Maria asked.

"Off and on. I was raised Catholic too," John shared.

"Really?"

"Really. But I haven't practiced Catholicism since I was a child. My parents attend a Baptist church now. I think I'm more spiritual than religious. I believe in Jesus, but I'm not that hung up on what denomination I attend. Religion is man made." John shifted the broom from his left hand to his right.

"So you're not a member here, but you volunteer to sweep?"

"I do. I spend an hour or so before Bible study doing little things that need to be done so I can partake of their dessert buffet guilt free," he laughed. "Besides, my mom raised us to do at least one good deed every day, so I know she's pleased to know that I volunteer at the church." Maria stared at John in silent adoration. "I sometimes attend the early morning worship service on Sunday. Pastor Frank doesn't care if we come in sweats, but I know my parents would skin my hide if they saw me in church in sweats. I'll wear jeans to the early morning Sunday service, but if I miss that service, I'm usually a bedside Baptist because the people who come to the eleven o'clock service dress to impress."

"Don't listen to him, Maria. They are not dressing to impress. You should dress decent when you go to church," Lucy teased. She scooped a forkful of pumpkin pie in her mouth.

"Pastor says that Jesus doesn't care what you wear as long as you are there," John said. "I see you two know each other."

"We just met upstairs," Lucy explained. Maria wondered if Lucy even remembered her from the Alpha Kappa Alpha informational tea.

"Maria is the student that I quoted in my last editorial rebuttal. Remember the one I was telling you about?"

"This is the girl with the big ring?" Lucy asked. "Let me see that ring. I heard about that satellite."

"I don't have it on right now."

"It is quite the sparkler," John whistled.

"It's not really that big."

"Yes, it really is that big," John corrected. "It's huge, Lucy. Is that pumpkin pie?"

"Yup. And it's good too," she smiled.

"Why didn't you bring me a slice? You know I love pumpkin pie!"

"I didn't realize you were here. I didn't see you. You were too busy being a janitor," she giggled.

"I'm doing the work of the Lord. Laugh if you want." John propped his broom against the wall. "I told you I'd be here. I'll be right back, ladies. I'm going to grab a slice before it's all gone. The ladies at this church make the best homemade pumpkin pie. It makes you want to jump up and slap your mama! Watch my broom."

Lucy grinned at Maria. "So you're a freshman, and you're engaged already? Your fiancée doesn't play. He took you off the market fast."

"Technically, we're not engaged. It's more like a promise ring, but without the promise."

"Let me get this straight. John told me that this superstar football player gave you a big ring that has all the white sorority girls fawning over it, and you aren't getting married?"

"It's complicated," Maria sighed. "Very complicated. How do you know John?" she asked, eager to change the subject.

"I spend a lot of time at the Black House too. I helped him when he pledged Kappa."

"John pledged Kappa?"

"Uh, huh. He pledged his freshman year. How do you know John?"

"He interviewed me for the article that he wrote in the student newspaper. I really don't know him that well."

"He's a good guy. No, he's a great guy," Lucy giggled. "In fact, I have a crush on him. Me and half the eligible women on campus," she whispered. "Some of my sorors aren't talking to me now because they think that I was the reason that John broke up with his girlfriend who's also my soror. But I didn't have anything to do with their break-up. He and I are really just friends."

"What are you girls giggling about?" John asked, his plate topped with two slices of pumpkin pie.

"How'd you get two slices?" Lucy whined.

"Because the ladies like me better. They see me pushing that broom with a fierce intensity and they want to encourage me to keep up the good work. You should try it sometime."

"I was telling Maria that I have a crush on you," Lucy blurted. "And that our friendship has caused me to be ostracized by my sorors."

Now it was John's turn to blush. "Because those chicken heads think that you are the reason that I broke up with Sharon. But Sharon knows that Sharon is the reason that I broke up with Sharon," he growled.

"Forgive him, Maria. He gets so emotional about the Penn drama," Lucy smiled.

"This campus is like a soap opera. Everybody is always in everybody else's business."

"That's why he hides down here sweeping the fellowship hall. Sharon is dating someone else now and she attends the Hour of Power with her new boyfriend," Lucy teased.

John seemed to inhale forkfuls of his pumpkin pie and rolled his eyes at Lucy.

"Sharon didn't realize that John and I were friends, so the third time I saw her at the Hour of Power, all snuggled up with this guy who's a first year law student, I invited John to come so he could see for himself. When he saw what I saw, he knew something was going on and confronted her. She was cold busted. And she was doing her dirt in the house of the Lord no doubt, so some of my sorors think that I broke some sorority code of honor by telling

John. Whatever. John is my boy. I couldn't watch her do that to him."

"Thank you so much for airing my dirty laundry so eloquently, Lucy."

"You're welcome."

"Maria and I are going to walk back to campus together. Are you staying for Bible study?"

"I always do. But I'll drive you back. I don't want you two walking in the dark."

"You'll lose your parking spot if you do that, and you know how crowded Bible study is," Lucy protested. "We'll be fine."

"I'll get another parking spot. I insist. Let's go."

John inhaled the last two bites of his pumpkin pie and tossed his plate in the trash near where his broom was propped. He reached for a jacket hung behind a door and led the girls outside through a back door. "I couldn't let you ladies walk back to campus in the dark. My father raised me better than that. If something happened to you, I'd never forgive myself. By the way, I heard your testimony, Lucy. Nice job."

"You heard it?"

"I told you I was going to be there to support you. I was sitting behind the piano."

Maria stared at him in amazement.

"It was really touching. And you rehearsed it with me, so I knew exactly what you were going to say, but it was still very touching. I'm proud of you. That took a lot of courage." John slowed his gait slightly. "By the way, I saw your girl, Sharon. That's why she and her crew left early. It took her a minute, but she finally noticed me sitting on the floor behind the piano," he laughed. "She's so vain. I'm sure she thinks that I was spying on her. She is so egocentric, but I'm not thinking about that girl. I was there for you. Before she noticed me, she actually teared up when she heard your testimony. I didn't think that heifer had any emotion."

"Be nice, John. We are on God's property," Lucy scolded.

"A heifer is a female cow. That's technically not a bad word. Now if I called her a female dog, that's another story." John opened the passenger side door of a large, navy blue Buick in mint condition. "This was my grandfather's car. He gave it to me when he died. It's eight years old, but it only has forty thousand miles on it. He basically only drove it to church on Sunday and the store, so she's got a lot of life left in her."

"Why are you defending Betsy, John?" Lucy asked.

"Because Maria is accustomed to riding around in a Ferrari," he explained.

"I'm really not," Maria defended.

"I heard about that custom Ferrari that Dante bought. It was in the paper. Plus, I saw the one he rented when he came up to visit you a few weeks ago. This is no Ferrari, but Betsy gets me where I need to go. Climb into your chariot, ladies."

Without an invitation, Lucy climbed into the passenger seat as John opened the rear passenger door for Maria.

"Buckle up for safety, ladies," John ordered. "I'll drop you both off at the student union, that way I can loop around the circle and get back to church quicker. Does that work for you?"

"That's perfect," Maria smiled. "I appreciate the ride."

The ride back to campus only took four minutes.

"John, we would have been fine walking. Now you're probably going to have to park in the hood," Lucy said.

"I'll be fine. I'll be back in four minutes. My same spot will probably be waiting for me. Now get out so I can grab one more slice of pie before Bible study starts," John laughed.

"It's so unfair. You can polish off three slices of pie and look like that. I even look at pie and I gain a pound," Lucy groaned.

"Me too," Maria laughed.

"Sucks to be a girl. Don't hate me because I'm a lean mean eating machine!" he laughed. "Maria, it was good to see you again. Lucy, I'll see you tomorrow at the Black House. Now get out, I have a date with some pumpkin pie."

The girls waved from the curb as John pulled away. Maria remembered that Lucy lived in the dorm across from the student union, Maria's dorm was adjacent and across the courtyard. Standing on the curb, Maria decided to button her sweater, wrapping the belt tightly around her waist.

"It was good to see you again, Lucy."

"You too. By the way, what were you doing on that side of town anyway?" Lucy asked as Maria bundled her sweater.

"I went to pick up some sore throat medicine," Maria shared. She patted her bulky sweater. "Oh no! I think I left the bag with my medicine at the church," she sighed as she watched John's large sedan turn the corner. "I put the bag on the table to button my sweater."

"You also left your cookies on the table," Lucy added. "I just thought you left them on purpose since I know that skinny girls like you don't really eat cookies," she chuckled. "You pretend to eat cookies."

"I was going to eat them," Maria laughed. "I just like to drink milk with cookies so I was going to eat them tonight. I don't eat cookies all the time, but I do eat cookies," she defended.

"That's too bad. I should have said something. I saw you

put them on the table and noticed that you didn't pick them up. I didn't see you put a bag down. Someone else will eat them. Those cookies are almost as good as the pumpkin pie. They won't go to waste."

In the cool night air, Maria could feel the tickle in her throat returning.

"I have a sore throat, and I bought some antiseptic so that I could gargle."

"The student union has antiseptic. Want me to wait while you go inside? I don't mind."

"That's okay. It's a special antiseptic. They don't have it in the student union, I already checked. I'll just gargle with warm salt water tonight. It doesn't hurt that bad."

"I'm sure your bag will be at the church tomorrow. They'll just put it in the church office. I hope one of the hospitality ladies finds it before one of the townies does. Because if a townie finds it, and the bag has the receipt inside, they'll return it and get the money."

"Well, the receipt is in the bag."

"I'm sure your rich boyfriend has you on an allowance, so you can just go buy another bottle of antiseptic."

Maria pursed her lips to respond, but her gaze shifted toward a large gaggle of girls descending the student union stairs, many wearing pink and green jackets identical to Lucy's.

"Skee wee!" a few of them screamed. Maria recognized the sorority girl cat call that the AKA's used to greet one another. "Lucy! Where've you been, girl?"

"Skee wee!" Lucy returned. "I'll be right there. Give me two seconds," she returned. "I'm going to go speak to my sorors, Maria. Will you be okay getting back to your dorm?"

"I'll be fine. I live right there," Maria pointed.

"Sounds good. Thanks for coming to Shiloh tonight," Lucy smiled and waved.

Maria watched as the girls encircled Lucy in a group hug, and a blanket of giggles.

The tingle in her throat intensified in the cool night air. Maria glanced at her watch. She hated gargling with warm salt water more than using the Dr. Tichener's. She gripped her aching throat. It would take me eight minutes to speed walk back to Shiloh. I could grab my medicine, gargle and be in my pajamas by eight o'clock. Or I could stay for Bible study and let John give me a ride home. If I knew his last name, I could call the church and ask them to give the bag to John for me. Yawning, Maria considered her options as the student union clock chimed on the half hour. Bible study had just started.

Chapter 17

Driving under the Influence

She caught him peering up the escalator in the crowded baggage claim area. She smiled and waved with her free hand. He pretended not to see her, his head searching the area like a livery driver trying to identify his fare. Maria clutched her throat. "Look, Teenie. He made a sign for you," she whispered. Scribbled in crayon, T E E N I E was spelled out in large block letters, each letter a different color crayon. He covered his face with the sign. The gesture made her smile. Her teeth had turned out beautifully. She was proud of her smile and couldn't wait for David to notice her wire free teeth.

At the bottom of the escalator, Teenie stood in front of him and tapped the sign, her new wheeled duffel creating a barrier between them.

"You made a sign, how cute," Teenie smiled.

"Oh, there you are," David faked. "I wanted to make sure that I would recognize you. Since you've been on campus with all of those Yale nerds, I didn't know if you'd morphed into a Yale nerd yourself."

With a fresh haircut, Teenie blushed at how handsome he was. He wore dark jeans and loafers without socks. Beneath a brown leather bomber jacket, he wore the Yale sweatshirt that Teenie had sent him. She playfully kicked him in the shin.

"Ouch!"

"I'm a Yale nerd? Now you look like a Yale nerd proudly wearing the sweatshirt that I sent you."

"I didn't want to hurt your feelings. By the way, you weren't supposed to mail it to me. You could have saved the postage and brought it with you."

"I wanted to pack a small bag, and the bulky sweatshirt wouldn't fit so I just dropped it in the mail."

"That was cool, it came last week. It was in my room when I got home yesterday. Why haven't you cashed the check that I sent you for the sweatshirt?"

"I lost it," Teenie lied.

"You're such a bad liar." Reaching into the pocket of his jacket, he pulled out two twenties and shoved them in her pocket. "Don't I at least get a hug, Yale nerd?"

Blushing again, Teenie wrapped her arms around David's neck. He smelled the same as she remembered. Wrapping his strong arms around her waist, he swiftly scooped her off the floor, along with her heavy backpack.

"David! Put me down!"

"Looks like you haven't gained the freshman fifteen yet. You feel like you weigh about the same as when I last swept you off your feet, even with that big backpack."

Tanisha swatted his arm as he put her down.

"You always smell so good," he inhaled. "Hey Maria, let me give you a hug too." David added; his embrace of Maria was swift, casual and friendly. "Let's find out which carousel will have your luggage."

"We didn't check anything. We both just brought duffels and our backpacks."

"Really? I'm impressed."

"We're only going to be home for four days."

"But girls usually over pack. My sister always brought home the biggest suitcase she owned anytime she came home. And do you really think you're going to do homework this weekend? Pleeeaaase!" he scoffed. "Those books are a prop for your parents. You'll be so busy seeing your friends who are home for Thanksgiving that you're not going to touch those books. And on the flight back to school, you'll be so tired from partying all weekend that you're going to sleep on the plane. Trust me, I did the same thing my freshman year too. I should have told you to just leave your books at school. It would have really lightened your load."

"I have a paper due on Monday, so I need to finish that. I'll study a little," Teenie objected.

"Yeah, okay. If you say so, Yale nerd," he winked.

Teenie punched him in his arm.

"Ouch! Stop punching me, you bully!"

"Stop calling me Yale nerd," she shot back.

"Give me those bags." David snatched Teenie's backpack from her shoulder and slung it over his. He did the same with Maria's backpack and carryon bag.

The airport was crowded as mini family reunions occurred all around them. A swarm of college sweatshirts hunkered around the baggage carousels chatting with excited parents and siblings. A uniformed man wearing a hat with ORD Security emblazoned across the top encouraged the passengers to move from the escalator area as a new wave of travelers descended into the busy baggage claim area.

"Are you okay pulling your bag, Teenie? I can take it if you want."

"I'm good."

"Let's get out of here. Today is the busiest travel day of the year, and they don't call O'Hare the busiest airport in the world for nothing. I still can't believe that you two didn't bring home any laundry.

"Why would we bring dirty clothes home?" Maria asked. "That's disgusting."

"Every time I come home, I always bring a duffel bag full of dirty clothes for my mom to hook up for me. It's my little gift to her."

"See, that's the difference between men and women. Only a guy would think to pack dirty clothes and travel with them. That's just gross." Teenie frowned. "And what makes you think that your mother enjoys doing your laundry?"

"I'm her baby boy. She loves taking care of me," he chuckled. With the bags slung on his shoulder, more people bumped into him. "Well if you ladies don't have to wait for any more bags, let's hit it before we get stampeded. Do you need to hit the head, Teenie Tiny Bladder?"

"I'm all set, thank you very much," Teenie blushed. "I'm not three years old."

"She told me that she went as soon as she got off the plane," Maria shared.

"Maria! That's none of his business, and thanks for putting my business in the street, big mouth!"

Like a running back pushing through the front line to clear a path for the quarterback, David walked toward an escalator. The girls had to walk swiftly to keep pace with him. "I know she did. She never met a bathroom she didn't like. And I know she probably hates to use the airplane bathroom."

"How'd you know that? She said she had to go when she was on the plane, but she held it until she landed because she didn't want to use the airplane bathroom."

David led the girls through the baggage claim area and through a urine scented tunnel, the gray carpet stained in several places. Orange construction cones littered the area where the carpet had been removed and the concrete floor shone through. He stopped at an elevator marked Parking. "I could have told you that. Just one of the many Teenie quirks that make her so adorable," he laughed over his shoulder. "You're at Penn, right, Maria? So how'd you two wind up on the same flight?" His lean frame carried the heavy backpacks and duffel with ease. He seemed to have gotten more muscular since she last saw him in August.

"We weren't. Maria flew out of Philly, and I flew out of New York, but our flights took off at the same time. See, in this weird thing called capitalism, they have more than one airline leaving from different cities and sometimes the flights land near the same time and at the same city. Go figure."

"I see you didn't leave your sarcasm at Yale."

"Not a chance. I never leave home without it."

"My flight landed thirty minutes ahead of Teenie's so I just hung out in the coffee shop when I landed."

"The car is right over there," he pointed. Teenie shivered in the open air garage.

"Where's your coat, Teenie?"

"It's in my duffel bag. I was hot on the plane. I'll be fine once we get in the car." She wrapped her scarf around her neck.

"It's chilly in this parking garage, but once you're in the sun, it doesn't feel as cold. It's supposed to snow on Friday."

"It was colder than this in Philly. And at least the sun is shining. It was gray in Philly when I left this morning. I can't wait to see the skyline!" Maria smiled.

"Do you want to see the skyline today? I was planning to take the tollway back to the suburbs, but if you want, I can detour through downtown." David looked at his watch. "As long as we clear through downtown before two o'clock, we'll miss rush hour traffic."

Maria and Teenie looked at each other. "Are you serious? You'd really take us through downtown. That would be so cool, because I really want some Garrett's popcorn," Teenie gushed. "But that's so out of your way, David."

"Then downtown it is." David clicked the key fob on the BMW.

"Did you get a new car?" Maria asked. "I thought you drove a Corvette."

"I do, but when Teenie asked me if you could ride with us from the airport I switched cars with my mom because I assumed that you guys would have some real luggage, and the 'Vette has a smaller trunk, so I drove Teenie's favorite car."

"Her favorite car?"

"Teenie loves this car. I gave her driving lessons in this car. Remember that, Teenie?" David asked as he placed the bags in the trunk.

"Of course I do."

"I told my mom that you wanted me to pick you up in the car that you learned to drive in."

Teenie's mouth hung open. "You told your mom that I learned to drive in her car?" she repeated. "You're kidding, right?"

"Gotcha!" David laughed. "Dr. Dudley would peel my head if she knew you'd been driving her car. She barely lets me and my dad drive it because we always forget to hit the button to readjust her seat and mirrors back to her setting. And I always leave the radio up too loud for her, so she gets blasted when she gets in the car."

"My dad and me," Teenie corrected. "She barely lets my dad and me drive her car. Always place the other person ahead of yourself, Mr. G.E.D. Howard Medical School is going to expel you if they hear you talking like Pookie from the West side."

"Teenie is the grammar police," Maria shrugged. "She does the same with me and my friends. I mean my friends and me," she self corrected.

Dr. Dudley? Dr. Dudley? Tanisha said the name silently to herself. Why does that name sound familiar?

"Your mom is a doctor too?" Maria asked. "When I was in high school I visited a Dr. Dudley, remember that, Teenie? She was really nice."

Dr. Dudley? Teenie stared at Maria as David closed the trunk. The bright light of recognition fought its way through the thick gray concrete, illuminating Teenie's face.

"I'm sure it's not the same one," David stammered quickly.

"Why is her last name Dudley and not Barton?" Teenie asked.

"Since both of my parents are doctors, it's easier for my mom to use her maiden name professionally so there's no confusion. At one point they worked at the same hospital, so it got confusing when they got calls from the paging service. Legally, her name is hyphenated." David walked to the passenger side and simultaneously opened both doors. Maria quickly climbed into the backseat.

"What's your mom's first name?" Teenie asked.

David closed Maria's door. "What's with all the questions and the sudden interest in my mom?" he smiled.

"I just want to know. What's her first name again?" Teenie stared into David's eyes. "When I met your parents, I can't remember what your dad called her."

"Her name is Elle. Actually, her real name is Elliot," he sighed as a plane flew overhead muffling his voice. "But no one calls her that. She goes by Elle. She was named Elliot after my grandfather. Dr. Elliot "Elle" Dudley-Barton is my mother," he said softly. "Are you satisfied, Sherlock?"

His words were muffled by the airplane and a car passing by going faster than the posted fifteen mile per hour speed limit for the parking garage. No matter. His answer only confirmed what she already knew.

Dr. Elliot Dudley, Billie Mae Peterson's psychiatrist, was David Barton's mother.

ABOUT THE AUTHOR

A native Chicagoan, JC lives in the Washingto D.C. area with her husband and their three children.

Other books by JC Conrad-Ellis:
Boys, Beauty & Betrayal
Camp Colorblind
Chemistry & Chaos
Dancing with God's Grace
Love, Secrets & Pearls

Visit JC Conrad-Ellis' website for interactive blogs:
www.blackdiamondseries.com

Follow JC on Twitter
@dearjcellis

SUNSHINE ON SUNDAY

In Sunshine on Sunday, Tanisha "Teenie" Carlson and the Black Diamond Series' girls are high school graduates, eager to embrace their independence! Armed with their trademark charisma, style and wit, the journey includes: college for some, heartache, new love, additions to the friendship circle, and a controversial discovery for one of the ladies.

With Lori Perkins serving as their navigational moral compass, Teenie, Maria, Rashanda, Justine, and Grace are poised to pave their own way linked arm in arm. Yet, while on their personal paths of self discovery, the ladies are surprised to learn that (like them) their mothers are also complex women in search of friendship and love. Readers will cheer when a parent reinvents herself and starts a new chapter in her own life.

Sunshine on Sunday is a love story woven together like a comforting patchwork quilt. Each patch of love (family, romantic, friendship and self love) is carefully stitched together to form the pattern that defines each girl's love story. Will the love patches and threads sewn while impressionable teens prove strong enough to comfort their fragile hearts?

www.ingramcontent.com/pod-product-compliance
Lightning Source LLC
Chambersburg PA
CBHW071738190726
48292CB00003B/798